FLOWERS
ON HER
GRAVE

BOOKS BY JENNIFER CHASE

Little Girls Sleeping
Her Last Whisper

JENNIFER CHASE

FLOWERS
ON HER
GRAVE

bookouture

Published by Bookouture in 2020

An imprint of Storyfire Ltd.
Carmelite House
50 Victoria Embankment
London EC4Y 0DZ

www.bookouture.com

ISBN: 978-1-78681-816-4
eBook ISBN: 978-1-78681-815-7

For Orrin and Eleanore—I miss you

PROLOGUE

Stepping from the main hiking trail, the park ranger took a moment in the shade to catch his breath and stomp the caked dirt from his hiking boots before beginning his search of the camping ground. Just as he was finishing the last dregs of his water, the static from his walkie-talkie interrupted the quiet of the forest around him.

"Rob, are you there yet? Over."

Pressing the button, he replied. "Just got here. Over."

"See anything? Over."

Looking around the campsite, he saw a pot with remnants of soup, two bottles of water, and a blue tent. Everything looked normal, until he saw some blue shreds of fabric tangled in the low-lying bushes. Curious, he walked over to them, leaned down, and pulled one of the long pieces of fabric out of the brush between his fingers. Something dark spattered the end of the fabric.

"Rob? You there? Over," headquarters asked again.

"I'll get back to you. Over," he said, securing the walkie-talkie to his belt.

"10-4. Out." And then the radio went quiet.

Rob turned, searching the nearby area. "Hello?" he called out. "Hello?" he said again—this time louder. "Cynthia? Cynthia Andrews?"

No response.

Rob scanned every tree and bush within the vicinity, but there was no sign of the missing grad student. Perhaps the girl's family was right to be concerned that she hadn't contacted them in several days.

He let out a sigh and watched as a light breeze swirled dust clouds on the dry earth in the distance. And that's when he saw it. The shredded remains of a tent. His first thought was a bear attack, but few inhabited this area. His hand twitched at the gun in his holster, readying himself for what, or who, he was about to encounter as he approached.

Camping gear was scattered around the area: a large canteen lying on its side; two extra gallons of water; several packets of freeze-dried foods; a small skillet and a boiling pot. Ten feet away there was an open journal lying next to a pink hoodie. He pulled out a small digital camera and took several photos to see if Cynthia's family recognized anything as hers—if it came to that. He'd watched enough forensic shows to understand documentation was extremely important for any type of search or investigation.

Reaching for the sweatshirt he flipped it over to find one of the sleeves stained with dark blood, almost brown in color. He dropped the garment on the ground in horror as the forest closed in and a flock of birds burst from the trees above him.

Eyes darting, he noticed large heavy footprints moving north accompanied by a set of smaller, barefoot prints heading in the same direction, as one followed the other—or chased.

He felt the hair rise on the back of his neck and down his arms as he followed the trail through clustered pine trees. Deep into the woodland the footprints disappeared, replaced by divots and drag marks, the obvious signs of a struggle in the dirt.

Where did they go?

The wind, picking up, whipped and whispered through the trees forcing a shower of pine needles and cones to drop around him. He spied an area where small branches had been broken and followed the trail into a clearing where he was surprised to find ropes tied around a large tree trunk in unusual knots.

Slowly, filled with dread, he walked around the tree.

What he saw on the other side would be burned into his memory forever, he thought. The excessive violence. The horrifying, gaping wounds. The terror in her glassy eyes. It took every ounce of strength he had to take in the devastating scene before him.

The young woman, barely clothed in a workout T-shirt that read "No Pain, No Gain" and a pair of panties, had been bound to the tree with ropes across her chest, hips, and thighs. Her arms were fixed above her head, which now flopped forward limply. In between the restraints were wounds, huge slices down each side of her stomach, allowing her intestines to spill out. It was unclear if the wounds were caused by her killer or wild animals. Chunks of her thighs and calves were missing.

Rob stepped back as her hair stirred in the wind and stuck against her face, caught in her slightly open mouth. He ran back to the original base camp and fumbled for his radio. "Dispatch, we need the police up at the first camp area from Dodge Ridge as soon as possible. We have… there's a…" He couldn't find the words. He cleared his throat and tried it again, "Dispatch, we have a dead body."

CHAPTER 1
Wednesday 0900 hours

The motto that had been drilled into me during basic training was to never show weakness or hesitation before going into battle. Every day a new complication would try to drag me down and expose my fears. A sound mind and a firm focus are a soldier's closest friends, so I treat them as though my life depends upon it.

"I really don't know what to say," Katie said, sitting in the oversized leather chair with her arms crossed in front of her. She knew her body language expressed hostility. That wasn't her intent, but now she was on the spot, she felt cornered.

She was in a neatly organized therapist's office decorated in every tone of beige, probably carefully chosen to soothe the clientele. Around her there were four large leather chairs instead of a traditional couch, and a small round coffee table with a box of Kleenex strategically placed nearer to the client. A floor-to-ceiling shelving unit covered one wall showing off large framed photographs—a family of five, a military man on location somewhere, a sweet little girl posing with her pony—a glass figurine, a small vase of fresh flowers and some brochures about trauma and loss.

"There are no right or wrong answers here," said the psychologist, Dr. Megan Carver, in a quiet voice. She came highly recommended, with considerable experience in treating clients with anxiety, depression, and post-traumatic stress disorder. She had warm, dark eyes and the relaxed way she wore her chestnut hair loosely pulled away from her face made her seem like a close friend ready to listen. "This is just a preliminary meeting to see if we make a good fit to work together. I can answer any questions or concerns you might have, and, if you feel comfortable and ready, then we can begin discussing what has brought you here."

It sounded so simple, but for Katie this request was more problematic than it seemed. Most things in her life were more complicated than they appeared. Lifting the lid on her carefully suppressed trauma might cause more harm than good, but it was the only way she could think of to make the terrifying recurring images stop, to keep her focus on her work and move on with her life. Deep down she knew there was no secret formula to stop the flashbacks and anxiety she suffered daily, but she had to try.

"May I ask how you found me?" said Dr. Carver.

Katie hesitated. Her nerves twitched to get up and leave, but an instinct told her to stay and hear what the doctor had to say. "I read your reviews and did a background search."

"I see," she said. "Credentials are important to you?"

"Of course. It can reveal a lot about someone—or not."

"What do you mean?"

"Well, if someone—I'm not saying you—exaggerated their credentials that says a lot to me about their ethics." Katie tried to soften her words, reminding herself that she wasn't interrogating a suspect at the Pine Valley Sheriff's Department.

The therapist looked at her notes. "It says here that you're a detective, newly appointed."

"Yes."

"And before that you did two tours in Afghanistan."

"Yes. I was part of a military K9 team."

"I see."

Katie noticed that the psychologist didn't react. Perhaps it was due to the many clients she had counseled over the years, nothing would seem shocking to her, but she calmly reread several pages of notes and took time to phrase her questions carefully.

"I'm here to help guide my clients, to help them to see where the anxiety is seeded and work collaboratively to eliminate the source and move on to a productive life." She gave a slight smile, keeping eye contact, and then politely waited for a response.

Katie let out a breath. Uncrossing her arms, she leaned forward. "Dr. Carver, I apologize if I seem uncooperative to you. I'm concerned that news of my visit here will get back to the sheriff's department, and… I simply can't have that. This is private, deeply personal and separate from my work, and I would like to keep it that way."

"Please be assured that whatever you say and whatever we talk about will not leave this room. It is completely confidential. None of the information we gather will ever be shared."

"Thank you. I'm paying for these sessions from my own pocket, and not through work insurance. That is very important to me."

"Of course. I understand," she said. "Now, tell me, have you confided in someone before coming here? Like… a family member or a friend?"

"You mean does anyone know I'm here today?"

Dr. Carver nodded.

Katie recalled recent conversations with both her uncle, who was the current Pine Valley Sheriff, and Chad, her oldest friend. "My uncle and my… I guess you could call him my boyfriend. We haven't talked in any detail, but they both, on separate occasions, have urged me to talk to someone about my experiences adjusting back into society after my tours."

"No closer family members?"

"My parents are both…" she began. "They are both deceased."

Dr. Carver studied Katie for a moment. "Tell me about a typical day for you."

"About work?"

"Just any day—what it's like for you, and how you handle these difficult feelings."

"I don't know…" Katie's voice trailed off.

Dr. Carver put down her notepad and kept Katie's gaze. "You don't have to say anything you don't want to. Just know that it's a safe place here. No judgment. Nothing leaves this room. Understand?"

Katie nodded. No matter how hard she tried to find fault with the psychologist, she couldn't; her discomfort was her own doing. The only time she was truly able to manage her symptoms was while she was at work. She'd never let anything get in the way of protecting the innocent, but for how long that would last, she didn't know. Her acute anxiety had a life of its own, and could strike at any time.

"In your own time," the therapist said patiently.

"Well…" Katie began. Her voice sounded hollow in the room and she was extremely self-conscious, but she pushed through her discomfort. "I'm a police detective and I've been recently promoted to head the cold case division at the Pine Valley Sheriff's Department. It's been challenging, but I love my work. I feel like I'm actually making a difference and helping families—giving closure to them."

"Do you work alone, or with a partner?"

Katie smiled. "The last two cases I've had a partner—Deputy McGaven—he was assigned from patrol."

"How was it working with someone?"

"It's good. We cover more ground, bounce theories around… it's nice there's someone who has your back." Katie looked down and realized that she was gripping the chair arms tightly and immediately loosened them.

"I see," she said. "How do you feel about working as part of a team?"

"I've always worked with someone. Either on police patrol, in the military, and now as a detective. It's the nature of the job."

"I'm sure that's a considerable amount of stress having the responsibility of someone else. How do you handle it?"

Katie felt the familiar tingling sensation under her skin and her body temperature rose. "I don't know… I just deal with it…"

"Explain a bit more to me."

"I don't know… it comes with the panic and anxiety. I usually acknowledge it and work through it, I guess. I have to in order to do my job."

"I see. What happens just before you begin to feel these symptoms?"

"I'm not sure," said Katie, her patience waning, suddenly overwhelmed by the urge to get up out of the comfortable chair and leave without a word—and never come back.

"Does it happen at home? While you are interviewing a suspect? Consoling a victim or their families?"

Katie was stumped at first. She had never thought much about where the anxious feeling came from. It was obvious that stress was the trigger, but she had had flashbacks on other occasions. She closed her eyes for a moment as the sounds and smells of the battlefield bombarded her mind and startled her senses. Taking a deep breath, she forced her focus to return and opened her eyes to find Dr. Carver patiently waiting for her to answer. "The easy answer is stress, of course. My symptoms creep up when I'm feeling tense… like when we're just about to close in on a suspect, or when I'm not sure what direction to take the investigation in." Katie stopped, shocked at herself for divulging such personal information to a complete stranger.

"Does it happen every time when obvious stress is involved?"

"No."

"Does it happen when it's not work related?"

"Sometimes."

"Is it when you're alone?"

"Well, I do live alone, if you don't count Cisco, my dog."

"Is he a therapy dog?"

"No, just my partner in Afghanistan. My uncle pulled some strings and was able to have him released and sent home to me when I left the army." She smiled, once again forcing her hands to ungrasp the armrests, feeling Dr. Carver's eyes on her.

"Katie. Is it okay to call you Katie, or do you prefer Ms. Scott?"

"Katie is fine."

"Katie, I think that's enough for now. I want you to go home and really think about what you want from these sessions and how you'd like to proceed—if at all. Journaling is helpful."

Katie remained quiet as many emotions and thoughts flooded her mind—from never coming back again, to telling the psychologist about the memories that had been impossible to shake.

Dr. Carver rose from her chair. "It was so nice to meet you, Katie." She handed Katie her card. "Please give me a call when you've figured out what you would like to do. I'll wait to hear from you."

Katie rose and took the card and noticed that there was a personal handwritten number on the back. "Okay, thank you."

"You have to figure out what *you* want to do, and whatever you decide, I'll be here," she said and smiled.

Katie took the flight of stairs down to the parking lot with the words *You have to figure out what* you *want to do* resonating in her mind. She wanted to brush off what the psychologist said, but the words haunted her. It was something so simple. How did she want to handle her stress and anxiety? She noticed that Dr. Carver was careful not to mention PTSD, but it was definitely on the table. No matter what Katie decided to do—it wasn't going to be easy.

CHAPTER 2

Wednesday 1350 hours

Katie had been summoned to a meeting with Sheriff Scott. Even though he was her uncle, it was an official order and she didn't expect any special treatment. She hurried through the administrative building, down the hallway, and straight into Deputy Sean McGaven at the door.

"Hey," he said. His tall build and cropped red hair accentuated his huge smile.

"Hi," Katie said. "Looks like it's another one of those meetings," she said breathlessly, excited by the chance of a new case.

"Do you know what it's about?" he said.

"Not a clue."

"Nothing?"

"Nope," she said.

The sheriff's receptionist waved them on into the office.

Katie opened the door expecting to see her uncle alone, but was surprised to see the undersheriff, Samuel Martinez, hovering behind him looking annoyed—jaw clenched, eyes on his watch. Katie quickly glanced at the clock on the wall; two minutes early. She'd never had much contact with him before, but the word around the department was that he was a stickler for the rules and quick to judge.

McGaven stood behind Katie and she didn't have to look at him to sense his similar surprise at the presence of the undersheriff.

"Ah, here they are," said Sheriff Scott as he took a seat at his desk.

"Are we late?" asked Katie.

"No, no, right on time," he said. "Please, have a seat. You both know Undersheriff Martinez."

"Yes, nice to see you, sir," said Katie.

"Sir." McGaven nodded in agreement.

"I promise, this will be brief," the sheriff began, as he pulled up a chair between them. "As you know, there are still negotiations in progress for the county budget. It's been tedious, and they don't seem to be getting anywhere. I had wanted to keep Deputy McGaven full-time working on cold cases with Detective Scott, but unfortunately, that won't be possible."

Katie was disappointed, but she knew that her uncle must have had something else in mind because Martinez looked edgy. He clearly wasn't pleased with the situation, or with her; there were a handful of people at the department who didn't like the seemingly special treatment Katie received—even if it was well-earned.

"So, I've decided..."

Kate braced herself for the fact that the cold case unit might be temporarily disbanded, or maybe even permanently.

"... that we will split McGaven's duties."

"What does that mean?" she asked.

"He will work patrol two days a week and the cold case unit two days a week. There will be a day every other week where he will work an extra shift, either patrol or cold cases—whichever has the greater need, decided by his patrol supervisor."

"That sounds great," said McGaven.

Katie thought it was reasonable and was glad that McGaven was going to work with her again. "Why do I get the feeling that there's something else?" she added, looking at her uncle.

"You will continue to write your weekly reports, but—" he replied.

"But," interrupted Martinez, "you will also send copies of those reports to me, Lieutenant Jackson of Patrol, and Sergeant Cannon of the internal affairs division."

"Internal affairs?" asked Katie, confused. Internal affairs were only involved in cases of investigations relating to incidents and possible suspicions of law-breaking and professional misconduct attributed to officers on the force. "I don't understand. Why?"

"It's only a formality, for a twelve-month probationary period."

Katie stared at Martinez and then at her uncle. "Have I done something wrong?"

"No, nothing like that," the sheriff said. "It's because the cold case unit is not operated by the same rules and regulations as the homicide and other detective units. You don't report to anyone except me. The policies and those in charge of the department's strict laws want to make sure that your ethics are kept in check."

"So I'm under investigation because I investigate cold cases?" she pushed, trying not to raise her voice.

"Think of it as another set of eyes making sure that cases are handled properly," said Martinez. He watched her closely and she couldn't help but notice that there was a slight happy note to his voice.

"I see," she managed to say.

McGaven remained quiet, letting everything sink in.

"Nothing has changed. You will still have to submit a weekly report of your progress. Now you will just have to submit to three additional people."

"On the days that McGaven is working patrol—is it still allowed that I bring Cisco with me when I leave the office?" she asked.

"Yes, everything stays the same," the sheriff emphasized.

"Try not to be reckless just because you have the dog with you," Martinez added.

He was referring to an instance where Cisco had once helped to save her, but that was under extraordinary circumstances. "Of course, I, and we, will be professional and operate by the exact letter of the law." She forced a smile over gritted teeth.

"Is there anything else?" the sheriff asked Martinez.

"No, that's all for now," he said.

"Okay, Scott, McGaven, you're dismissed."

Katie got up and headed to the door followed closely by McGaven. She hurried back down the hallway and then descended the stairs to the basement. When she was safely out of earshot, she turned to McGaven and said, "Well, I guess that's that. Like we don't already have enough obstacles on our cold cases."

"Don't fixate on the red tape. Let's just concentrate on working the evidence," he said.

Katie forced a smile. She loved working with McGaven. "You're right. Nothing has really changed. When will I next see you in the office?"

"Looks like Friday," he said.

"Great. I'll see what kinds of cases I can dig up. Be safe out there."

"Same to you." He smiled and walked in the opposite direction, heading back to patrol.

CHAPTER 3
Thursday 1030 hours

Katie sat at one of the two desks in her office at the end of the hall, tacked on to the forensic division because the detective division was already at capacity before she joined. Her cold case unit consisted of several empty rooms filled with filing cabinets containing every unsolved case in the department's history. The quiet solitude of the basement was the perfect environment for Katie to mull over evidence and talk aloud to herself without disruption. Over time, she'd brought several indoor plants and an air purifier to clear the dank smell that had lingered there since her first day.

Grabbing a pile of eight files that had been selected by the sheriff for her attention, she flicked through them. Which case to pursue was ultimately Katie's decision, based on the evidence, people of interest, and type of case, but he liked to have a say sometimes. Not all cold cases were homicides, but they were the most pressing, followed by rapes, burglaries and arson.

As Katie thumbed through hundreds of pages of interviews, forensic reports, photographs and autopsy reports, the words began to run together in her head. She couldn't get her mind in sync with the fact that internal affairs were going to oversee everything she did. She assumed that it must have something to do with the politics of who was going to run for sheriff next, when her uncle retired. To her, the thought of someone else being sheriff seemed impossible, but she knew of at least two other high-ranked personnel that vied for his position—and the undersheriff was one of them.

Katie stood up from her desk, stretched and had just decided to go on the hunt for some coffee when the phone on her desk rang.

She snatched up the receiver. "Detective Scott."

"Hello?" said a very shaky woman's voice on the other end.

"This is Detective Scott, may I help you?"

"Is this the cold case unit?"

"Yes, it is."

"My name is Mrs. Lenore Stiles."

The name sounded familiar, but she just couldn't place it. "What can I do for you, Mrs. Stiles?"

"I make this call every year," she said. "My son, Sam Stiles, disappeared on this day five years ago. It's his birthday. He worked at Palmer Auto Repair and had left early, not feeling well. Well, I won't bore you with details you already have, but I wanted to know if there were any new developments on his case."

Katie's gut tightened as she took in the deep sadness in the woman's voice—a mother who lost her son and never got closure. "Mrs. Stiles, I've been recently assigned to the cold case unit and I can assure you that if we have anything new in his case, we will contact you."

"Detective Scott," she said slowly. "I'm not a well woman…"

Katie closed her eyes in grief, remembering how horrible it was to lose her own parents and feeling lucky to at least have known what happened to them. Mrs. Stiles didn't have that luxury.

"I've been through a lot since that day," she said. "Mr. Stiles couldn't take the stress and he passed away two years ago from a stroke—never knowing what happened to his only son."

"I'm so sorry for your loss, Mrs. Stiles. Please accept the department's deepest condolences," said Katie, not knowing what else to say. She didn't want to sound scripted and uncaring, but the woman's pain was almost more than she could bear and she needed to remain professional.

"Please, Detective, can you give a dying woman her last wish? Find out what happened to Sam."

The words stung Katie's chest. She wanted more than anything to ease this woman's pain and bring closure. "I'm not familiar with your son's case, but I promise I will look into it personally."

"Thank you. That's all I can ask," she said, her voice suddenly winded and weak with relief.

Katie took her phone number and address. "If I have any questions, is there a good time to contact you?"

"Anytime—day or night. I don't sleep much."

"Thank you for your call, Mrs. Stiles. I'll be in touch soon."

Katie slowly returned the phone to the cradle on her desk.

She couldn't help but feel deeply connected to every case she worked. How could some detectives remain detached? How could you ever receive a call like that and react as if it was just another day on the job? She got up from her desk and stepped into the hallway. She looked to the left and could hear the forensic manager, John, moving around in the examination area. Other than that, it was quiet.

Across the hall, she punched in #4546 on the keypad, flipped on the light, and was immediately greeted by the familiar musty smell of old paper. It took her less than two minutes to find the file: Stiles, Samuel John. It was large and heavy.

Back in her office, Katie forgot about her need for a coffee fix and put her lunch break on hold as she began to deconstruct the case. She pulled everything from the packet and put the paperwork in chronological piles, beginning with the first missing person's report taken by a Deputy Kristy Daniels after a welfare check had been requested. Stiles's boss, Dennis Palmer Senior, had called the police after he couldn't reach him for three days and when no one had heard from him. According to the police report, Sam Stiles, thirty-four years old, had left work early on a Tuesday afternoon complaining that he didn't feel well. It was unusual for him to miss work but his boss wasn't concerned. Stiles was then currently single, lived alone, and had few friends. His parents were the only family listed, no siblings or other relatives documented. When he didn't show up for work the next day, his boss and co-workers weren't immediately alarmed and didn't go check on him. It was not until the third day missing that Stiles's boss put a call into the police department.

Katie made notes as she worked; names, places, times, anything missing or in need of further inquiry. When Deputy Daniels arrived at Stiles's apartment, 2722 Diamond Street—Apt. 16, she found no one home, but the sliding door was unlocked. Upon searching the apartment, there were no signs of foul play and everything looked to be in order. She noted that there was food out on the counter—deli meat, mayonnaise, loaf of bread, and a tomato that had been sliced. A knife and small plate beside them. Judging by the decomposition, the food had been out for a couple of days. Neighbors were interviewed and no one had seen Stiles or heard anything suspicious or noteworthy.

Katie pulled out a stack of eight-by-ten photographs of his apartment, which had been taken a few days after the initial report. The images depicted the apartment in order and the food found on the kitchen counter. It was noted that Stiles's wallet and keys were there, but his car was missing.

Katie searched the rest of the paperwork to find out if the car had been recovered—there was no indication it had been. She made a few more notes. A Detective Paul Patton was then assigned the case. She noted that he wasn't on the roster anymore. After placing a few calls and contacting the department's human resources, she found out that he was recently retired, but still living nearby.

At the back of the file it was noted that Stiles liked to frequent a couple of the local bars and had been arrested twice for assault.

There were several names that Katie had to run down, but she was going to start at the beginning and first track down the deputy who had answered the call for a welfare check.

Something about the recorded account of what happened to Sam Stiles seemed out of place to Katie. Everything was too neat and tidy. Something bad had happened to Sam Stiles—Katie would bet her job on it.

CHAPTER 4

Thursday 1445 hours

A few calls and Katie was able to track down former Deputy Kristy Daniels, who was now Sergeant Daniels, and she had agreed to meet her at Bobby's, the local diner, to talk about Sam Stiles's missing person's report.

Katie parked her unmarked police sedan in the parking lot, spotting the Pine Valley patrol vehicle already there alongside only two other cars. It was mid-afternoon, so the diner would be mostly deserted. She grabbed her file containing her notes, a photocopy of the Stiles report and a blank notepad, made sure her detective's badge and firearm were secure underneath her beige suit jacket, and then she entered the diner.

A woman with short blonde hair and a solemn expression, dressed in a deputy sheriff's uniform, sat at the back of the diner facing the entrance. She looked up and nodded in acknowledgment as Katie approached.

"Sergeant Daniels?" Katie asked.

"Detective Scott," she replied stiffly.

Katie tried to lighten the mood as she sat down. "My parents and I used to come here all the time when I was a kid. Best sundaes in town."

The sergeant nodded. "Well, the food is okay, but the coffee is strong and freshly brewed twenty-four hours a day."

Katie remembered what it was like working patrol for the Sacramento Police Department for a little more than two years; it was difficult finding establishments that had fresh coffee and clean restrooms in the middle of the night.

The waitress stood at the table. "What can I get for you?"

"I'll have an iced tea. Thank you."

The waitress left.

Katie thought she'd get right to the point. "I'm looking into the Samuel Stiles case after I received a phone call from his elderly mother this morning."

The sergeant watched Katie with some caution. "I remember catching that call," she said, eventually.

"I know it was a long time ago, but I wondered if you could tell me about it in your own words. Was there anything that seemed strange or stuck out to you?"

The waitress returned with a large iced tea and refilled the sergeant's coffee before retreating back into the kitchen to chat with another waitress.

"That's funny you should ask."

"Why is that?" Katie said as she watched the officer pour cream and two sugar packets into her coffee.

"I had only been off training probation barely two weeks. It was my first missing person's call, so I was pretty amped," she said. "Truthfully, I was a bit nervous."

"I read your report, but I wanted to hear it from you."

"I remember going to the auto shop."

"Palmer Auto Repair," stated Katie.

"Yes. I talked with the owner, Palmer senior. It was a father and son operation with two other employees at the time—five in total counting Stiles. Anyway, Palmer senior said that Stiles didn't show up for work and wasn't answering his phone." She took another sip of coffee, pausing a moment to recall the memory. "I thought the two employees were acting a bit suspicious."

"What do you mean?"

"Shifty, watching me, but acting like they weren't. Know what I mean?"

Katie nodded. She had seen her fair share of shifty individuals when she was on patrol. "I didn't see any background run on them from the file—or notes."

"I think the detective..."

"Detective Patton," Katie added.

"Yeah, I think he ran backgrounds, but there was nothing to show if I remember correctly, you'll have to ask him." She shifted in her seat and adjusted her gun belt.

"He's retired now. I'll have to track him down," Katie said.

"He's still in the area and he's a really easy-going guy. He'll remember this case, had an amazing memory for details—and barely had to look at his notes to jog his memory." The sergeant laughed.

Katie made some notes. "So Stiles had left work early because he wasn't feeling well."

"Yeah, they said three days previous he left because he wasn't feeling well and went home."

"Did they think he was actually sick?" Katie asked.

"They said he wasn't concentrating on the work and used the restroom several times. It seemed legitimate."

"Okay."

"So since no one could reach him and he hadn't shown up for work, I went to his residence. It was a small apartment on... I think it was on Diamond Street."

Katie nodded.

"When I got there, his car wasn't there, but I knocked on the door several times. No answer. I looked inside through the window and everything looked fine. I tried the front door and it was locked. There was a small sliding door that entered into the small dining area and it was unlocked. I kept knocking and saying his name."

Katie wrote notes detailing the officer's approach, which matched the report. Her thoughts were that Stiles might have always left the slider unlocked or he just forgot that day. Maybe he didn't use the front door and entered and exited through the slider.

"I decided to go inside since it was a welfare check. I let Dispatch know what I was doing and I heard another deputy respond that he was in the area. I pulled open the sliding door and called for him again. There was nothing out of place and no unusual smells."

Katie knew that she meant the smell of a deceased person. There was no mistaking that stench.

"Would you like anything else?" the waitress interrupted.

"No, thank you. Not right now," the sergeant replied.

"Did it look like anyone had been there recently?"

"See, that's the thing. It looked like no one had been there in a week, maybe more. That's why I thought it was strange that there was stuff on the kitchen counter to make a sandwich. It was obvious that it had been there for more than a couple of days. There was something strange about it."

"I saw the photos," Katie said. She shuffled through her file and pulled out one of the photographs of the half-made sandwich.

Sergeant Daniels took a look at the photos again to refresh her recollection. "See," she said, "the knife and bread are almost symmetrical. And look at how the tomato was perfectly sliced and left, it's more like a photo shoot."

Katie looked at the image again. The sergeant was correct in her assessment—the items looked like they were arranged, not natural.

"I don't know. It seemed like it was staged to look like Stiles had been there and made a sandwich and then..."

"And then disappeared," Katie finished her sentence.

"Yeah."

"Did CSI come out?"

"They didn't."

"What do you mean? The photographs," Katie said.

"I took them. I had one of those disposable cameras in my patrol car. Overzealous, I guess, still being a rookie. Trying too hard to impress."

"I don't think so… it showed good instincts," Katie said. "It's easy to dismiss things when nothing comes of it."

The sergeant relaxed a bit, warming to Katie's inquiry. She obviously realized that Katie wanted to solve the case as much as she had. "Well, nothing did come out of it."

"What did the rest of the apartment look like?"

"Organized. Neat. No dishes in the sink. Clothes hung up in the closet. That kind of thing."

"Bed made?"

"I think so… I'm not sure."

"So it didn't look like someone coming home and crashing out sick for a few days. Were there delivery containers? Evidence of watching TV in the living room. Maybe sleeping on the couch? That kind of thing." Katie tried to picture it in her mind.

"Exactly. I didn't realize at the time, but everything seemed like he had just left. But…"

"But what?"

"His keys and wallet were on a table next to the front door."

Katie shuffled through the photos but there weren't any taken that showed the front door area.

"Thinking back now, it did seem like he hadn't been home. I was still a rookie, but even so, the apartment did seem unnatural… staged."

Katie quickly read through her notes. "Well, I think I have everything I need. If I have any questions, I'll call you."

Sergeant Daniels reached into her pocket and retrieved a business card. She quickly wrote a number on the back. "Here's my cell."

"Thank you," said Katie as she took the card and gathered her notes and photocopies of the case.

"Detective Scott?"

Katie turned to the sergeant.

"Let me know if you find him," she said sincerely.

She nodded. "I will. Thank you again."

CHAPTER 5
Thursday 1645 hours

The valley view from the mountain was breathtaking and Katie never tired of it. It took almost an hour to drive the windy gravel and dirt road to Detective Paul Patton's house. She was able to find his phone number and address from Human Resources on his exit interview a few years ago from the sheriff's department.

Katie was a bit hesitant contacting him due to her previous experiences with some of the department's detectives, but Detective Patton was friendly and agreeable on the phone, inviting her up to his cabin to discuss the case in more detail.

As Katie made the final turn into his driveway, she saw a small custom log house with a large front porch which she thought must have a stunning view of the valley between the pines and oaks clustered along the ridge behind her.

Katie steered her car to park next to a brown pickup truck, taking a moment to gather her thoughts. Her gut told her Sam Stiles never made it home that day. From when he left the auto garage but before he arrived at his apartment, he had vanished.

Opening the car door, Katie grabbed her notes and copies of the file and was immediately confronted by the strong, wonderful aroma of pine. The slight breeze caught the scent and carried it around with the loose leaves, an outdoor fragrance that remained forever etched in Katie's memory. No matter where her life carried her, she would always remember the small things about living in Pine Valley, taking them with her wherever she went.

She walked around the pickup truck and glanced in the bed filled with dark blue tarps, camping gear, maintenance items, carefully coiled extension cords and some type of air compressor.

She jumped as something wet touched her hand. Down by her knees a stocky yellow Labrador retriever was giving her the once-over. He looked old with a mostly greyish-white face and seemed quite mellow about his security detail.

"Hey, boy," she said and gave him a pet on top of the head. "Aren't you a handsome guy."

"Tank, come here," a man's voice called out, and the dog instantly turned and trotted back to his owner.

Katie noticed that the front of the property was just as neat and organized as the inside of his truck. Firewood was cut and perfectly stacked. Several large half barrels were filled with late-season vegetables—each had a carefully constructed barrier made of chicken wire to keep any wild animals from foraging.

"Detective Scott, I presume," said the man. He was heavyset; his thick grey hair still kept in a short uniform style, and wore jeans and a red flannel long-sleeved shirt.

"Yes, but please call me Katie."

"Paul Patton," he said, extending his hand in greeting.

"Detective?" she said.

"No, I'm just Paul now. When I retired I hung up that part of my life."

"Nice to meet you, Paul." Katie noticed his grip was firm but a respectful squeeze. He had several deep ridged scars on the back of his hands.

"Likewise. Just made some lemonade iced tea," he said walking back to the house. "Would you like some?"

"Sounds great." Katie thought his home was beautiful and quiet. It was a nice place to retire after dealing with homicides and chasing bad guys for a career.

"C'mon inside," he said and hovered at the door waiting for Katie to enter.

Katie looked around the home. She'd expected it all to be in brown tones, large game heads on the wall, and everything made of leather and dark accentuations, but inside it was decorated with a palette of cool colors of blue and green with accents of raw wood. It was quite enchanting and gave a sense of tranquility just as the outdoors—there was no other way to describe it. She realized that it must have taken a painstaking amount of time to create this lovely home.

"What a beautiful place," Katie said.

"Thank you. It's been years in the making—to create what we wanted," he said.

Katie nodded and followed Paul into the large kitchen area of clean white cabinets and stainless steel appliances. The counters were slightly cluttered with small appliances and pottery items that held all sorts of accessories and utensils.

Paul brought a glass pitcher filled with iced tea and set it down on the counter. Katie took a seat at the bar and watched as he poured her a large glass of tea filled with ice. He slid it over to her and then filled his own glass.

"Thank you," she said and took a nice long drink. "This is fantastic. Lemon and mint… no wait, it's spearmint."

The dog moseyed around her and then lay on the floor nearby.

"You know your stuff."

"I have several kinds at my house. It's one of the things that I love about having enough room to grow fresh herbs and vegetables."

Paul came around the counter and took a seat next to Katie. "So, you want to ask me about the Sam Stiles case."

"Yes. Thank you for seeing me so quickly."

"For you, it's my pleasure."

Katie wasn't sure what he meant by that statement. "I'm sorry…"

He laughed. "I know your uncle well, we go way back. Too many years to say."

"Oh," she said, smiling. Her uncle had many close friends who would do just about anything for him.

"He talks about you all the time. I see him once or twice a month for poker. A bunch of old guys talking about the ol' days."

"Well, I still appreciate you seeing me today."

"I can imagine that you want to dig into this case, but I have to tell you, we worked this case hard for a couple of weeks and didn't turn up much. There was no evidence to speak of—only witnesses and people who knew him. Leads were mostly driven by accounts, not forensics."

"You seem to remember it well."

"After you called I dug into one of the boxes where I keep all of my cases—historical stuff. I thought I might write a book someday." He took a long drink of tea. "Silly, I know, but useful now to refresh my memory."

"I saw in your report that Sam's boss and co-workers at Palmer Auto thought that he might have fallen victim to some shady characters because he gambled—possibly owed some money." She pulled out her report and skimmed through areas where she highlighted portions of interest. "And you questioned," she flipped several pages, "the Golden Owl bar owner, Patrick McDermott."

"Oh yes, McDermott—he's dead now—died last year. He owned several businesses around Pine Valley including a few restaurants and a strip mall. But he loved the bar scene and would spend most of his time there. People knew him well. He didn't have a family. The bar was his family. But it doesn't matter, the bar is closed, and McDermott is dead."

"He said that he hadn't seen Stiles for a couple of weeks. Do you think that was true?" she said.

"Look, everyone knew McDermott. Many cops also frequented that same bar."

"Was there illegal activity?"

"Just the usual stuff—gambling on a pool game or playing liars dice at the bar. Nothing that would warrant a hitman to come after you if you owed money. No, nothing like that," he said.

Katie couldn't help but notice that Paul seemed agitated by the question and didn't hold eye contact with her. She made a mental note, but pressed on. "You stated in the report that you canvassed all the places that Stiles either had contact with, or was known to some of the patrons."

"Yeah, we spent more time tracking down leads from family and friends—it turned up absolutely nothing. No one had seen him or heard from him. It was like he just vanished."

Katie hesitated but asked, "Do you think that he was killed?"

Paul took a breath and fiddled with the placemat underneath his iced tea. "I think it's quite possible that when he left work that day he ran into someone, not someone he knew, per se, but someone who had crime in mind. Maybe he was robbed? Maybe he was carjacked? Maybe he went to buy drugs? Though there was no evidence of him using. Anything could have happened to him. These are just theories, not backed up by any evidence. We didn't have much to work with."

"Something had to have happened to him before he made it home," Katie said. "I saw the photos of his apartment that the deputy took and I have to say that it does look suspicious... the items left on the kitchen counter appeared staged. His wallet and keys left behind... it was like someone had put them there to make it look like he had come home—and left again."

Paul got up and went into the kitchen to refill his drink. "Would you like some more?"

"I'm good. Thank you."

He filled his glass, rattling the ice cubes. This time he stood in the kitchen and leaned against the counter. "I followed the Toymaker case and those little girls you found last year. You have a gift, Detective Scott. I was glad that the sheriff decided to make the cold case unit a reality."

Katie appreciated the compliment, but it made her a bit uncomfortable—she was just doing her job and she knew that she still had a lot more to learn. "I'm realizing that working cold cases is not only about working all the evidence with a fresh perspective and using your gut instincts, but it also involves having a little bit of luck on your side."

He laughed. "So true. I had many that drove me crazy until there was the smallest thing that broke the case wide open."

Tank got up and made his way to the kitchen where he noisily lapped up water.

"So, I'm getting the feeling you think there's more to this case than just a missing person. And whoever took him went to his apartment, arranged the sandwich-making items on the counter, left his wallet and keys to make it look like he had come home," Paul said, watching Katie carefully, like he wanted to catch her in a lie.

"I don't want to jump to any conclusions. I want to look at everything and follow leads that you may or may not have accomplished." She was careful how she worded her answer not to make him defensive. "Five years have passed. There could be a number of things that could shed some light on why Stiles went missing. Someone coming forward…"

"I'm beginning to understand what Sheriff Scott sees in you." He walked back around and sat down next to Katie again. "We followed every lead that came to us, but everything came back to Palmer Auto and the parents."

"Parents?"

"Don't seem so shocked. Believe me, I've been fooled a time or two by some of the nicest people that murdered their five-year-old little girl or smothered a mother-in-law with a pillow. I've been fooled. We're only human."

Katie recalled her conversation with Mrs. Stiles; her fading health, a widow, just wanting to have some closure on her only son. "Mrs. Stiles called me today wanting to know if there had been any new leads on her son's case. It was his birthday…"

"Those are the hardest calls, I know."

"Mr. Stiles died a couple of years ago and she's not well herself."

"I remember the parents calling on the victim's birthday. They were optimistic and strong at first, but the more time went by you could see the pain and deep sorrow on their faces as they lost hope. They knew that their son was most likely dead—but…"

"But what?"

"But they kept hopeful—that's all anyone can do."

"If you were going to pick up this cold case—what would be something that you would do this time? Anything any different?"

"Thinking back, I remember feeling someone wasn't telling the truth—or the whole truth—at the auto shop. I didn't catch anyone in a lie and no one had any real criminal record, but I just had this feeling like they were hiding something."

"What did you do?"

"What could I do? I followed through with questions and they seemed to be telling the truth. I remember thinking that maybe Stiles never came to work that morning… maybe they were covering their tracks."

The same thought had crossed Katie's mind.

"I saw here that you spoke to some of the customers."

"Yeah, we were able to track them down and they all said that Stiles was there."

"Did they say anything that seemed…"

"Out of sorts? Weird? Not usual?"

Katie laughed. "Well, something like that."

"All three customers were new. It was their first time using Palmer Auto Repair. That alone seemed a bit odd, but I spoke with all of them and they verified the work with receipts."

Katie finished her iced tea. It would be getting dark soon and she wanted to get a start on the drive home along the slow winding road she had to take.

"Looks like you have your work cut out for you," he said.

"I think so, but if it was easy everyone would be a cold case detective," she said. "Well, I think that I have everything I need—for now." She stood up and gathered her things. "Thank you again for seeing me, and the wonderful iced tea."

"Wait just a moment," he said and hurried out of the kitchen area, disappearing down the hall. He returned in about five minutes holding a plain manila folder. Handing the thin file to her, he said, "Here. This is something that might help you."

Taking it, she replied, "What is it?"

"Whenever I was off work, sitting at the bar blowing off some steam, I would write down my personal thoughts about a case. It wasn't official, but it helped me offload and to come up with story-lines for novels when I retired. I don't know… it might help you."

"Thank you. I think anything at this point would be helpful," she said. It was a little unorthodox, but something was better than nothing.

"Best of luck, Detective Scott," he said. "If you need anything else on the case, please don't hesitate to call me if you think I could help."

"I will. Thanks again."

It was twilight by the time she left, giving an orange-colored glow to the trees as she drove home. Katie took the sharp corners a bit too fast as her mind wandered back to the conversation with the detective. He seemed to be holding back on something—but why? She was beginning to realize that cops didn't like to answer questions about their cases, particularly the ones they'd failed to solve. That was only normal, she guessed. For now, she would file the suspicious behavior in the back of her mind.

The daylight waned and the brilliant reddish orange filtered through the trees flickering like a light show as she coasted down the gravel track back to the main road. A fox skirted across Katie's path causing her to slow her vehicle just at the same time her cell phone rang. She pulled to the side of the road.

"Detective Scott."

"Hey. You at work?" said Chad.

"I'm cruising down the back roads right now."

"Work related?"

"Of course."

"You have plans for dinner tomorrow?" he asked.

"Maybe," she said, shyly.

"I was thinking a light dinner at Carlo's Bistro."

"That sounds nice." She smiled and couldn't imagine her life in Pine Valley without Chad, the childhood friend who had been her rock after she had returned home from her two tours in Afghanistan. She'd never thought that she would see him again, but he had come back to town around the same time in search of a firefighter position.

"Katie?" he said interrupting her thoughts.

"Yes."

"Call me when you get home."

"Talk to you then," she said and hung up.

CHAPTER 6
Friday 0700 hours

Military dogs tread quietly at your side waiting for your command—sometimes leading the pack. Loyal. Silent. Forever bonded. They are regal with intelligence and never wanting to be anywhere else except right at your side stealing your heart in the process. Their destiny has been imprinted in their DNA to protect, serve, and to find the bad guy—at all costs—even if it means giving their own life to save others.

The building was two stories high and sat on the edge of the six acre K9 training facility for the Pine Valley Sheriff's Department—which also doubled as one of SWAT's training areas. With two main doors on either side and different levels of moveable windows, the structure was a fun house of surprises designed to engage working K9s to find specific drugs or the perpetrator.

Katie led her very excited German shepherd, Cisco, toward the main entrance of the training building. The early morning sunlight glanced off the dog's shiny jet-black coat. With high-pitched whines and alert amber eyes, Cisco readied himself and waited for Katie's commands.

Katie and Cisco had been a military K9 team in the army on both of her combat tours in Afghanistan. Cisco had been credited with detecting the locations of dozens of explosive devices, while participating in over a hundred patrols clearing routes for the team. Cisco was a special dog and Katie was extremely lucky to be able to bring him home. Their K9 bond remained unshakeable.

She unsnapped the leash and dropped it to the ground. Cisco instinctively went into training mode and took his position at her left side; ears forward, nose and tail lowered, alert to anything unusual.

Katie approached the building with trepidation as if it were a real-life situation. She hurried to the side of the entrance and kneeled down, pressing her back against the wall. Dressed in army fatigue pants and a long-sleeved T-shirt, she reached for the weapon in her leg holster. Pointing it ahead, she inched along the wall and Cisco copied her, hugging close to her side until they reached the corner. Katie stopped, Cisco too—waiting.

When she knew the coast was clear, Katie sprinted to the entrance and flung out the door, sheltering to one side as she shouted, "Sheriff's Office, come out or I'll send in the dog!"

No response.

"You're surrounded. Come out now or we'll send in the dog!" she pushed.

Cisco barked, eyes locked on the doorway.

Katie moved to the opening and entered slowly with Cisco at her side. She wanted Cisco to search the building, so "*Voran*," she commanded in German. It was traditional to train German shepherds in the language for both police and military dogs. Cisco knew German, English, and hand commands.

The dog ran deeper into the building, systematically searching the bottom floor. His excited panting was only interrupted by intense moments where he caught a scent and put his nose to work. Just before the staircase at the far end, Katie called out "*Platz*," and then, "*Bleib*." Cisco immediately downed in his position, belly touching the floor, and waited.

Katie looked behind her and then glanced up the stairs, still focused and training her gun in the direction she moved. She slowly climbed the stairs. "*Fuss*," she instructed Cisco to heel at her side. The team ascended the stairs until they reached the top platform. Katie checked the immediate area from the left to right before deploying Cisco. She said, "*Voran*," again to search the second level.

Cisco bolted—his nails scraping against the plywood flooring, then rapid barking. Katie hurried to catch up and found him barking at a closed closet. She knew that the training decoy was hiding in the closet.

"Come out with your hands up," she ordered.

Cisco still belted out deep barks.

"Come out now!" she yelled.

The door slowly moved.

"*Platz*," and then "*Bleib*." The dog obeyed, eyes fixed, immediately stopping barking and dropping to his position on the floor.

Katie still followed protocol and inched to the cabinet, waiting a few seconds, and then flung open the door. Inside, the decoy, dressed in a full bite-suit, raised his hands in the air and inched out.

"Turn around, keep your hands on your head," Katie ordered.

The decoy obeyed.

Just as Katie pretended to put the handcuffs on the trainer, he bolted backward knocking Katie off her feet. Her gun flew from her hand and clattered across the floor. The decoy reached to grab Katie, now unarmed and vulnerable, but Cisco sprang into action with incredible speed and agility, clamping down on the decoy's arm, throwing him off balance.

Katie fell to the ground while Cisco kept his grip, as the decoy's body was flung around as he struggled to escape. Moments later, the suited man hit the floor.

Katie yelled, "*Aus!*"

The dog instantly released his grip and trotted next to Katie, still keeping a keen eye on the decoy.

"Good boy," she said.

"Damn, what a hard bite," exclaimed the man with pain in his voice. He walked up to Katie and offered her a hand up. "Sorry for hitting you so hard. Our usual K9 guys weigh twice as much as you."

Katie laughed. "No problem. It did take me by surprise—and that's good to keep me on my toes. No special treatment here…"

Katie hurried down the stairs and out the front open door towards Sergeant Blake Hardy; Cisco stayed beside her carrying his favorite yellow ball as if he had won the lottery. Hardy was in charge and oversaw the K9 unit for the sheriff's department. It was clear by his gait and appearance that he had been a cop for his entire career. His greyish crew cut and intense stare sealed the first impression.

"That's one happy dog," he said.

Still a bit winded, Katie said, "He loves everything about training."

"Have you been working him outside of the training area?"

"I've been taking him on some trailing and scent exercises behind my property, just to keep him engaged," she said.

"I bet it's hard for a war hero to sit at home and relax." He faced Katie but kept his attention on Cisco.

Katie laughed. "It is, but I love training too."

"How's it going with the cold cases?"

Katie was surprised that the sergeant was interested. He usually kept things brief and only about dog training. "It's tough and challenging, but I'm enjoying it. No two days are ever the same."

The sergeant looked up and nodded at the decoy approaching from the building. "How'd it go?" His demeanor reverted back to business.

"Great bite. Even harder than Nitro."

"That's impressive."

"Hear that, Cisco?" Katie said.

The dog responded with shaking the ball and gave a slight grumble.

Katie turned to leave; she needed to get changed for work. "Thank you, Sergeant, for letting us train."

"Anytime," he said and gave a quick nod.

CHAPTER 7
Friday 0845 hours

After securing Cisco at the police kennel, Katie changed into a tan suit in the locker room and headed to the forensic division to move forward on the Sam Stiles case. She made her way down to the basement and stood in front of the entrance, swiped her identification, and waited for the door to unlock.

As always when she entered the forensics area, she was hit with the sense of being in a soundproof bunker. She pushed forward and took a deep breath of the recirculated air cleaned through layers of industrial HEPA filters and the high-tech filtration allowing the forensic division to stay as uncontaminated as possible. She couldn't think of a cleaner, quieter, more convenient place to work.

On the way to her office she passed the main forensic examination room, filled with scanning electron microscopes and computers. As usual, she saw John hunched over a microscope in dark cargo pants and a black T-shirt which showed his arm tattoos. Most people would never guess that he used to be part of the military as a Navy Seal.

Katie didn't want to disturb him, so she smiled and moved on down the hallway. To her surprise, her door was ajar. She sucked in a breath, but was quickly relieved to see her partner, Deputy McGaven, sitting at his desk tapping away at the computer keyboard; conducting background research was one of his strengths in their partnership.

"Hey," she said.

He looked up and smiled. "Morning. You running late?" McGaven looked different in plain clothes rather than his deputy uniform. His white dress shirt was neatly ironed and he wore a dark maroon tie, looking like a sharp detective.

Katie put her briefcase down on her desk. "No," she said with a slight sarcastic, but playful tone. "I'm not late. I've been training with Cisco since about 7.00 a.m. this morning. And I had to change." She shed her suit jacket and hooked it over her office chair.

"Ah," he said.

She looked at the whiteboard in the corner, which was empty now that all the leads for her last case had been taken down. She sighed.

"What's up?" McGaven said.

"Nothing."

"C'mon, what's up?"

"Just had a moment, remembering all the working profiles and information for the Payton case."

"Yeah, I noticed that blank slate too when I came in, back to square one."

"So," she began changing the subject, "what are you so fired up about?" She glanced at the Stiles file, now open on his desk.

"I assumed that this was the case that we're going to be working on and then I saw your sticky note. And well, I've been searching the backgrounds on some of the most likely suspects."

"Like?"

"Like, the clowns that Stiles worked with. Five years ago, Palmer Auto Repair was run by father and son, Dennis senior and junior, with two employees, Derek Von Der Brennen and Sal Redino."

Katie pulled her chair around and sat down next to him. "Sounds like something out of a sitcom. Who works there now?"

"Same with father and son, Dennis senior and junior, with same two employees."

"What's the story on these guys?"

"Not much. Just some petty stuff. Trespassing. Theft. Nothing that pops out."

Katie leaned back. "Maybe we're going about this all wrong. We still have to talk to these guys and see if their stories change at all—we might get lucky and someone might slip up or come forward with some new information."

"I don't see these guys having much of a conscience even if they were involved in Stiles's disappearance."

"People are people. And everyone after a certain length of time wants to confess—get it off their chest," she said.

A knock at the door made both officers look up to see a pretty brunette woman with short hair in the doorway, carrying several folders and a rolled up map. "Hi," she said.

"Hi, Denise," said Katie.

"Here's your maps and some more background on those names you emailed me," she said coyly when she looked at McGaven.

"Okay, you two," Katie teased. "Save it for after work."

McGaven blushed and stood up quickly to take the files from her. Denise worked in the record's division and had been extremely helpful with extra background checks and searches through social media. She had recently been dating McGaven, which made Katie happy because they were both exceptional co-workers and nice people. She hoped their relationship would endure the intensity of the workplace.

"Thanks, Denise," said Katie as she took the maps from McGaven. "Bye." She laughed.

"Bye," said McGaven in a quiet intimate whisper.

"Bye," she replied, and left.

"Oh, that reminds me," Katie said. "You and Denise are going to my uncle's anniversary party. Right?"

"Of course. There's food, right?" he said.

"Of course," she said.

"Then I'm there—we're there."

"Okay, can we get back to work?" laughed Katie. "So," she said as she unrolled the street map of the neighborhood where Palmer Auto and Sam Stiles's apartment were located. The distance between them, she estimated, was about three miles.

"The garage on Terrace Avenue and his apartment on Diamond Street were closer than I first thought," said McGaven. "I've patrolled that area many times. Not much goes on there."

Katie tacked the maps up on the outside of the cupboard doors so they both could see them easily. "You're right. The report initially said that they did a canvass from the garage to his apartment. Actually, the deputy who caught the call did the canvass. Found nothing. I think she was expecting to find his car."

"Looks like there are two ways he would have gone home,' said McGaven, tracing his finger along the map.

"That's true if he *was* going home, but I don't think he made it," she said. Thumbing through the original file, she retrieved the photographs that Deputy Daniels had taken of his kitchen and the miscellaneous photos of his car and place of work. "The only evidence we have is this," she said and taped up the photographs of the sandwich on his kitchen counter. "He drove a navy blue late model Honda four-door."

"Okay, what do we have between point A and point B?"

"Wait a minute, something is missing," she said and sat at her desk opening her laptop. "I remember seeing in the file from one of the people questioned that there had been some type of road work that day." Her screen came into view. She quickly went to the California Division of Road Operations and searched through their database at the approximate dates five years ago. "During that entire week, they were repaving the roads down Main Street, which passed Terrace Avenue where the auto garage is located. It looks like there was some type of issue with the drainage too."

"So if Stiles really did go home sick like he said, then he would've had to go a different, roundabout, route."

"And then double back." Katie frowned.

"Street maps are like puzzles, everything has to fit."

Katie stood up and gazed at the photographs and the street maps. "What do we really have here?" she said, more to herself. "What are some of the main points of interest? It would be of interest to Stiles."

"Bowling alley. Cleaners. Apartments. Two gas stations. Discount grocery store… High end condos…" began McGaven.

"There are too many directions and ways for him to leave the auto garage… north… south…" she grumbled.

The desk phone rang.

"Saved by the bell," he said.

Katie grabbed up the phone. "Detective Scott."

"Detective," came a feeble voice. "This is Mrs. Stiles."

"Yes, Mrs. Stiles, what can I do for you?" She dreaded having to speak to her without any new information.

"After we spoke, I remembered that I had some of Sam's things packed away. Garrison House Rental Agency was nice enough to deliver them to me about a month after Sam went missing, and after the police were done with their investigation at his apartment."

Katie turned to McGaven who had been watching her and she raised her eyebrows, as if to say *we might have some new clues.* "Do you still have these boxes?"

"Yes, I went downstairs to check."

"Has anyone looked in these boxes?"

"No, they were already sealed when I received them and I've never opened them."

"May I have your permission to come over and look inside them?" she asked.

"Of course. Do you think it will help?" Her voice faded a bit.

"Anything could help. I'm going through everything in this case and looking at each report and piece of evidence."

"Thank you, Detective," she said as her voice cracked. It was clear that she was still devastated about the disappearance of her son and her health was fading.

"Would it be okay if my partner and I came out today?"

"Yes, anytime."

Katie was quiet during the drive to Mrs. Stiles's home. She drove down the familiar streets and cut through other roads to get to the opposite end of town.

"What's on your mind, Detective?" said McGaven. His face was serious as if he had some thoughts that were worth mulling over too.

"I was thinking about the rental agency."

"And?"

"They seemed to be pretty efficient and quick to return Stiles's stuff."

"Fair question. But remember, they weren't going to receive any more rent without a tenant."

"Mrs. Stiles could have paid for a few months... It seems so final, like they already knew." She took a turn in the road faster than she should have and the sedan bounced and bucked. "Something seems off, that's all."

Bracing himself with his hand against the dash, he said, "Checking out Mrs. Stiles's house will put some things to rest—maybe even that gut instinct of yours too."

Katie smiled. "You're probably right." She leaned forward to read addresses. "I think that's it." She eased the vehicle to the side of the road and parked.

The neighborhood was one of the older ones in the Pine Valley area. Many of the homes were built in the 1940s and 1950s era.

This particular area of homes had been kept up and updated through the years. The Stiles's home was painted a dark turquoise blue with white trim. It was a boxy design with a flat roof and painted shutters giving it more of a beach cottage feel. The front yard had blooming flowers with a meandering vine travelling along a trellis and over the quaint gate entrance.

Katie had a difficult time seeing Sam Stiles growing up here, but she guarded herself and tried to keep an open mind because nothing was ever as it first appeared to be.

Katie and McGaven exited the vehicle, both taking in details about the neighborhood, gathering information. The ground was wet as it was evident that the sprinkler had been operating only about an hour ago. Stepping up to the front porch, Katie knocked on the door. There were small potted plants and succulents in various colored planters arranged around the small entrance. A couple of goofy yard ornaments grinned at them from the flower beds: a cat with a flag in its paw and a garden gnome with brightly painted clothes.

The door opened. An elderly woman with white hair rolled in tight curls stood at the threshold. She was dressed in a comfortable yellow running outfit and had on white sneakers.

"Mrs. Stiles?" asked Katie.

"Yes," she replied.

"Hello. I'm Detective Scott and this is Deputy McGaven."

"Yes, of course," she said as her voice slightly wavered. "Please, come in."

"Thank you," Katie said.

As Katie and McGaven entered the home, they found it was decorated as one might imagine how an alone older woman would embellish her home. Numerous knick-knacks, outdated plaid furniture, and crochet blankets were displayed throughout. It was cluttered, but organized and clean.

"Mrs. Stiles, thank you for allowing us to come over on such short notice," Katie said.

"It's no trouble. Please, follow me. I'm afraid that I'm not much help moving the boxes."

"No problem. That's why I brought McGaven."

They followed the elderly woman through the house, down the hallway, down a short flight of stairs, and then into a small room. There was a door leading outside, which she unlocked, opened, and passed through. The side yard was bleak, not as lovely as the front. There was a small building that Katie assumed was once a garage or an old storage building.

Mrs. Stiles turned to Katie and handed her a single key dangling on a chain. "Here's the key to the side door. All of Sammy's belongings are in moving boxes and have his name on them. Please feel free to look in anything you like."

Katie took the key and said, "Thank you. We'll return this when we're done." She wanted to wait and see if they found anything before asking Mrs. Stiles more questions.

"Please take anything you need for the investigation. I… I… hope it helps you," she said and then turned away.

Katie knew that her grief was heavy, leaving her lonely without any type of closure, not knowing what had happened to her only son. It made it even more imperative that the entire investigation found out what happened to Sam Stiles.

McGaven followed Katie to the side of the building; she quickly unlocked the door and stepped inside.

There were boxes from floor to ceiling labeled: Christmas ornaments; old dishes; fancy linen and tablecloths; tools.

"Oh wow," said Katie. "Do you see Sam's name?"

McGaven with his height could see more boxes than Katie could. He moved a few things and said, "Here they are."

Medium-sized moving boxes with "Sammy" and his address written on the sides came into view.

"How many are there?" she asked, eying the cobwebs above their heads, wondering if there were large spiders hiding all around them.

"I would say about ten or twelve."

"Okay, let's get started." Katie shed her jacket and rolled up her blouse sleeves.

McGaven grabbed two boxes and quickly cut the sealed tape with his pocket knife. "At least it looks like no one has been in them since they were packed up."

Katie opened the first box not sure what to expect. Inside, there were newspaper wrapped items from his bedroom—photographs, personal items, bathroom toiletries, and a box of cigars. She let out a sigh realizing that they were most likely only going to find throwaway personal items.

"Just stuff from a junk drawer and a dresser," said McGaven. "It's weird going through someone's personal items."

"You've never executed a search warrant before?"

"Yeah, but this is different. It just feels wrong."

"I know what you mean, but let's be thorough."

Katie and McGaven spent over half an hour going through the boxes.

Katie looked in another box near the end of their search and discovered a group of letters and postcards. "Wait, here's something."

McGaven immediately stood next to her. "Letters?"

"Yeah, and some postcards from Hawaii and… Lake Tahoe and it looks like Canada. Some are from Mr. and Mrs. Stiles, but here are a number of them from a Natalie Cross. I think we should take these back to the office. But let's keep searching."

Katie found several folded paper grocery bags in a plastic basket and took one and put the letters inside. She kept searching, not sure what she was looking for.

"Here's a photo of a woman," said McGaven. "She's pretty. Possibly Natalie Cross?"

"Here," she said. "Put that in the bag."

Katie came to a box that had some jewelry: a man's watch, a bolo tie, Puka shell necklace, and an antique diamond ring. "Wow, this is the kind of ring you propose with. Probably a family heirloom. I should give it to Mrs. Stiles for safekeeping." She felt sad because a proposal was never going to happen. "Wait…" she said. In a small black box there was a single key with a black rubber top.

"What is that?"

"A padlock key. I don't recall seeing anything from the photographs in his apartment that would need a key like this."

"It could be for anything."

"This is one of those really heavy-duty ones, like would be used for a storage unit. It says, 'Strong Lock'."

"I haven't seen any paperwork, bank statements, registration for his car, or bookkeeping items that might indicate if he paid for a storage facility," said McGaven.

"I haven't either," she said.

Katie and McGaven finished sifting through the boxes and then restacked them neatly.

She grabbed the bag with the letters, photograph of family members and one unknown woman, and key. "Well, it's more than we had earlier this morning. I'll let Mrs. Stiles know we're leaving and what we're taking with us." She had the letters, photo, key, and ring.

Katie hurried back to the house and opened the back door. "Hello? Mrs. Stiles?" She waited. "Hello?"

"Yes," came a feeble voice. "Please come up, Detective."

Katie navigated the stairs and was in the living room in a moment. Mrs. Stiles was sitting and having some tea. "Mrs. Stiles, can I ask you a few questions?"

"Of course."

She showed her a photo of Natalie Cross. "Do you know this woman? Or, have you ever seen her before? Please, take your time."

Mrs. Stiles stared at the photograph for several moments, but she shook her head. "No, I've never seen her before. Pretty girl."

"How about these letters?"

Thumbing slowly through the pile, she smiled. "My husband and I sent Sammy these letters and postcards when we went on our trips. Mr. Stiles loved to travel."

Katie smiled. "It seems that your son was a bit sentimental keeping these letters."

She handed back the letters, and said, "He was. Most people didn't know that. He was a sensitive boy."

"What about this ring?"

There was a glimmer in Mrs. Stiles's eyes and it was clear that she had recognized it. "That was my mother's wedding ring and I gave it to Sammy to keep until he found the right girl."

"I will leave it with you. It shouldn't be in storage boxes."

"Thank you, Detective."

"Mrs. Stiles, we're leaving now and I'm going to take these letters and photograph. Oh, and also this key."

"Of course, my dear. Whatever you need to conduct your investigation."

Katie felt the entire situation pull at her heart. She leaned down and touched Mrs. Stiles's hand. "I'll let you know the minute we know anything."

CHAPTER 8
Saturday 1615 hours

Katie rushed out the front door all dressed up for her uncle's anniversary party. She was arriving early, per her uncle's request, and Chad was going to meet her there after he was off shift at the fire department. Leaving Cisco behind, she carefully navigated her way across her driveway in heels to her Jeep.

She turned the key and her SUV roared to life. Backing down the long driveway, her thoughts wandered to the cold case—as usual. She played with various theories and ideas that rattled around in her mind. Did Sam Stiles meet an untimely death? Did he have an elaborate plan to leave and obtain a new identity? Who was Natalie Cross? Was his illness that day just an excuse, a ruse, or a convenience?

Before she put her Jeep into drive, she glanced in her rearview mirror to make sure her makeup was still in place—which it was. Dresses and high heels made her a bit self-conscious, but this was a special occasion and she knew that her aunt would love to see her dressed up.

Katie drove the back roads to her uncle's home. She always preferred the longer route because it was picturesque and allowed her to calm her nerves and empty her mind of whatever was plaguing her. It amazed her that she hadn't had a single episode of anxiety or any of the dark feelings that had been so prominent during the Amanda Payton case.

Are things finally changing just because I spoke with a therapist?
Would life begin to move forward again—in a healthy way?

She felt strongly that she could work through her flashbacks and anxiety. It wasn't because of her visit with the therapist; she felt it was because she had *chosen* to meet her trauma head on and then work through it. There was an entire life ahead of her and she had accomplished so much in a short period of time. It was time to slow down, take a breath, and enjoy the process.

Easing back her speed around a couple of sharp corners, where pine trees butted up against the roadway, she carefully made her turn. The wind had picked up, causing the tree limbs to dance in the headlights.

As she made another sharp turn, she approached her uncle's large, ornate gate which was wide open. There were only a couple of cars already there parked down the side of the property. A white van was stationed close to the front door, which said "Festive Caterers." Two women dressed in black pants and white chef's jackets were replenishing food from their refrigerated cargo area.

Katie found a vacant spot to park, sitting in the darkness for a moment listening to the rhythmic tapping of the engine as it cooled. Something nagged at her. She couldn't pinpoint where this invasive feeling was coming from—but something seemed out of order. She remembered one time her uncle told her that being a cop was always going to make you suspicious and test you on how much you could trust any person or situation.

Shaking that weird feeling, Katie grabbed her clutch purse and got out of her vehicle. She felt the cool breeze in her face and across her feet in the open-toed shoes. The driveway was slightly bumpy and she felt the pebbly surface beneath the balls of her feet.

Even though most guests hadn't arrived yet, she heard a few voices, chatting, and laughing, coming from inside. It struck her that so many people wanted to celebrate the happy marriage of ten years between her uncle and aunt. It made her smile. She didn't know what her relationship with Chad would bring, but she hoped that it would stand the test of time just as it had for her Uncle Wayne and Aunt Claire.

Katie walked to the front door where the large double doors were propped open and the smell of food wafted towards her.

Taking a deep breath, she crossed the threshold and entered the house. She stood for a moment at the top of the five wooden stairs before descending into the large living room. The decorations were tasteful and sparse with silvery accents next to a half dozen vases of white roses, peonies, and orchids.

"There she is," said Aunt Claire. "I thought we were going to have to send out a patrol to bring you here." Her infectious smile and genuine hospitality exuded her true personality. Her short coiffed blonde hair accented her perfect bone structure and dark eyes. She was beautiful and didn't need makeup or expensive dresses to prove it.

"Happy anniversary," Katie said giving her a hug.

"Thank you, sweetheart."

"Aunt Claire. You look amazing," said Katie admiring her fitted white dress.

"You took the words right out my mouth. Katie, my dear, you really need to show off your fab figure more often. Blue suits you. Those boxy suits just don't do you justice." She took Katie by the hand and steered her to the refreshment table. "I'm going to leave you here to get started, but I'll be back soon. I have to check on a few things in the kitchen before the rest of the guests arrive."

"Okay," said Katie.

"Oh," she said turning towards her, "where's that handsome fireman?"

"He'll be here later. He had to finish a shift."

"Good. I can't wait to see him. You go and relax. I know your uncle wanted to chat with you before the party." With that said, she moved to the kitchen, slightly adjusting flowers as she went.

A well-dressed bartender stood behind a temporary table doubling as a bar. "What can I get for you?" he asked with a pleasant smile.

"I'll have a glass of white wine please." She watched the young man pour her a glass and then hand it to her. "Thank you."

"There you are," said her uncle as he wrestled with his tie. He looked extremely regal and handsome in his dark suit.

"Let me help you," she said and tied it for him. "You'd think that you've never done this before. Remember, you've already met and married the woman of your dreams." Katie smiled.

"Only by the grace of God. Why would she want an old sheriff like me?"

"Are you serious?" she said. "You *are* really nervous. Don't worry, you look handsome and the only woman for you has already said yes. This is the party ten years later." She giggled.

"Come with me," he said walking through the living room and outside on the patio. It was quiet and, since there weren't any of the guests yet, it was private.

Katie was curious as she followed him outside, exiting through a double set of French doors. She had never seen her uncle so nervous before. He was the strong leader, the pillar of the community who would command an entire department of police officers under any emergency. His calm intelligent demeanor was what the entire town respected him for.

The garden outside had been decorated with white lights, which accented the beautiful flowering vines and blooming rose bushes. The fragrance was as wonderful as the scenery.

Sheriff Scott glanced around them to make sure that no one was nearby. "I have something to show you. I would have had you with me when I bought it, but I saw it and immediately thought of Claire."

"What is it?" Katie's curiosity was at an all-time high.

Her uncle pulled a black velvet box out of his suit jacket. He slowly opened it and revealed a necklace with pearls, diamonds, and green garnets.

"Oh," she said. "It's gorgeous. Claire will love it."

"I thought of her when I saw the green garnets. We were on vacation once and she had made mention that she really loved them."

"Uncle Wayne, you definitely hit this one out of the park. Just relax and enjoy your party."

He returned the box to his pocket. "Now," he began, "how are you? I know that we haven't been on our monthly fieldtrip and burger run this month."

"I know. I think there's going to be a seascape and landscape painting exhibit downtown next month."

"Nice sidestep," he said.

"What do you mean?"

He leaned against the railing looking a bit more relaxed when the conversation turned to police work. "I know you weren't happy about the new arrangement and the fact that you have to carbon copy other departments about your investigations. But trust me, this so-called probationary period will be over soon."

"I hope so."

"I saw that you decided to reopen the Sam Stiles case. Good choice," he said.

"Well, it wasn't my first choice, but his mom called on his birthday. How could I say no?" Katie looked out at the flowers and the twinkling lights.

"Those are the toughest, I know. I think you will have good luck with this case and solve it."

"I believe that there was foul play—that's just my theory—at least right now."

"How was Paul?" he said, quickly changing the conversation.

"You mean Detective Patton?"

He nodded.

"He's fine. Kind of an interesting character living alone up in that large cabin."

"He's had a bit of a rough time after his wife passed suddenly."

Katie thought about how the house and yard were beautifully decorated. "It must be difficult for him, everything around him must remind him of her." She thought a moment before she asked, "What's your take on him?"

"What do you mean?"

"Well, was he a good cop? Well liked? Had he a reputation for solving and closing cases? Just stuff like that," she said.

"He was a good cop. I always thought he would have wanted to be something else… besides a cop."

"What made you think that?" She remembered the file folder he gave her with notes that were more appropriate for a background for a novel or screenplay. It still seemed odd to her that he gave her those. It was almost as if he was trying to tell her something. What it was—she didn't know.

"Things he said and implied. He never really liked being on patrol—he was more pessimistic than the rest of us. But things changed a bit when he made detective. It suited him more."

"I could see that," she said.

"Between you and me, I always felt like there was something else going on in his life that he wasn't sharing."

"What do you mean? Something illegal?" she said.

"No, nothing like that. I always got the feeling that he was dealing with something difficult that he wasn't willing to confide with anyone."

Katie thought about her conversation with him, and remembered that she too had the feeling that he was anxious about something. She'd dismissed it as being protective over a case that he had investigated.

There were voices at the entrance as guests began to arrive.

"Oh, I better go be the good host," he said, giving Katie a kiss on the cheek. "And don't think that I didn't notice that you bought a new dress. That firefighter of yours is not going to know what hit him."

"Uncle Wayne…" Katie said, embarrassed.

As most of the guests arrived, Katie recognized many people. Some were from the department, either on current duty or retired, while others were longtime family friends. People were standing enjoying their drinks and others had small plates of appetizers.

Katie smiled and nodded a hello to several sheriff's department personnel—including the top brass—as she made her way back outside to find McGaven and Denise enjoying some hors d'oeuvres. They were acting cute and feeding each other samples from their plates.

"Hello, you two," said Katie, guessing that they didn't care if anyone at the department knew they were dating.

"Katie," said Denise. "Wow, that dress is… you look beautiful." She leaned in and hugged her friend.

"I second that *wow*. Where's my partner?" joked McGaven.

"You're very kind, thank you. I'm glad that you both could make it."

"This is incredible, such fabulous food," said Denise enjoying another bite.

Katie noticed her uncle seemed to have disappeared and wasn't making his rounds through the crowd.

"You have to try this little puff pastry," said Denise and gave Katie some.

Politely, she took a bite. "Wow, you're not kidding. This is *really* good."

"Where's Chad?" McGaven asked.

"He's going to be a little bit late finishing a shift," she said. "Well, I'm going to find my uncle, otherwise I'm going to eat all those puff pastry goodies."

"We'll talk to you later," said Denise cuddling in with McGaven.

Katie was still excited that her partner and friend were dating. They made the cutest couple: McGaven so tall like an all-American farm boy, while Denise was petite and full of enthusiasm, and they seemed to be getting along really well.

She moved through the crowd noticing that the volume level had begun to rise since she had arrived—most likely due to the consumption of alcohol and the festive celebration.

Someone touched her arm and she expected to see Chad, but instead she saw John, the Pine Valley PD forensic supervisor, staring at her. "I wanted to say hello before there was a line of people waiting to talk to you," he said with good humor. He was dressed in slacks and a dark green long-sleeved shirt. His intense blue eyes locked on hers.

"John, it's so nice to see you here. What, a night off from crime scenes?" she asked.

"My crew can handle it, but they know they can call me if needed."

"Always available." She smiled.

"Yes, *available* I am," he said with emphasis. "You look beautiful."

"Thank you." Katie tried not to let her slight embarrassment show as she felt her temperature rise. She turned to the entrance just as Chad walked in. Her pulse quickened at the sight of him and his eyes on her.

John noticed too. He smiled and said, "I'll see you later," and disappeared into the crowd. She watched him and wondered how he dealt with the memories of being a Navy Seal, but felt glad he'd switched careers as there was no one better to run a forensic unit.

"Hi," Chad said and kissed her. "Sorry I'm late."

"You're not at all. I think the party is just getting started."

They moved through the crowd stopping periodically to say hello to old friends and new, shaking hands as well as giving brief hugs. With relief, Katie noticed that her uncle had rejoined his guests at last.

At one point, Katie and Chad passed by a large display case filled with the sheriff's collection of antique guns, and stopped to admire it with some other guests. There were several western guns, some Colt revolvers, pepperboxes, and Derringers. Most of them were circa 1830s, and a couple of them had some silver adornment with one-of-a-kind etching. Her uncle also had a pair of hooked fighting knives from the seventeen hundreds in there.

"How long has your uncle been collecting?" asked Chad.

"I'm not completely sure, but certainly since he became a police officer. He's very particular about what he puts in there."

"It's an amazing way of documenting history."

"Definitely," she said.

"Wow, look at those knives," said a guest. "I'd hate to be up against someone with one of those."

"I believe those are Spanish fighting knives," said Katie.

"Are they for decoration, or were they actually used to fight?" the guest asked.

"From what I understand," she said, "they were actually used in honor fights."

"That's the last thing that any cop needs when responding to a call," said Chad.

"You're not kidding," said McGaven as he walked up behind them and joined in on their conversation. "But maybe we should make it a part of our weapon arsenal, just in case."

Everyone laughed, except Katie. She had been watching her uncle as he approached and knew something was wrong.

"Uncle Wayne," Kate said as she hugged him tightly the moment she could get to him. She could smell whiskey on his breath. He wasn't usually much of a drinker, even when he was celebrating.

"So great to have you here, my gorgeous Katie." He then extended his hand to Chad. "Glad you could make it."

"Thank you for inviting me, Sheriff," he said.

Katie leaned in. "Are you feeling okay?"

"Me? Of course. Maybe just a bit tired. Go enjoy yourselves."

CHAPTER 9

Katie and Chad moved back through the crowd sipping new drinks and nibbling on appetizers. She tried to put all concerns for her uncle and thoughts of the cold case to the back of her mind. She just wanted to enjoy the party. It was a celebration!

A small quartet played outside on the patio, beautiful with the blooming garden in the background and following the same theme as the decorations from inside of the house.

"Well, Detective Scott," Chad began as he took her by the waist, holding her tight, "I think a dance is in order."

Katie didn't object as they joined several couples in a slow sway to the music.

"Excuse me, may I have your attention please," interrupted her uncle. He waited a moment until everyone was quiet before continuing. Katie and Chad moved to the French doors to hear what he was going to say.

"First, I want to thank you all for being here tonight to celebrate this special occasion." He wrapped his arm around Claire's waist. "What am I saying? It's an absolute miracle that we've been married for ten years."

There were soft chuckles throughout the crowd.

"Seriously, I won't make this sappy or long, but it means a lot to me that you all are sharing our special day. I couldn't imagine my life without this amazing woman at my side. I love you, Claire," he said and kissed her.

Everyone clapped and yelled their well wishes.

"Oh, and one more thing," the sheriff said, "I would like for all of you to witness." He pulled the velvet box from the inside of his jacket. He opened it and said, "To the most amazing and beautiful woman that I've ever known. This is to celebrate and honor our ten-year marriage." He pulled out the necklace and the crowd gasped.

Claire put her hand to her mouth in surprise as she held back the tears. "Oh, it's beautiful."

He put the necklace around her neck and gave her a kiss, mouthing, "I love you."

The guests cheered and clapped again before dispersing to enjoy themselves.

"They make a great couple," said Chad.

"They really do," Katie said, believing for a moment that she was beginning to discover what true happiness was like.

The evening pushed on and everyone seemed to enjoy the party and each other. Katie had never laughed as much as she had talking with everyone. Even her feet didn't hurt as much as she thought they would in her high strappy heels.

Amped up from all of the conversations and positive energy throughout the party, Katie took a moment alone to gaze at the garden in the backyard. With the evening light and tiny strings of white lights around the patio, the twisty blooming vines with the delicate white flowers looked magical. The fragrance coming from honeysuckle, roses, and lilacs was intoxicating.

Chad came up and wrapped his arms around her waist. They didn't speak but enjoyed the moment where they were—together. They both were relaxed and happy. It was a moment that Katie could only describe as pure bliss.

"GET OUT!" yelled her uncle from inside the house. Katie heard several gasps and then the party went quiet. "I said, get out!" he yelled again.

Katie broke away from Chad and ran through the crowd to find her uncle face to face with the guy she'd spoken to regarding the Stiles cold case—retired detective Paul Patton. Paul looked different—not the hospitable ex-detective widower with a nice Labrador retriever having iced tea with her.

What was going on?

"Fine," Patton seethed. "But, we *all* know the truth."

"You couldn't handle the job, and now you've chosen tonight of all nights to air your grievances. Go home, Paul—just go home." Suddenly realizing the crowd of stunned faces around him, the sheriff tried to regain his calm and diffuse the tension.

McGaven and John inched closer in case something more happened.

"Secrets have a way of spilling out when you least expect it," Patton seethed, grabbing a tumbler and hurling it at the display cabinet beside them, shattering the glass from both the tumbler and the front of cabinet.

McGaven pounced. "C'mon, it's time to go," he said, grabbing Patton's arm and dragging him out of the party through a sea of astonished guests.

Katie's uncle turned to the crowd and said calmly, "I'm sorry for the interruption, folks. I guess some people can't handle their alcohol. But please, both Claire and I want you to enjoy the rest of the party."

Katie dashed to the pantry to find a broom and dustpan to sweep up the glass. Her aunt assisted her. "Katie, honey, you don't have to do that."

"It's no problem. I don't want anyone to step in it. The faster it gets cleaned up, the faster everyone can get back to enjoying themselves like it never happened."

She looked around as she returned to the main area and saw her uncle talking with a group of four people. "Uncle Wayne, may I see you for a moment," she said, taking his arm and gently steering him into his study at the end of the hall.

"Uncle Wayne, what's going on?"

He took a breath. "I'll explain later."

She put her hand on his arm. "No. Tell me now. What was that all about?"

"Okay."

Katie watched her uncle carefully. His balance was off, his face pale, and perspiration was heavy on his forehead. She waited patiently for him to explain.

"Paul has always been moody. He could be happy and content one moment and then pissed off at the next."

"I thought you told me he was a good cop?"

"He was… but there was always something up with him. It was like every time something good happened at the department, or when I got a promotion, he mocked it saying stupid things like that would never happen to anyone else."

"What did he mean by that?" she asked.

"Like I said before, he seemed like police work was beneath him. Like he could have done anything else."

"What did he mean by *we all know the truth?*"

"I don't know. He came in cursing up a blue streak and saying that I don't deserve everything that has been given to me…"

"Sounds more like he's jealous. Has he ever acted like this before?"

"No, never to this degree. Never so openly. I care about the guy, but to come here to my house and disrupt my celebration—I draw the line right there."

Katie studied her uncle. *Was there more to their rift?*

"I know that look, Katie," he said. "Everything is fine, I assure you. Now c'mon, let's go back to the party. Everyone has probably already forgotten about that stupid outburst by now." He smiled and led Katie out of the study.

The party continued, but there was a change in the air that made Katie feel like she wanted nothing more than to go home and fall into bed. Chad led her to the foyer where her uncle and aunt were saying some goodbyes to guests. She noticed that her uncle still looked pale.

"Uncle Wayne, Aunt Claire, this was lovely. Happy, happy anniversary to you both," she said and hugged each of them. "We're still on for a run at 7.00 a.m. and then a quick breakfast on me, right?"

"Of course," he said.

"I can't wait. I'll need a run to burn some calories of this fabulous food," said Claire.

"Uncle Wayne, are you feeling okay?" Katie asked.

"I'm fine. I think some of those seafood puffed balls upset my stomach, that's all."

Katie and Chad said good night and left.

CHAPTER 10

Sunday 0650 hours

After a good night's sleep, Katie returned to her uncle's house just before 7.00 a.m. in her jogging gear. Everything looked neat and orderly, the driveway now empty, caterers packed up, and the mini orchestra was gone. It looked as if no one had ever been there. She wondered if her uncle had stayed up late to clean up. She rang the doorbell, stretching her hamstrings to warm up as she waited.

Minutes passed, but no one answered.

Confused, she walked around to the back of the house and peered in through the French doors. The front room was neat and tidy, but the lights were off. She tried the doors, but they were locked. It was possible they had slept in after a long evening—maybe her uncle really was sick.

Katie looked at her cell phone but there were no text messages from either one of them. She decided to try the front door one more time and rang the doorbell again, for longer this time, pressing her ear against the door. She heard movement—it sounded as if something was being dragged across the floor. Her mind went into worst-case scenario mode. Cop or no cop, she sensed something was wrong.

She slammed on the door with her fist. "Uncle Wayne? You in there?"

More shuffling on the other side of the door.

"Uncle Wayne?" her voice wavered.

The door slowly unlocked and it opened a crack. Her uncle stood there, barefoot in his sweats and a white T-shirt. He was disheveled and looked as if he had aged twenty years overnight. He didn't speak—his eyes a thousand miles away. He was clearly in shock.

"What's going on?" she said.

He opened the door wider to reveal his shirt was covered in bright red blood—spattered and smeared, his hands and forearms bloody.

Katie rushed inside. "What happened? Are you alright?" Her first thought was someone had broken in and her uncle had been attacked, but there wasn't any sign of a forced entry.

"I… didn't… there was…" he muttered.

"Uncle Wayne, sit down," she said and guided him to the couch, quickly checking him over to see if he had been seriously injured. But the blood didn't appear to be his. "Are you hurt?"

He tried to speak, but his words didn't make sense. "So much… everywhere… I…"

"Uncle Wayne, where is Claire? Is she here?"

He didn't say anything, but kept glancing to the far side of the house where the bedrooms were located.

"Stay here, okay?" she said, trying not to let her voice tremble. "*Okay?*"

He finally looked at her and slowly nodded.

It pained Katie to see her uncle in this condition and so many horrible things ran through her mind. She needed to see if Claire was okay, but the blood on her uncle's shirt made her waver as she pushed various images from the battlefield out of her mind. There was no doubt something terrible had happened here last night, and she needed to know what, despite the imaginary fumes of expelled ammunition, dust, and inexplicable heat that suddenly slammed her senses.

No… not now… not again.

She swallowed hard and fought the dizziness. Her throat dry. Her hands sweaty. And her legs felt strangely rubbery, with every step making the floor feel uneven.

No... she willed.

She made it to the corner at the end of the hallway. It was dark still, the dull, cold light of the overcast morning barely making it through the skylights. She ran her hand along the wall looking for the light switch, fumbling around until she flipped the lever upward and a low wattage bulb lit up the hallway.

There were three bedrooms in the house, two of them ahead of her, one was a spare bedroom and the other doubled as her uncle's office. Both of those doors were open and Katie could see clearly into them. Vacant. She peered through the hallway bathroom and it was empty as well.

The lights above her flickered, stopping her in her tracks. "Aunt Claire?" she said. "Hello?"

Katie hurried around the corner and stopped, staring in disbelief. There was blood smeared on the outside of the master bedroom door. Red handprints sliding down towards the floor. Katie's heart pounded in her chest. She realized that she hadn't taken a breath in a while—causing her vision to darken as if she was going to pass out.

"Claire," she managed to say between a few deep breaths.

Squeezing her eyes shut and leaning against the wall, she tried to push away the memories of war that assailed her. She willed herself to steady her breathing and planted her feet to wait out the panic for a moment.

When she was ready, Katie reopened her eyes, blinking a few times to focus her view on the bloody smear in front of her. She carefully moved forward, mindful not to touch anything that might later become evidence. Even under such stress, she was still programed to follow protocol.

She slowly turned the knob and pushed the door open. The king-sized bed wasn't made, but the sheet and comforter had been casually flipped back as if her aunt and uncle had just awakened and got out of bed.

"Aunt Claire?" she said again into the silence.

Turning back, she made her way further down the long hallway to the last remaining room, the large laundry room at the end of the hall. The door was open but the light was off. Just before she reached the doorway, she looked down to see a pair of small, bloody footprints in the carpet, barely visible in the low light.

No... Aunt Claire... please no...

Katie's feet were glued to the floor, but she knew she had to see what was in the room. Leaning in, she flipped the switch and froze as the bright light illuminated the room—unable to move—unable to breathe. Katie sank to the floor managing only a strangled, agonized cry.

Why...?

Lying on the floor, against the dryer, amongst the freshly pressed laundry and tubs of colorful detergent, lay the lifeless body of her aunt. Her pale yellow nightgown was soaked in blood. Three long gashes down each side of her torso. Blood had splashed everywhere. Katie looked in the sink and froze at the sight of the murder weapon, wet with crimson blood.

Fighting for her sanity against her anxiety and insurmountable grief, Katie tried with all of her strength to try and piece together what could have happened to this kind, caring woman. With a jolt, she realized her beautiful Aunt Claire was still wearing her anniversary necklace.

"I didn't do it..." came a strained whisper from behind her. "I would never..."

Her uncle's voice startled her. She turned quickly and saw him standing there with his eyes glued to his wife's lifeless body.

"I... swear... I didn't do it..."

"Uncle Wayne, please," Katie said.

"She... was... like this when..."

"Please," she said and guided her uncle out of the room and carefully down the hallway. "I know what I saw." She finally turned to face him and said, "Why is one of your Spanish fighting knives in the sink?"

CHAPTER 11

Sunday 0950 hours

Sheriff Scott's house was blocked off with every emergency vehicle that Pine Valley had at its disposal. After the 911 call from Katie hit the airways, the news media mobile units were dispatched as well. They were being held back with curious neighbors until the investigation was completed. There would be a news conference later that afternoon.

The emergency personnel hurried about their duties along with several extra patrol vehicles that were eager to get first-hand news of what had happened.

As Claire's body was removed by gurney and slid into the morgue van, every face working the area was solemn and those who knew her personally broke down in tears.

Detective Bryan Hamilton was assigned to the homicide. It wasn't the type of murder case that any detective wanted at the department, but they assigned him only because he had the most experience.

Katie sat with her uncle who was inconsolable at the sight of the dark body bag containing his wife of ten years. Katie had cried so much that her face felt strangely tight. She was numb—emotionally and physically. She had been through difficult times in her lifetime and on the battlefield, but this was something more than the death of a loved one; her aunt had been murdered in cold blood.

Detective Hamilton entered the living room and spoke to a few of the officers securing the scene, giving John from forensics some instructions that Katie couldn't quite hear. She'd worked with Hamilton on the Amanda Payton case and it was no secret he had strong feelings about her being the sheriff's niece, but as they locked eyes across the room she felt his sincere condolence, wordlessly passed from one cop to another. She'd never noticed the kindness in his eyes before, or the slight greying through his dark hair, and it was clear that he took care of himself at the gym. She was slightly surprised that he was assigned this case, but it did make her feel better that he was new to the sheriff's office and would hopefully be unbiased during the investigation.

"Sheriff, I'd like to ask you a few questions here if that's alright. Are you up for it?" he asked and then turned to Katie. "Does he need any medical treatment?"

"No, that's not his blood," Katie barely managed to say.

"Sir, can you tell me what happened?"

Without looking at the detective, the sheriff spoke of the events in a monotone voice. "I didn't feel very well last night."

"Can you tell me what happened this morning?" the detective gently pushed.

"I felt strange when I went to bed, could barely keep my eyes open. It was like I had taken a sedative."

Katie wanted to interrupt but remained quiet.

"So you're saying that you'd had too much to drink?"

"No," he said. "Didn't feel well during the party." His voice was strangely even and droning.

"Party?" he asked, looking at Katie.

"It was my aunt and uncle's ten-year anniversary party last night," she answered.

"What do you remember next?"

"Claire told me to go to bed and that she would be along soon."

"What time was this?"

"About 12.30 a.m."

"What happened next?"

"I don't know," he said.

"What do you remember? When did you find your wife?" The detective took notes.

"I woke up some time later, groggy. I had fallen asleep in my clothes, so I got up and changed. The clock read 4.57 a.m."

"Was your wife beside you?"

"No."

"What did you do next?"

"I washed my face. Got a drink of water."

The detective patiently waited.

"I saw that Claire hadn't come to bed, so I called her name."

"Did she answer?"

"No. I went out the door and at first I didn't notice the footprints because the hallway was dark. I…" He stopped a moment to catch his breath before continuing. "I called her name again… I walked into the laundry room and switched on the light… and that's when I saw her…" He could barely finish his sentence.

Katie squeezed his arm for support, fighting back the tears.

"What about the knife?" the detective asked.

"I… saw my fighting knife on the floor. I couldn't… didn't understand."

"What did you do?"

"I picked it up, and then realized what I had done, so I carefully set it in the sink."

"Detective Hamilton, do we have to do this right now?" asked Katie.

"We're trying to piece together what happened. You know that it's best that we ask questions right away. Sir, can you answer a few more?"

The sheriff nodded.

"Did you notice if you left anything unlocked or open last night? Could there have been anyone left in the house from the party?"

"No, I don't think so."

"I can confirm that. When I came over this morning, everything was locked," Katie said.

"Is there anyone who would want to hurt Mrs. Scott?"

"No, everyone loved her."

"What about you, Sheriff? Have you received any threats lately?"

"Not that I know of."

"Any case you worked on, a perp you put away, or someone in the political arena?"

"Well… sure… I guess… anyone in my position would have people who resent them…"

"Detective Paul Patton crashed the party and had words with my uncle," said Katie.

"Patton?" the detective asked.

"Yes, he's been retired for about four years," the sheriff explained. "He was complacent during his last years on the job and his wife died suddenly. He complained about some of his last investigations because I took him off the cases."

"I see," said the detective as he made notes. "I'll be speaking with him as well."

Katie watched as the undersheriff appeared on the property outside and began speaking with some of the police officers—he wasn't happy and appeared to have some heavy words with the deputies as well as John.

McGaven burst through the front door and ignored the deputy who was supposed to log in everyone who entered the crime scene area. "Katie, sir," he said but was unable to express any further words.

"Deputy McGaven, could you please take Detective Scott outside? I'll be out shortly to ask her a few questions," said Detective Hamilton.

"C'mon," said McGaven.

Katie hesitated, not wanting to leave her uncle's side.

"It's okay," her uncle assured her. The look on his face was heart-wrenching as she walked away.

*

Katie sat down on one of the benches on the patio. The sun had broken through the morning clouds but even the warmth and fragrance of the flowers didn't make her feel any better. She held her tears back, afraid if she started crying again, she would never stop.

McGaven sat next to her. "I don't know what to say, Katie. I'm so sorry from the bottom of my heart."

"Thanks, McGaven. It's been a nightmare—I saw… I saw her body. It was the worst I've seen… even on the battlefield." She looked away.

"Whatever you and the sheriff need, I'm here, and Denise too. *Anything* you need."

Katie couldn't respond and kept her eyes on the ground.

McGaven squeezed her hand. "I'm not kidding. Anything you need. We can stay with you, take care of Cisco, or just be there if you don't want to be alone. Okay?" he said.

Katie looked up at him. She did feel lucky that she had a great partner and friend. "Yeah, I'm not sure what's going on yet. Or what my uncle will need." Her voice was raspy.

She looked inside and saw John examining and photographing her uncle's display cabinet and the space where the Spanish fighting knife should have been. She pictured in her mind the bloody antique in the sink, blood swirling down the drain. Katie knew without a shadow of a doubt that her uncle didn't commit this horrific crime.

"Detective Scott," said Hamilton.

"Please, call me Katie."

He nodded. "I just have a few questions for you, but I may have more later on. You up for it?"

"Of course." Her voice was weak.

McGaven remained quiet and acted as a friendly support during the interrogation.

"What time did you leave the party last night?" the detective asked.

"Around 11.15 p.m., maybe 11.20 p.m."

"How many people were still here—approximately."

"I don't know. Maybe twenty people. There were a few more outside."

"Did you hear what was said between your uncle and Detective Patton?"

"Everybody did. He said something to the effect 'we all know the truth'."

"Did you notice anyone paying exceptionally close attention to your aunt? Did you notice or hear her maybe have words with anyone?"

"No, nothing like that. It was a celebration. Everyone was having a great time."

Detective Hamilton made a few more notes. "Would you happen to know where your aunt kept the guest list?"

"I… don't…" Katie began. "Oh wait, she uses—used—that table in the corner of the living room as a desk. That would be the best place to find her guest list and anything else you might need."

"What time did you arrive here this morning?"

"A few minutes before 7.00 a.m."

"And why was that?"

"We have this tradition that after family events, like holidays and parties, the next morning we would go for a run and then have breakfast together." Katie grew weary as she tried to see what was going on with her uncle inside the house.

"I think that's enough for now."

"Okay," she said as she stood up, noticing that her legs were shaking.

All three of them looked up at the sound of loud voices and movement coming from the living room. Moments later, the undersheriff and one of the lieutenants were leading Katie's uncle out of the house in handcuffs.

"Why are they arresting him?" said Katie, trying to push through to help her uncle.

"Wait, it's just protocol right now," Hamilton said and blocked her path. "They'll release him shortly I'm sure. We'll call you directly to let you know what you need to do."

"This is ridiculous. My uncle didn't kill his wife." She looked at the detective. "You're crazy if you think he did!"

Detective Hamilton paused a moment, choosing his words carefully. "What I think doesn't matter at this moment. I need to get all the facts and evidence first. I'll be in touch."

CHAPTER 12

Sunday 1430 hours

Katie sat on the couch with her legs drawn up and Cisco glued to her side. The dog wasn't going to leave her no matter the circumstances—it was obvious he sensed her deep grief and sadness.

McGaven pottered in the kitchen, trying to put together something for Katie to eat, but she wasn't hungry. She still couldn't get the image of her aunt's body and her uncle being carted off to jail out of her mind—an agonizing loop of endless images running through her mind.

She wanted more than anything to work the crime scene. If they didn't find a viable suspect immediately, all the evidence would land back on her uncle.

"C'mon, Katie, you need to eat," said McGaven. "You've had my eggs before and I've improved them."

"No thanks. Maybe some tea would be nice."

Cisco pushed his long nose against her hand, demanding to be scratched behind the ears.

"Don't you have to report for your shift?" she asked.

"Not until later, the sergeant understands." He began shuffling things to plug in the kettle. Opening the cabinet, he said, "What kind of tea?"

"Anything that doesn't have caffeine, I guess."

A car drove up the driveway and the engine turned off. Cisco jumped to his feet and began barking, high-pitched to indicate that he knew the person.

McGaven went to the door and was greeted by Chad dressed in his uniform of navy pants and shirt with his surname, Ferguson, on the front. "Hey, McGaven," he said in passing as he rushed inside to Katie. Without saying another word, he hugged her tight.

"I'm so sorry. I didn't hear until later. We were in training exercises all morning," he said. Looking at Katie, "Why didn't you call me?" he said softly.

"I had to stay at the house for a while with my uncle, and then they forced me to go home. I'm sorry. I was going to call you later. I wasn't really thinking."

"It's okay," he said. "I'm still in shock. When I heard, I kept thinking *why?*"

McGaven brought the tea to Katie.

"Thank you," she said.

"What can I do?" Chad asked.

"Nothing really. I don't know what they are going to do with my uncle."

McGaven and Chad stayed around for another hour fussing over Katie and talking shop in hushed voices.

"You know," Katie said, "I think I'm going to take a nap. You guys don't need to be here. McGaven, you need to get ready for work. And Chad, I'll call you in a couple of hours, okay?"

"Are you sure?" he said. "I don't mind hanging out."

"No, I'm just going to sleep."

Hesitantly, Chad and McGaven finally left. She waited to hear their cars back down the driveway and leave, looked at her watch and then got up from the couch. She figured that John had had plenty of time to document and process the scene by now. She needed to get over to her uncle's house and see if she could find out something that would point to another person—something that John and Hamilton might have missed.

She opened a small drawer from the end table and retrieved the spare key to her uncle's house.

Cisco circled around her, feeling her energy.

"C'mon, Cisco, I may need your help."

As Katie reached her uncle's house, she found the gates closed with yellow crime scene tape draped across them. She punched in the four digit code and drove up the driveway. Instead of parking in her usual location, she opted to pull up towards the back of the house where her car wouldn't be spotted by patrol, or anyone else that happened to come by.

Katie opened her car door and got out; she decided to leave Cisco in the passenger seat until she needed him. Her cell phone buzzed. It was a text from Nick, her ex-army sergeant, who had moved to the area after she had located his brother for him. It was nice having him about an hour away. They shared a bond that no one else understood, but they had seen more, lost more, and both suffered from PTSD.

His text said:

I heard. Call me when you're ready.

It made her smile. If anyone knew and understood what she was going through at that exact moment—it was Nick. She really wanted to see him, but it would have to wait.

Katie didn't want to go and see the crime scene again, but she knew it was the only way that she could help in the case. The longer the investigation lasted, the less opportunities she would have. It was now, or never. She slipped on a pair of non-latex gloves and paper protectors over her running shoes. No matter what she did, she definitely didn't want to contaminate the scene.

Standing on the patio, she closed her eyes and opened all her senses. She wanted to calm her racing heart and focus on her search as if it was just another crime scene. She used this technique often when she was going into battle or on special searches with Cisco. It facilitated any important search to dump useless stuff carried with us every day and to focus on one task. If she thought too much about her aunt, she would fall apart. That wasn't going to help anyone.

Her attention caught the sound of the small chirping of the sparrows throughout the garden. There was barely any wind through the backyard and the fragrances of the blooming flowers from last night were lighter now than they had been at the party.

She opened her eyes after a couple of minutes, immediately noticing that the patio had been swept recently—she wondered if it had been last night, or after the crime scene team had traipsed all around the house.

There were four possible entries into the house besides the front door. Two sets of French doors, a back door from the laundry room, and a side door into the garage. The most obvious route would be the laundry room outer door.

Looking around carefully and listening for anyone approaching the driveway, Katie walked to the laundry room entrance. She knew that John was thorough in his searches, but she wanted to familiarize herself with the scene because she knew that Detective Hamilton wasn't going to let her read over any of his report.

The entrance was what some people would consider a mud room—where you could enter your house if you were dirty from some outdoor activity. You could simply step into the laundry room, shed your clothes, and either wash them or soak them in the sink without bringing mess into the house. Two empty turquoise pots stood sentry on each side of the door on a narrow cement walkway that ran all the way around the house and ended at the door entering into the garage. Someone could have easily entered the house from here.

Katie looked up along the eaves to find a security camera directed from the garage toward the driveway. She knew that her uncle felt safe in his home and wasn't consistent about setting the cameras or the alarm. It had been part of the house when he purchased it a little over nine years ago, and, most likely, it hadn't been updated or switched on—but she would check.

She walked slowly along the path; nothing appeared out of place and there were no markers indicating John had found evidence here. At the laundry room door, she inserted the key and opened the door. Waiting a moment just in case the alarm sounded.

In full daylight, the blood had dried to a darker color making it appear more like paint or some type of oil. At least that was what Katie tried to make herself believe. She entered, leaving the door open behind her in case Cisco began barking. Zigzagging around the dried bloody patches, Katie moved through the laundry room and headed to the master bedroom, keen to get out of there as quickly as possible.

Everywhere she looked she saw black patches around doorways, on knobs and various items in the bedroom where John had dusted for prints now leaving behind charcoal smudges. As she'd concluded before, there was no blood in the bedroom, near the bed, or in the adjoining bathroom. The bedding had now been removed, including the pillows, and towels and various toiletries had been stripped from the bathroom for forensic testing.

Katie ran through what her uncle had said about waking up and searching for Claire. She stepped back to the bed and where her uncle would have stood up—assuming the left side, where his things littered the nightstand. She turned right toward the bathroom and then looked at the bedroom door.

Remembering what her uncle looked like at the party and how pale he was—she wondered if he had been slipped something to make him feel ill or something that would make him sleep. It was all theory and conjecture until they tested his blood, but she wondered where the glass was that her uncle said he had drunk from—until she remembered that it was probably cleared up by the caterers.

Reluctantly, Katie went back to the laundry room and tried to retrace Claire's last moments of life. She felt a knot in her throat and more than a little dizzy as she opened the washer and found some tablecloths from the party still in there. It made sense that she was up late taking care of some of the cleaning.

Did someone break in, or have a key? Did they already have her uncle's antique knife, or were those slashes done post mortem? Were they still lying in wait to attack again?

Katie imagined that someone had surprised her, that her aunt yelled or screamed, but her uncle was too deeply asleep, possibly from a drug he had been given. So, her aunt ran to the bedroom door to alert him. By the amount of blood on the bedroom door, the floor, and around the baseboards, Katie assumed that this was where the attack first occurred. But her aunt still had enough strength to run back down the hallway to the laundry room—evident by her bloody footprints.

Once back at the laundry room, Katie closed the door and saw there were more bloody smudges on the doorknob and around the cupboard doors. Her aunt must've tried to barricade herself in there, but it didn't work. The person fought their way in and finished the job—an obvious overkill.

Katie took a few more minutes to search around the washer and dryer in case there was anything that had been missed or kicked underneath. There was nothing. Frustrated and feeling even more defeated, Katie searched down the wall on the other side of the outside door. There were two heavy hooks where you could hang a coat or an umbrella. On the floor, just barely past the backside of the washer, was a piece of partially unraveled thread about two inches long—it looked to be a heavy piece of threading from clothing, something that was heavyweight like an outdoor jacket or a rugged shirt. Katie picked it up. It could have been a clue or it could have been lying there for two years. She knew that her aunt was extremely clean and had a precise schedule when she did heavier housework, like windows, baseboards, cleaning behind furniture and appliances. It was unlikely that she would have missed the thread.

Katie had an idea. There was nothing more that she could do inside the house, so she exited the laundry room and made sure it was locked securely. Jogging back to her Jeep, she opened the passenger door and Cisco jumped out, circling around her and stretching his legs.

"Sorry, buddy, for leaving you, but you have to do me a favor," she said.

Cisco's ears perked and he kept his eager eyes fixed on Katie.

She had done some trailing and tracking with him, so he knew how to follow the trail. Kneeling down in front of the dog, she presented the twine in front of him. Curiously, he sniffed the piece. His snort indicated he'd picked up a scent. Standing back up, Katie gave the command to search, "*Such.*"

Cisco gave a pleasant bark, performed a partial spin and took off towards the backyard. There was no way of knowing if he would find anything, but it was worth a shot so she followed him along the cement pathway.

Cisco's demeanor changed when he was on the trail of something. Head down, tail down, nose grazing the ground, he had picked up a definite scent. There was no distracting him—the stiffness in his body was evident. He was going to find whatever it was he was supposed to find.

Katie jogged behind him as they made the turn around the house and headed toward a coiled hose on the ground. The dog began to dig at the hose and then he sat for Katie, panting—waiting for her.

"Good boy," she said, patting him on the side.

Katie carefully moved the hose and didn't see anything initially—until she saw a small piece of blue fabric about an inch and half long and quarter inch wide. It seemed an odd place for it—but Cisco had picked up on a similar scent.

At first, Katie thought it was a piece out of a pair of blue jeans or denim shirt, but it was much thicker and denser. Standing up, she saw a slightly bent nail sticking out of the siding about three and half feet from the ground, though she wasn't sure what it was for, possibly part of a decoration. Looking closely, she discovered that there were light blue threads caught on the nail similar to the section under the hose. She slipped off her paper evidence booties.

"Good boy, Cisco," she said again.

The dog stood up and began barking, blocking Katie from moving from her position.

"What are you doing here?" said the voice.

CHAPTER 13

Sunday 1545 hours

Katie turned around, startled by the man's voice. She was relieved when she saw who it was, but still kept her composure as she slipped the two pieces of potential evidence along with her gloves into her back pocket.

"Katie, what are you doing here?" John said again. His expression didn't seem to indicate that he was surprised to see her there, just the need to ask.

"I came back to see if I could find anything," she said, matter of fact.

"Like what?"

"Something that would completely prove that my uncle isn't a killer," she said, trying hard not to make her voice waver when she thought about her aunt.

"I see. And?" He moved closer to her.

"I haven't found anything." She instinctively moved a little bit away from him. There was something about him that she could never quite pinpoint, but she felt a strange gravitational pull towards him whenever he was nearby.

"Are you sure about that?" he said.

"Of course."

"What do you think happened here?"

Katie wasn't sure if she should spill the beans and tell him what she thought had transpired in the house. She was about to say something, but then decided against it. Finally she said, "What are you doing back here?"

"I left behind some buckets in front that I had unloaded and didn't use. I saw your Jeep."

"Oh."

"Look, I can't imagine how you must be feeling right now. I wish there was something that I could do to take the edge off of what you've been through today. Some words of wisdom. But I'm just deeply sorry."

Cisco lost interest in the conversation and trotted around looking for something more interesting to sniff.

"Thank you. I appreciate that, but we need to find out who did this… and why."

John for the first time averted his gaze from her.

"What? What's wrong?" she asked.

"I'm not going to lie to you, but all the evidence seems to point to…"

"To my uncle—I figured that. But what would his motive be?" Katie kept her emotions in check, but turned to make her way back to the Jeep.

"You have to let everyone do their job," he said gently. "No one wants to railroad him. It's clear that he didn't do it, at least in my opinion, but that's not how things work. You know that."

She knew that John was right, but it still stung when he said it. The thought of losing what remained of the last of her family made her physically ill. She wasn't going to let that happen—no matter what.

"Katie," he said but she didn't slow down. "Katie, wait. Can you wait a second," he said and gently touched her arm.

She turned to face him.

"Look, I know there's nothing that I can do to stop you from investigating, but no one is going to hear it from me. Understand?"

She nodded.

"I may not have known you that long, but I do know that you'll never rest until you find out who murdered your aunt—no matter what happens."

Katie steadied herself and took a breath. "I… I will do what I have to. John, he's my only family. I can't let it go down like this without a fight." Her voice caught in her throat.

"I know," he said softly.

"I would never ask you to do anything against department rules."

"You don't have to ask," he said.

"What do you mean?"

"You need *anything*, I will help you," he said.

Katie knew that he meant what he said and he wasn't going to interrogate her to find out what she had been doing. She looked down.

"I mean it, Katie. I will not tell you again."

She regarded him for a moment and thought about how good a leader he must've been as a Seal. He returned her gaze. Finally visually breaking away, she said, "C'mon, Cisco, let's go."

The dog obediently jumped in to the Jeep and waited.

Katie looked back at John again and gave a faint smile and an affirmative nod before she got back into her vehicle and drove away.

CHAPTER 14

Monday 0755 hours

An emergency meeting was called into play first thing in the morning. Katie knew that it was coming, but was surprised that she had received a phone call from the assistant to the undersheriff telling her to attend that special meeting at 8 a.m. sharp. It wasn't a request—it was an order.

Katie sat in the sheriff's office waiting for everyone to arrive. She couldn't help but notice that Undersheriff Martinez had already moved her uncle's things from the desk, including his personal photographs, which were now neatly stacked in the corner. *That didn't take him long*, she thought.

At a few minutes to the hour, people started arriving—some she knew would be there—but others were a bit of a surprise. It seemed that there was some type of investigation going on with someone from internal affairs. Only two participants acknowledged Katie's presence and that was McGaven and John. Detective Hamilton, Lieutenant Moss from internal affairs, and Deputies Henderson and Gates wouldn't look her in the eye, and Martinez was no less than frosty towards her. Had they already convicted the sheriff in their minds? McGaven sat next to her and gave her a reassuring look she knew well from working with him for the past six months.

As they all packed in close together, the undersheriff gave stern instructions to the secretary that under no circumstances should they be interrupted. "Well, it looks like everyone is here.

Let's get started," he said, visibly carrying his stress in his jaw and hunched shoulders.

Everyone remained quiet, their collective opinions and feelings wrapped into one giant problem. Now they all sat together wondering what was going to happen next.

"As all of you know, we are dealing with a tragic incident and murder that doesn't look like it will be resolved immediately." Katie wanted to scream, but was forced to sit quietly and let this man make her uncle out to be a killer. "We've all taken a hit when one of our own falls victim to such a tragedy—under these unfortunate circumstances I will be standing in as sheriff. We have to stick together and move through this trying time with professionalism and with teamwork. I wanted all of you together so you could hear what I had to say to each one of you. Detective Hamilton, you're heading this homicide investigation of Claire Scott."

Katie twitched at the mention of her aunt's name.

"I expect the same hard work and doggedness in this investigation as in any homicide—no matter what the outcome. We have to prepare for the worst and hope for the best."

No way did he just say that.

"Yes, sir," Hamilton said and nodded that he fully understood what was at stake. He glanced to Katie with a stern look, as if to say, *don't screw up my case.*

"I don't have to tell you that the media are out in full force and they are just getting started. I do not want anyone speaking to the press or relaying any information to anyone outside this office— no family members, no wives, no buddies at the bar—no one. I hope I make myself crystal clear."

There was still a stilted silence, but most nodded in agreement.

"Deputy Henderson, since you've handled many press conferences in the past, I want you to coordinate with me on details. And Deputy Gates, since you were the first to arrive at the homicide at Sheriff Scott's home, you have a particularly important job. I would like for you to coordinate all of our tips and hotline information regarding this case…"

Is this guy for real?

"Everything pertaining to this case will be updated daily to me and to Lieutenant Moss in IA. Of course, I will keep the mayor up to date as well," he said.

A couple of the officers made notes. Martinez turned to John, who remained still and seemed to be taking in everything that was being said. "John, you don't know how important your job is to this case."

"I have an idea," John said.

Ignoring his trivial remark, Martinez continued, "This homicide takes priority and everything—I mean *everything* collected from that crime scene needs to be tested. Care and skill need to be the objective."

"Of course," John said. Katie tried to read him but he kept a poker face to everyone in the room.

"Deputy McGaven, I realize that you've been given a special work schedule and I don't want to change such things now. So continue to work your half-time patrol, and half-time cold case unit."

"Yes, sir," McGaven replied.

"Some things will be discussed and most likely changed in the future, but for now that schedule will remain the same."

Katie tensed when he said *changed in the future*—red flag number one.

Did that mean the cold case unit would be disbanded?

It looked as if Martinez was done with his orders and he was going to dismiss everyone, but he dramatically paused and then focused on Katie. "Ms. Scott," he addressed.

Katie immediately noticed that he didn't address her as detective—red flag number two…

"I want to give you my sincere condolences for your aunt. I know that this must be an incredibly difficult time for you," he said.

Katie thought the words were nice, but the intent behind them was different altogether.

"It is completely within your right to take some time off."

"That won't be necessary," she said. "I'd like to get back to the case I was working on." She was proud of her resolve that her voice was strong and didn't crack.

Martinez scrutinized her for a moment, as if he was deciding if she was just telling him what he wanted to hear—or not. "I want to impress that it will not be held against you if you need bereavement time."

"Thank you. I appreciate that, but I want to stay busy and productive," she said.

He raised his chin and studied her again. "Of course, I've been fully updated on the case you're working on." He looked around the room. "Any questions?"

A long quiet pause fell over the room.

"Well then, you're all dismissed."

Everyone rose from their seats, and Katie tried to exit as fast as she could.

"Oh, Ms. Scott, not you."

Here we go…

McGaven hesitated and whispered to Katie, "I'll wait for you outside."

She nodded.

Turning to Martinez, she waited as the room emptied.

"Take a seat," he said.

"No thanks, I'll stand if that's okay."

Martinez didn't seem to care, but he had something to say and didn't want the rest of the group privy to his comments.

Katie waited and maintained her relative calm.

"Ms. Scott," he said.

There it was again…

"I wasn't for the creation of an official cold case unit. I felt that it could be handled within the detective division on a rotation basis, but Sheriff Scott adamantly expressed that you would be the perfect person to head it," he said and leaned on the corner of the desk. "Okay, I can live with that. And I can live with the fact that you're using our resources to work an ex-military dog at our K9 training facilities. But what I can't, and won't, sit back and take is the blatant disregard for direct orders, protocol, and proper investigative procedures, such as with the Payton and Compton cases."

"I see," said Katie, trying not to allow her sarcasm to seep into her words.

"No, I don't think you do see," he said. "I'm in charge now, for how long depends upon the investigation." He stood and took a step toward Katie. "I would suggest that you don't step out of line—because I would hate to see you demoted all the way back to a patrol officer or front desk duty."

She gulped back her response, careful not to step out of line.

"I know how impetuous you are and I know how much you want to be involved in your aunt's homicide case—but I warn you—don't do it. Understand?"

"Yes, sir," she said, never wavering her tone or averting her gaze.

He waited another dramatic pause before he said, "Great. As long as we understand each other. Just investigate your cold case and report back to us. You're dismissed."

CHAPTER 15

Monday 0930 hours

Katie didn't immediately return to her office, even though she knew McGaven was waiting for her. Instead, she decided to take a fifteen-minute walk around the police compound and over to the K9 training area to let off some steam and regain her objectivity and focus. She walked at a comfortable pace taking deep breaths until she felt better. The tightness in her chest lessened. The dryness of her tongue and the inside of her mouth receded. Her surefooted pace helped switch her back to cold case mode and put her uncle out of the scenario—at least for a few hours. There was nothing that she could do for him at the moment, except to be strong, so there was no reason to agonize and stress about it. By the end of the day, she should hear where her uncle was going to be sleeping—home or jail.

As Katie returned to the sheriff's office building, her attitude had improved and her face felt flushed like she had gone on a five-mile run. By the time she buzzed herself into the forensic basement, she felt back to normal—or as close as possible.

The examination areas were deserted, and that was fine with her. She made her way to her office and found McGaven already digging into the information highway trying to get some more new leads for the Stiles case.

"Hi," Katie said.

McGaven looked up and studied her for a moment. "You okay?"

"As good as I can be."

"What did he say?"

"Oh you know, the usual: 'Don't step out of line, stay away from your aunt's homicide investigation… or else'."

"Or else?"

"I'm paraphrasing."

McGaven frowned, which was unlike him. "What are you going to do?"

Katie let out a sarcastic laugh. It felt good to relieve some of the pressure—and the deep grief that was going to take a long time to heal. "I'm going to work this cold case and stay out of it."

"No you're not," he said calmly. "I know you're not going to let things go and rely solely on Detective Hamilton's expertise. He's not a bad detective or anything, but I think he's…" McGaven didn't finish his sentence.

"It's okay. I know what you mean." Katie pulled out a file with notes including Patton's notes for his potential novel. There was nothing more she could do about her uncle until the end of the day. She kept telling herself that.

"Katie," he said, "maybe you should take off and go home to rest."

"I can't rest. It's better that I concentrate on something productive—and important. We need to find out what happened to Sam Stiles. Have you found out anything more on Dennis Palmer, both junior and senior?"

"I did a real estate search. The business owns the wrecking yard over on highway 10."

"I don't know where that is," she said.

"You know where that goofy sign is with the guy asking for your old, non-running car?"

"Of course. But that's not called Palmer Wrecking Yard."

"No, it's called…" he reread his notes to get the correct name, "County Recycling and Automotive. That's where the real money is made—not changing someone's oil or doing tune ups."

"Interesting. Does either dad or son own anything else? Businesses or land?"

"Senior owns two small houses on the eastern side of town—both paid for. I'm sure that his son lives in one of them."

Katie studied the maps they had tacked up earlier. "We need to get a larger map, maybe a county one." She thought for a moment. "It would only take someone about ten to fifteen minutes to drive to the wrecking yard from Stiles's apartment."

"Meaning?"

"I'm not sure yet. What about the two employees, Derek Von Der Brennen and Sal Redino?"

"No big deal. Minor offenses. Trespass. Burglary, but no conviction. There doesn't seem to be any violent charges."

"Okay. But that doesn't really mean anything, except they may have not been caught."

"I bet you hate that you can't really begin a criminal profile yet."

"Yes, *but* we can do a victimology of Sam Stiles and create a backward profile of sorts by finding out where he would be the most vulnerable—and when and where he could fall victim to a crime."

"I like it," he said and smiled.

"There's more in my bag of tricks—just stick around to see," she said.

Katie wasn't verbalizing the obvious. One possible theory was that Stiles owed money to the Palmers. They made up the story that Stiles went home sick, got rid of his car through the wrecking yard and buried his body somewhere on the large deserted property. She knew that was just a speculation, but it still niggled in the back of her mind. There were too many documented cases that unfortunately ended this way.

McGaven studied the recycling and automotive area from the aerial maps he was able to bring up on the computer. "This is interesting. Look at how much extra land they have adjacent to the business."

Katie scrutinized the area. "Yeah, I wonder why they don't use it. Or even lease it out. Land is quite expensive in California, even in rural places like that."

"So what do you think?"

"I think it's time we had a chat with the Palmers."

Katie rode silently in the passenger seat. It was easier for her to sit, lost in her own world, while McGaven drove. She paid no attention to the road signs, pedestrians and cars moving about. Her thoughts were focused on who would want to frame her uncle—and the devastating loss of her aunt. The more she thought about it, the more she realized that there were potentially many people who would want to hurt her uncle, or see him jailed.

"I've been thinking too," said McGaven. His voice turned serious, interrupting Katie's thoughts.

She turned and looked at him. "About?"

"Well, it's true that the higher you climb in a professional standing, the more people resent you, even people who had been friends the entire time."

"What are you saying? Are you talking about my uncle?"

"Well yeah. I figured you were trying to figure out who would try and frame your uncle for murder," he said.

Katie was surprised that McGaven could read her that well. In fact, it was a little unnerving.

"What?" he said. "I think I've gotten to know you some—how you think. And I know what I would be trying to do in the same situation."

Katie smiled. They had been through quite a bit together in the short time she had known him. "What do you think?"

"You're forgetting that I was here at the sheriff's department during the entire time that you were in Afghanistan. And, I know a few things."

"Like?"

"Sheriff Scott has been more than an outstanding sheriff. He's one of the guys—meaning that the deputies know that he's looking out for them no matter what. Not all sheriffs are like that anymore." He took a right turn and then stopped at a traffic light. "What that means is there are people who have something against him—for political reasons, jealousy reasons, criminal reasons, you name it."

"Every single person he put away would have a motive," she said.

"Not to mention people who have been passed over for his positions, not just for sheriff; he was a pretty amazing detective."

"I appreciate you thinking about this…"

"Of course, Sheriff Scott is the man."

Katie smiled as best she could. She was torn—also wanting to be strong and hold back the tears.

McGaven slowed the vehicle and pulled into Palmer Auto Repair. There were two cars in the garage stalls and another parked to the far right side of the property.

"Here we go," said Katie as she got out of the car before McGaven cut the engine.

She quickly assessed the area. There were two employees working on the two vehicles—she assumed to be Brennen and Redino. No sign of either Palmer.

McGaven shut the driver's door and followed her.

"Excuse me?" she said.

No one answered. She walked into the automotive stall.

"Excuse me?" she said again.

"Yeah," came a voice from under a hood. "You can check in at the office."

"Okay, thanks."

Katie eyed the tiny office at the right, door open, a small counter adorned with advertisements for motor oil, engine parts, and octane boosters. She saw the back of a balding head of someone shuffling paperwork—and assumed it was the senior Palmer. He was adjusting his glasses and organizing the receipts and invoices.

"Excuse me, Mr. Palmer?" said Katie.

McGaven opted to stay near the work area where he could watch the employees and be within earshot of Katie's conversation.

"That's me—at least, it was when I woke up this morning," he said, still not looking up from his paperwork.

"Mr. Palmer, I'm Detective Scott from the sheriff's department."

He immediately looked at her, studying her badge and holstered weapon. "What can I do for you, Detective?"

"We're looking into the disappearance of Samuel Stiles," she said watching his reaction closely.

"I haven't heard that name in a while. It's been, what, about five years now?"

"We're following up leads and anyone who knew Mr. Stiles."

"He was a great mechanic—meticulously work-ethic oriented. I think he was taking care of his parents. That's not something that is taught at tech school, you know."

"What do you remember about that day—the day he left early?"

Mr. Palmer paused a moment before answering. "It was a Monday, I remember, because Mondays are hectic. There's always a pile of mail and invoices needing reconciling from the weekend. There were more appointments than actual time."

"What do you remember about Mr. Stiles?"

He shook his head. "I don't know. I wasn't paying too much attention to the mechanics that day. The morning was backlogged."

"When he said he was going home—how did he appear to you?"

"I don't know, kinda quiet, I guess. He never had been off sick before—so I couldn't complain. Things happen, you know."

"Did you see him leave? Did he get into his car? Or did someone pick him up?"

"I didn't see him leave. Just assumed he drove his car because it was gone."

"Would you mind if we took a quick look around?" she asked.

"Sure, go ahead. Whatcha looking for? Maybe I can help."

Katie turned away, but not until after she had scanned the small office. There wasn't anything that seemed sketchy or out of place. "No, we just wanted to get a feel for his last day here and possibly which direction he went."

"Help yourself," he said.

Katie watched his movement and pauses in speech, but he seemed genuine. There was no hostility towards her. He didn't have much to say about Stiles, but it was five years ago. Mr. Palmer didn't seem to exhibit certain pauses that might mean he wanted to keep his story straight, and he didn't have averting eye contact to think about how he wanted to answer the question.

She approached McGaven who hadn't moved from his position where he could see everything that was going on around the garage. There really wasn't much to see.

"I want to go around back," she said.

He nodded.

Katie noticed that the two employees were watching them—it wasn't clear if it was just curiosity—or something else. She walked around the side of the building through some overgrown weeds. There was a cleared spot about two-foot square where there was a turned over crate to sit on and a mound of smoked cigarette butts. It was obviously a place where employees took their breaks.

She kept walking. Turning, she didn't see McGaven. He was most likely keeping an eye on the boys working under the hoods.

As she made her way around the back, she found piles of recycled tires and wooden crates, the type that were usually packed underneath larger car parts. She looked closer, but nothing seemed out of the ordinary. Not knowing what she was going to find, if anything, she made sure that she inspected each item carefully. Two large dumpsters were located at the other corner, one for regular recyclables and the other for garbage. The back door led out to an alleyway and the screen door was a heavy-duty metal. But what caught her attention was a large portable storage container—the kind that was normally used at the shipping yards. This one was approximately twenty feet long. She approached the large door, which was locked with a Strong Lock padlock and her mind reeled to the key they found in Stiles's personal things. She touched the padlock and made sure that it was secured and slowly took the key from her pocket. She had taken the key just in case there happened to be an opportunity to see if it fit a particular lock. Carefully she inserted it, but it was clear that it wasn't the right key. That would have been too easy.

"What are you doing here?" a voice demanded.

CHAPTER 16

Monday 1235 hours

Katie slowly turned around as her fingertips brushed by her Glock. The voice behind her didn't sound like anyone she had seen or heard at the auto garage. Her eyes landed on the younger version of Mr. Palmer—it was obviously his son. Where he had materialized from wasn't clear.

"Mr. Palmer?" she said, trying to change the tone of the interaction to civil and not accusatory.

"Yeah, that's right," he snarled. "You a cop?"

"I'm Detective Scott from the sheriff's department."

"What do you want?"

McGaven rounded the building and came up behind Palmer junior, looking, as usual, like a huge roadblock because of his height.

"My partner and I are looking into the disappearance of Samuel Stiles."

He didn't say anything, but was aware that McGaven blocked his exit.

"He worked here for about two years?"

"Yeah, I think that sounds right," he said.

"How much did you know about him?" she asked, knowing instantly that this guy wouldn't give up any information even if he had something to say.

He shrugged at the question.

"We're trying to retrace his steps when he left that day."

"Oh."

"Did you see him leave? Did he drive or did someone pick him up?"

"Dunno. I was working on an engine of a '74 Camaro."

"You seem to have a good memory from five years ago."

"Believe me, if you ever rebuilt an engine you would remember it."

"You wouldn't happen to remember what day of the week it was?" She watched him carefully.

"Yeah, sure."

"And?"

"It was the middle of the week—Wednesday, I think."

"You don't seem so sure."

"Look, I work all the time. Every day blends into the next," he said. "Like now, I need to get to work."

"Of course," Katie replied. "Thank you for your help."

Palmer junior grumbled as he made his way around McGaven who remained silent the entire time.

Katie walked back to the car with McGaven. They didn't speak to one another until they were back inside the vehicle pulling out of the parking area of the garage.

"They were a nice group," said Katie with sarcasm.

"Do you think they're hiding something?"

"Yes, but I'm not so sure it's about Stiles."

"Okay."

"Okay what?" she asked.

"How can you tell?"

"I watched senior closely. There weren't any hesitations, or rehearsed answers."

"Maybe he's a psychopath?"

"Not likely. Even psychopaths have some truth when they are trying to convince you of something." Katie searched her phone for the wrecking yard. She brought up the map and then used the GPS. "Here, let's get a look at the recycling and wrecking yard."

"On it," he said and made travel preparations to head in that direction. "If the Palmers are the owners of the wrecking yard, then why are they both at the auto garage?"

"I was thinking the same thing." She looked in the side mirror and watched a black truck pull out of a driveway and take its place behind them. She could make out just part of the license plate number: XLG_3. "Maybe their names are just for the record and they have nothing to do with the place?"

"There wasn't any mention of it in the original report?"

"Nope," she said, still watching the heavy-duty truck keep an exact distance of two car lengths behind them. When McGaven turned down a road, the truck soon trailed. "Detective Patton didn't seem to mention that."

"Maybe he didn't know?" he suggested.

"No, I would bet on the fact he knew," she said.

"Hmmm."

"Hmmm what?"

"What's that you said recently?" he asked.

"What?"

"The plot thickens?"

"Like a plot that Detective Patton conjured up for one of his novels."

*

The long unpaved road seemed to go on forever as the unmarked police sedan sped along. Katie had to admit she was feeling better—but it was only due to the fact that she was in investigative mode in unchartered territory. She tried to keep the image of her aunt out of her mind, no matter how hard it was. Her weary heart was with her Uncle Wayne; she knew she needed to be well minded enough to be able to help him.

"We passed that stupid sign a while ago," said McGaven.

Katie searched up ahead, straining her eyes to see. "I think we need to get a better vantage. Make a left up there."

McGaven turned up a narrow road and they immediately climbed, but the thoroughfare was in good shape and didn't need a 4-wheel drive vehicle to access it.

"Where's this?" she said surveying the area.

"Not sure. Never been here before."

"Maybe some type of county access."

"Could be."

"Since we don't have a real reason to be on the property—and we don't want to show all our cards at once—let's find a place with some camouflage and see what we can with binoculars," she said.

"And if we find something?"

"Then," she said, "we'll decide if a search warrant is needed or find some other pretext to be looking around there."

"Undercover?" he asked with some enthusiasm.

"Great idea."

"What about Martinez or internal affairs?"

"What about them?" she said with a sour expression.

"If we do anything that deviates from standard protocol during an investigation—in this case a missing person's cold case—we'll get reprimanded. Don't we have to have prior permission?"

"I didn't hear him say that."

"You know they're going to be watching us like hawks—looking for anything to justify taking away the cold case unit."

Katie saw a group of trees that would be perfect for them to park and scope out the property down below. "Not until something big happens with my uncle. But yes, they've already decided they are going to disband it. It's just a matter of when," she said sourly. "Martinez told me specifically that he was against it from the beginning."

"Oh shit. That totally sucks."

"Maybe so, but I'm not going to give up without a fight, for the unit and my uncle." She felt tears begin to well up but pushed them away. Her grief was beginning to take her on a roller coaster ride.

"You have to stop doing that."

"Doing what?"

"Carrying the weight of the world on your shoulders. There are other people who will help you. You're not alone, Katie."

"I don't want to be responsible for someone getting put on leave—or worse—fired."

McGaven pulled in between several trees. They were off the road enough in case someone was to drive by. "Let other people decide what they want to do."

Katie laid her hand on McGaven's arm. "Thank you."

He smiled.

Both officers were out of the car in seconds and McGaven opened the trunk to retrieve a pair of binoculars.

Katie quickly surveyed the immediate area, making sure that there wasn't anything that would hinder their long-distance search of the auto wrecking yard, while McGaven readied himself in prime position. The trees acted as cover camouflage, but the land below was readily visible.

"Okay," began McGaven, "it's not as big as I originally thought. Maybe the Internet maps were wrong or extremely outdated?"

"Why?"

"It appears to be about one quarter of what we saw on the map back at the office. I can see the vacant land next to them. There are defined fence lines and some pretty serious-looking security cameras."

"Cameras? Are you sure that they aren't connected to the wrecking yard because of different types of metals? Some are quite valuable."

McGaven panned back and forth for a few minutes without saying anything. "Wait a minute."

Katie heard his voice change and knew that he had found something.

"I can barely make out the name."

"What?"

"I think it's 'lye'."

"Lye." Katie's mind searched as to why an auto wreckers or salvage yard would use lye. "Would they use it to clean some of the metals? Let me look."

McGaven gave the binoculars to Katie. She quickly brought up the eye pieces to her own eyes, readjusted the focus, and slowly scanned the area. She saw the organized piles of various types of metals that were being recycled. There were areas that had different parts of cars along with entire cars lined up in rows. An area toward the back of the property had several giant piles of tires.

"See what I mean," he said.

"Sodium hydroxide, right?"

"Yeah."

"There's a huge amount of bags—enough to fill a big truck. What are they using it for?" she said.

"That's disturbing."

Katie scanned the area and everything else appeared to belong in an auto salvage yard. As she moved north of the property, she saw what McGaven was talking about with the fence line. It was wire fencing but there were small cameras fixed to the top of the corners.

"Can you see the cameras?" he asked.

"Yeah. It doesn't make sense to have them at that property. Maybe they're going to lease out the land to marijuana growers? There are huge crops popping up everywhere and many business owners are renting the land."

"That's true, but it looks different."

Katie lowered the binoculars and turned to McGaven. "It's weird, but I think we just need to file it under 'not enough information yet'."

McGaven laughed.

"What?"

"I don't know how you do it."

"What are you talking about?" she asked with a little annoyance in her voice.

"How can you juggle all these things right now?"

Katie didn't want to answer that, and she didn't want to think about the obvious things plaguing her.

"You know you're going to have to grieve—you're not super-woman," he pushed, but in a caring way.

"Of course I know that," she snapped. "Sorry. It's just that a weird piece of land with security cameras doesn't bring us any closer to finding out what happened to Sam Stiles."

"No, but it does give us more information about his employ-ers," he said. "And that's a start. This doesn't make sense now, but something will turn up during the investigation that will make sense of this."

Katie walked back to the car. "You know, McGaven, you sometimes make perfect sense," she said, smiling, then she stated, "I'm hungry. And I want to make another stop too."

"Thank you, Mrs. Stiles, for seeing us on such short notice," Katie said. She didn't think she needed more information, but this case was complex and she wanted to find out who Sam Stiles really was.

"Of course, anything that I can do to help," she said.

"Well," Katie began, "I want to get to know Sam a bit better."

"What do you mean, Detective?" Her voice was shakier than before as Katie watched her with curiosity.

Katie spied more than a half dozen prescription bottles lined up on the counter. There was a small pile of western novels along with a neatly gathered bundle of old newspapers.

"It would be really helpful to know more about him, what he was like." Katie forced a smile, glancing at McGaven in the upholstered chair nearby.

"Well, he was always a good boy. He rarely got in trouble and it wasn't ever for anything serious," she said. Then she closed her eyes, as if it helped her to remember fond memories. "He didn't have any siblings; I couldn't have any more children. I had two miscarriages and then it was going to be very dangerous for my health. Anyway, Sammy was used to entertaining himself, playing, watching TV. He was sensitive to others, their feelings. He brought us a lot of joy and now—"

"Mrs. Stiles," Katie interrupted so Mrs. Stiles didn't have to go there. "Do you remember any of his friends?"

"Oh, he had a lot of friends, but as he got older I couldn't tell you their names or anything. He had an incredible appreciation for music. He listened to all kinds of music and wanted to form his own band. I really don't know if…" Her voice wandered.

"Right before he disappeared, did he seem upset or different in any way?"

"I keep thinking about that day."

"Why?" Katie said.

"Well, he had been in an even better mood, very upbeat, almost childlike, as if he had a secret, but it was a wonderful secret."

"Did he say that he had something to tell you?"

"No, but I got the feeling there was something he wanted to share."

"Was he usually up front with you and shared things?"

"Most of the time. He took his duties as a son to heart, making sure Mr. Stiles and I were doing well and we were able to afford our medications. That was very important to him."

"How often did you speak with him?" asked Katie.

"Oh, about three to five times a week."

"Did he ever confide in anything that was bothering him or that he was having some trouble?" Katie was careful not to ask if someone wanted him dead.

"Detective Scott, my Sammy was an open book much like he was when he was a kid. No, he seemed fine, and if anything, he was happier than usual."

CHAPTER 17
Monday 2000 hours

Katie hung up the phone, stunned and swimming in deep sadness. She was trying so hard to hold everything together, to stay strong for her uncle's sake. She took a deep breath. Lawrence Ameretti, her uncle's criminal attorney, who had come highly recommended, had just updated her on the status of his case. Her uncle wasn't coming home today. Intense negotiations were underway and Ameretti assured her that he would do everything he could to get her uncle released with an ankle tracking device. That was all she knew for now.

Katie answered the soft knock at the door at exactly 8 p.m. Nick Haines was right on time as she knew he would be, just as she knew that he would answer her request for help. She would have done the same if the situation was reversed. He gave Katie a big hug. "Oh, Scotty, life isn't fair," he said and then took a step inside. Limping slightly on his prosthetic leg as he entered, he gave Cisco a pat and quick scratch behind the ears before moving into the kitchen and living room to sit down.

Nick had been Katie's sergeant in the army—he was the reason that she made it through the tough and terrible times and became a stronger person. Recently, after his honorable discharge, he had asked Katie to find his estranged brother and now he was mending old family wounds living just outside the county area. He was healing too, both physically and psychologically.

"Thanks for being here," she said and shut the door.

"I knew it was only a matter of time the moment I heard about your aunt," he said with his slight southern drawl.

"I've been thinking about this ever since I found her," she said stiffly not wanting to let her emotions tumble out. "I don't want to get any of my colleagues involved—I know they would, especially McGaven and John. This isn't their fight."

Katie moved to the kitchen counter and took a seat on one of the bar stools. She knew it was easier for Nick to navigate the taller chairs.

Nick took a seat next to her and waited for her to talk.

"I need to shadow the homicide investigation without anyone knowing."

"What's your idea?" he asked.

"I can't do anything that would indicate that I'm investigating this case."

"You need to get into the police database?" he asked. His training and expertise was in IT and he could do just about anything related to computers, software, security systems, and firewalls.

"No. I don't think that it will come down to that. I just need to know what Detective Hamilton is doing—and not doing."

"Sounds easy enough."

Katie had been avoiding his gaze. In the low lighting, it was easy to not see his long prominent scar down his cheek. It gave him a fierceness, a warrior appearance—at least, that was what she initially thought when she had first met him.

"Scotty, spit it out."

"I can't stand this waiting and not knowing if the detective in charge of the case is doing everything possible—and not just building a case around my uncle. I'm trying to stay focused on my case load but I'm having a difficult time sleeping," she said. "I need you to shadow the detective in charge of the case."

"To what level?"

"I want to know everything he knows, or thinks he knows."

Nick leaned back, obviously thinking about what Katie was asking from him. "You know I'm good at these types of things, but I have to tell you, if this detective is any good at his job, he'll start putting together that a guy with a bum leg has been following him."

"I know…" Katie said softly. "But he has no idea who you are; he's never even seen you before."

"Tell you what."

Katie looked at him.

"I'll let this pass—just this once, under the circumstances."

"What?" she said with a smile. As she watched him, she realized how much she had missed him since she had been home. He was a part of her family from another place and time.

"You have a specialized team at your disposal and don't even know it. In fact, I mean a *real* specialized team with amazing attributes."

"What are you talking about?" Her interest was now piqued.

"What I'm talking about," he mimicked in good humor. "You've got me, now that's a given, but you have Jimmy and Nadine too." Katie's sergeant had relocated with his estranged brother Jimmy and his wife, Nadine.

"I can't ask—" Katie didn't finish her sentence because Nick interrupted her.

"You can and you will. Look, you know that Jimmy is an expert in all the F/X stuff with movie makeup and special effects. But, Nadine has been doing insurance investigations and she's amazing at details and dealing with people." He leaned down and petted Cisco who had padded over quietly and rested his head on Nick's good leg.

"Oh," was all that Katie could say. She'd never thought about that.

"Oh?" he laughed. "Scotty, you need to allow others to help. I'm here. I'll always be here when you need me—that's the code we share. But Jimmy and Nadine are just an extension of me—so that makes them within the code too."

"But Nadine has the baby."

"So, that wonderful little bundle, Jessie, has a father and uncle too. We'll just work it out."

Katie didn't answer straight away. She knew he was right; they could be her eyes and ears as she continued to investigate the Stiles case. She didn't want anyone to have any idea that she was following the homicide case or that she had any inside knowledge. She felt that ugly familiar tightness in her throat and chest, and her arms began to tingle.

Nick reached out and took her hand. "Relax, breathe easy," he said.

Katie fought the tears. She felt a mess. No one else had ever seen her physical symptoms of anxiety before, but Nick completely understood them; he suffered his own demons too.

"I'm sorry..." she whispered.

Cisco spun his body round and squeezed next to her, feeling her stress and discomfort.

"You don't have to be sorry. You're safe. You're with friends here—Cisco included, I see," he laughed in spite of himself, trying to lighten the mood. "You can't go this alone—we have to acknowledge and have the awareness of what's triggering these nasty little symptoms."

Katie breathed slowly and began to feel better—and more herself. She knew that she had been carrying an extra huge baggage from the trauma of her aunt's murder.

"There you go... you're getting color back in your cheeks."

"I've never done that before," she said.

"What? Had a panic attack?"

"Not in front of anyone."

"This calls for something to drink."

"What—wine or beer?"

"Well, I was actually thinking of something more calming and healthy, like tea."

"Oh," she said and laughed. "It's funny to hear you say let's have some tea." She laughed again.

"Hey, it's not the manliest drink option, but I'm actually growing to like some of the teas." He sorted through her cabinet and found a box of tea that suited him.

"I like it."

"Scotty, I just knew you would." He plugged in a teapot and prepared cups.

Katie realized how lucky she was having amazing friends from both of her worlds of hometown and army.

Nick sat down again. "You haven't said anything, so I'm going to just jump out there and ask."

Katie waited for the feeling in her weak legs and sweating palms to cease and desist. The anxiety hadn't completely dissipated.

"What's the status on the sheriff?"

"It's complicated," she sighed. "He's not coming home tonight, maybe tomorrow with an ankle tracking device. But he doesn't want to go home. Would you?"

"He should come here to be with you."

"That's what the attorney is trying to do," she said.

"Good. The right thing will happen. Just patience now…" He prepared the tea. "We've got a plan now. Everyone has a part and we're going to get to the truth… I promise."

CHAPTER 18

Tuesday 0845 hours

Katie finished tacking the county street map on the cabinets in the office space then reorganized the rest of the information they had about Samuel Stiles: location of his work, apartment, parents' house, Palmers' houses, and added the auto wrecking yard. She stood back and studied it, but realized that everything appeared disjointed and random.

She exhaled forcefully.

"What's up?" said McGaven as he raised his eyes from the computer he had been so engrossed in.

"This is just a random mess," she said.

"What do you mean? Those are facts. It's a part of our job to find the facts, interpret the facts, and then find the bad guy. Or in this case, find the missing person."

"Thank you for your input," she said sourly.

"Hey, I'm on your side."

"I'm sorry. Didn't sleep well—woke up a million times just to listen to Cisco snoring and enjoying a wonderful doggie dream."

"Would you have slept better having doggie dreams?"

Katie laughed. "Definitely. Wouldn't you?"

She took the photographs that the deputy had taken of the food on the kitchen counter and attached them on the board in a random order. That was it. There was nothing more they could put on their suspect story board.

Katie stepped back. It still didn't bring out any revelation or new lead. She stepped to the whiteboard and began to write a victimology for Stiles. A victimology helped investigations by making a timeline, of sorts, of where and when a victim might expose themselves to becoming a possible crime victim—along with who they were as a person. As simple as it sounded, it could be a helpful tool used by investigators to look at different case scenarios or to move the investigation in another direction.

Auto mechanic (aspiring musician)
Single
Only child
Caring parent: sensitive kid, entertained himself, cared about parents, kept in contact 3–5 times a week. Seemed happier than normal—like he had a good secret.
No indication of drug/alcohol user—none was found in his apartment.
No police record
No pets
Lived alone
Liked to gamble—frequented nearby bar (now closed down) no indication he had gambled there but friendly pool betting
Seemed to be involved with a Natalie Cross (unable to find any information about her) alias?
Letters—from parents just the usual travel letter. The letters from Natalie were light and were written from someone getting to know the other person. There was no indication of who she was, where she lived, or what she did for a living. The return address was an apartment building downtown that she no longer lived in and there was no forwarding address. Dead end. For now.
Photo of Natalie Cross
Padlock key
Antique diamond ring?

"Who are you really, Sam Stiles?" she said staring at her limited list.

"Who, indeed," replied McGaven.

"Only two things that stand out are his gambling and this mystery woman, Natalie Cross—besides that he seemed like a nice and well-liked guy."

"We should keep digging."

"The key we found didn't fit the storage unit at Palmers—but that would have been five years ago and they might've changed the lock since then. And it would have been just too easy. How are you coming with those other storage units?" she said.

"I'm going to make some calls, but I wanted to start with the ones near his usual commutes first." McGaven got up and took some small yellow sticky notes to mark the locations of storage facilities. There were four in the basic area—two were along the driving route he would take every day.

"Okay. It's a long shot. Give them a call. I'm going to read through those letters and take a closer look at Detective Patton's personal notes," she said. "I still don't even know what he had to do with my aunt's murder," she muttered. "What do both cases have to do with each other? Or, is it just a coincidence?"

Katie read through everything she could, finding it difficult to concentrate as she listened to McGaven talk to managers of storage places. The letters from Stiles's apartment were from his parents when they had first met—kept sentimentally, she guessed. There were two letters from Natalie Cross when she was visiting her friends in New York. Nothing insightful, but just updating on what she had been doing on her visit.

McGaven hung up the phone, disappointed. "I knew that would be too easy. No one had ever rented a storage unit under the name Sam Stiles or Samuel Stiles. I know it's been five years, but there could be some type of trail—when he rented, who might have bought the locker, anything."

Katie continued to stare at the evolving wall evidence. "Wait a minute. You said you asked them to search for a unit with the name Sam Stiles, right?"

"Yes."

"Try Natalie Cross."

McGaven picked up the phone and talked to the same people again and found one who said that Natalie Cross had a unit rented in that name, but it was due to be auctioned off that Saturday. "Thank you," he said and hung up. "We got a hit! At the ABC Storage on High Street, locker #H37 rented by a Natalie Cross has gone into default. It was supposed to have been auctioned a month ago, but something got mixed up and it's going to be auctioned *this* Saturday."

Katie grabbed her jacket and cell phone and the padlock key they had found among Stiles's things from his mom's house. "Let's go."

Kate sat quietly in the car, lost in her thoughts about last night's conversation with Nick. In the light of day, she wondered if she was doing the right thing—the best thing for her uncle. The more Katie thought about the sheriff, the heavier her heart felt as she flashed through the worst-case scenarios. She had to mindfully change her thoughts otherwise her anxiety symptoms would flare up with a vengeance, paralyzing her with extreme fear. Rubbing her fingers against her palms, she tried to halt the process.

"It's just up here," McGaven said.

The huge ABC Storage sign was impossible to miss. McGaven eased the vehicle into the main, though small, parking lot in front of the office. The facility was fairly large and covered several acres. There were units with outside access and heavy cement buildings where the interior units were available.

McGaven and Katie entered the office to find a man in his sixties with shaggy grey hair and an equally ragged beard waiting behind the counter. As he saw them approach, he straightened his wire-rimmed glasses, clearly pegging them for cops at first sight.

"Deputy McGaven, I presume," he said.

"Yes, and this is Detective Scott. We're working the missing person's case I spoke about on the phone."

"Ah, nice to meet you both," he said, giving them the once-over, scrutinizing their badges and guns—the guns in particular.

"And you are?" McGaven asked.

"Hugo Martin, I own this place, whether I like it or not. I've got a bit of a staff shortage at the moment so I've been manning the desk most of the time. That's why some of the storage units haven't been auctioned out yet."

"Mr. Martin, may we see the paperwork on the unit for Natalie Cross?" Katie said.

"You can call me Hugo, Detective."

Katie smiled. "Hugo."

"I figured after you called that you'd come in, so I pulled the file and made a photocopy for you." He pulled some paperwork from a drawer behind the counter and handed it to Katie.

"Thank you," she said, running her eyes over the contact information. The emergency contact was Sam Stiles. She turned the paper toward McGaven so he could see. "When was the last payment made?"

"Let's see here," he said as he tapped at the keyboard. "Looks like more than three months ago it was defaulted on."

"How did she pay?"

"She would pay for six months in advance with a credit card."

"Do you have a photocopy of her driver's license?" she asked.

"Yep, give me a sec." He shuffled some papers and then photocopied the woman's driver's license copy for them.

"We have a key," Katie stated.

"Oh, the lock has already been cut off and we put a master lock on it until the auction." He closed up his register, locked the filing cabinet, and shuffled around the counter. "Follow me," he said and made his way out the door.

Katie and McGaven followed the elderly man in silence. Katie couldn't help but think they might be about to make a major break in the case— Natalie Cross hadn't turned up in the original investigation.

They followed Hugo around two buildings until they came to block H. He unlocked the outside door and then propped it open with a large rock. Flipping a switch, the fluorescent bulbs inside flickered to life, one area at a time. The old man continued down the hallway making the first right, and passed three units until he came to #37 on the left side.

"Here we are," he said, opening the large padlock, leaning down and pulling up the door to reveal a half-full unit. Boxes were stacked four high across the entire back wall. In front, a dismantled bed frame, mattress, two night stands, exercise bike, two dilapidated dressers, and several bags filled with artificial flowers.

Katie and McGaven peered inside.

"Leave it like you found it, and if you need to take anything for your investigation, just let me know what it is," said the owner.

"Thank you, Hugo," said Katie.

"Hope y'all find what you're looking for," he said as he walked away, his voice echoing strangely down the cement hallway.

Katie shuddered. It was like walking into a tomb. She wanted to get through the search as quickly as possible.

"Well?" said McGaven. "At least there's not much to look through."

"At least there's that," she said softly.

"You okay?"

"Yeah." She was feeling weak, melancholy; fatigue setting into her body. She wasn't sure why, but it was hard to keep her concentration on the case. She thought back to her conversation with Dr. Carver, and how she'd confessed to loving working as a team—it focused her mind a little. She smiled reassuringly at McGaven, holding up to the weak light the sheet Natalie Cross had filled out when she signed up for a unit. She tried the phone number listed, but it had been disconnected. "Phone number is no good. You weren't able to get anything on her background?"

"No, not yet—didn't have time before we ran over here."

Looking at the date on the sheet, she calculated that it was before Stiles went missing by nearly a month. It seemed strange. Why would she rent this storage unit for her stuff? Was she going to move in with Stiles?

McGaven was hard at work going through drawers in the dressers and nightstands, so Katie headed to the back, squeezing past the exercise bike to get to the boxes. Inside the first she found paperback books, old school papers, craft projects, Christmas ornaments, and a few miscellaneous clothing items. McGaven soon joined her and began searching the boxes from the other end.

After twenty minutes, they'd opened almost every box and found nothing. Until Katie happened upon a thick pack of papers folded in thirds with a rubber band around them slipped down the side of one. They were escrow papers for a house at 412 Garden Lane.

"Hey, here's something," she alerted McGaven. The house had been purchased by Natalie Cross, full price, paid in cash: a two bedroom, twelve hundred square foot home with seventeen acres. There was a page of inspection notes taken before the escrow closed—but didn't match Natalie's signature at the bottom. "What do you make of these notes? The title company and escrow paperwork are the original notarized copy," she said.

"Why would these papers be here, and not at the home?" he said.

"Maybe this was just a temporary holding area? Maybe she was hiding it? For what, I don't know."

"It could be for any reason."

"Hmm… I agree," she said. "It says something about land developing or separate parcels." She read the original paperwork. "Seventeen acres. You could divide that into parcels and make some money." She thought about the vacant part of land at the auto wreckers.

"I don't think there's anything else here," McGaven said.

"I think you're right unless she hid something," she mused.

McGaven looked around and began searching all the furniture more closely, looking for hiding places. Katie took the drawers out of the dressers and flipped them upside down. She reached her hands inside the empty slot and felt something taped on the back. "Got something…" She used her fingernail to scrape the sides and then pulled the envelope out.

"Money?" he said. "Contract?" he guessed.

"No," she said pulling the flap out and slipping the single piece of paper out. "It's… it's a marriage license."

"Let me guess… Natalie Cross and Sam Stiles?"

"Yes. But look at this. They were married the same day he went missing."

"Didn't see that coming."

"We need to get over to the house on Garden Way."

CHAPTER 19

Tuesday 1330 hours

Katie felt a surge of adrenalin as they raced toward the house. McGaven drove faster than usual. Neither spoke as they sped through narrow roads and then took a shortcut on the highway to reach the Garden Way cut off. It was a long rural road with mostly larger parcels of land and older homes—averaging five and ten acre sections.

"Is that it?" Katie asked. She leaned forward, trying to read the dirt-covered sign.

"I think so," he said, slowing his speed.

Most of the mailboxes were large, well-worn and missing numbers. The trees obscured some of the properties and it was difficult to see the houses, which were set back from the road. McGaven pulled the car to the side of the street and parked. They hadn't passed any other vehicles. They were alone.

Katie was first out of the car. Listening and slowly turning, she explored her surroundings; the warm breeze hit her face and the soft sounds rustled through the trees. She hesitated for a moment, taking everything in as if she were on a battlefield. It was clear to her they were getting close to something.

McGaven peered through the fence and trees trying to get a better look at the house. "No car."

"Let's go knock on the door," she said.

Katie led them up an old cement pathway to the gravel driveway which wound around the house. Scattered along the path were pieces of old mail and flyers. Katie unclipped her gun, keeping it lowered but ready. McGaven made eye contact with her and, without saying a word, pulled out his weapon too.

They inched toward the front door, across layers of decomposing leaves that covered the porch, and over a chipped pet food bowl by an old bag of garbage. Katie pushed it gently with her boot. It felt heavy and a foul smell seeped out from within. McGaven's face went pale. Katie pulled out the penknife she always carried with her and carefully sliced the bag several inches, enough to see what the contents were. Holding her breath in anticipation, she watched as typical kitchen garbage tumbled out. Behind the moldy food, which had turned to a dark slushy consistency, and an empty dishwashing detergent bottle, was a severed human hand.

Katie gasped and took a step backward. McGaven with her. It appeared to be a woman's left hand, shriveled and waxy, remnants of pink fingernail polish on the tip of the blackened nails. There was a simple gold wedding band on the ring finger.

"Do you think?..." McGaven said softly.

"Don't know until it's examined," she said. "But... it's most likely hers."

Katie knocked loudly. She opened the flimsy screen door and knocked again on the front door. She tried the doorknob and it was locked. "Go around the house and I'll go around the other way. I'll meet you in the back." She gestured.

McGaven nodded as Katie retraced her steps to peer inside the windows. She couldn't see anything through the thick layer of dirt and grime, so continued back to the driveway, moving with stealth and alertness, taking in everything around her.

She met McGaven at the back door. He shook his head. On the ground near the back door, there were pieces of heavy electrical tape, rope, and a kitchen towel covered with large dark marks.

"Can you see in that window?" she asked McGaven because it was too high for her to see inside and McGaven was taller. Up on his toes, he peered inside for a moment then slowly moved backward. His face told an entire story.

"What?" she asked.

"It's the bedroom," he said. "There's a body on the bed."

Taking two steps backward, she lurched and stomp-kicked the back door, shattering it on the hinges. It cracked, but didn't fully release. She kicked it again and the door opened. Katie rushed over the threshold and was immediately hit with the stench of death. She tried to ignore it. She heard McGaven cough behind her.

There were remnants of severely spoiled food on the kitchen counter and small dining table with some basic white dishes stacked as if waiting to be set for dinner. Katie led the way toward the bedroom as the stench intensified. She covered her mouth and nose with one hand and kept her breathing shallow. She almost tripped over a dead cat on the floor in the hallway, stretched out and bloated like a macabre balloon animal, but she pushed on, knowing a worse sight awaited her in the bedroom.

Lying on the bed were the decomposing remains of a woman wearing a sundress. Both her hands were missing and the side of her skull was caved in. Her body was black and putrefied, the gases and purge fluid all leaked out over time causing the body to collapse. All that was left of her was the pretty dress over fermenting flesh and bone.

"Is it her?" McGaven said. His voice was hoarse but he tried to keep himself professional and focused.

"I can't say for sure, even with the photo on her driver's license. Don't touch anything, but let's walk back through the house."

"The big question," said McGaven, when they were back outside, gulping in fresh air, "is where is Sam Stiles?"

Katie walked farther out into the backyard. She didn't answer right away, gazing out at the large acreage, deep in thought.

Slowly she turned and walked back to McGaven. "He's here," she finally said.

"Here? Where?"

"Removing that woman's hands is a sign. It's a warning. The woman in there hasn't been dead for five years. I'm no medical examiner, but I would guess she's been dead months, not years."

"What about Stiles?"

"I think he *was* killed the day he left."

"So you're saying, let me get this straight, that Stiles and Natalie got married the same day he supposedly disappeared. He was murdered, we don't know why or where his body is, but his new bride was murdered years later."

"Well, yeah, but we don't have all the evidence yet."

McGaven thought about it and looked around the property. "Why kill Natalie? Why leave a calling card by severing her hands?"

"The garbage bag was obviously left by mistake. Why, I cannot figure out."

"So what you're saying, you think someone came here specifically wanting to kill the couple."

"I may be off by a little, but this is what I think happened: Natalie and Stiles got married, low-key, probably at the court house and, for whatever reason—it's easy to check—he didn't show up at the house. Maybe she went on an errand? Maybe Stiles went out to get something for her? I think Stiles met with a violent end—just theorizing he owed the mob money from gambling. Or something like that. But Natalie never knew what happened to him, but stayed here, but again, for some reason, the killers came back and murdered her—it's got the hallmarks of a mob-style hit. I know it sounds a little rattled when I explain it." Katie thought for a moment. "I can't imagine how devastating it must have been for Natalie not knowing—she probably searched for him."

"We really don't know exactly what happened but..." he said.

"But...?" Katie gazed out at the acreage.

"You getting that gut thing again?" he said.

"That brings me back to… I think Sam Stiles is here. It makes sense. No one would ever find him. The couple obviously got married without telling anyone. He's here. The more I think about it—it's the perfect way to get rid of his body. He didn't run off. He's here," she said adamantly.

"Where? Here?" McGaven said.

"No… here," she said and gestured to the large seventeen-acre parcel.

"You know once we call in the police and forensics that they aren't going to search that area," he said.

"Yeah, I know, but they would if we found something that would provoke a search," she said.

"What are you thinking?"

"Bring Cisco to sweep the area, and if there's nothing then no big deal," she said.

Nodding, he said, "I like it. Just to make sure, because when *they* arrive, we're off the case."

"Exactly, and Sam Stiles will never be found."

"It's a gamble."

"It's not a gamble when you're conducting due diligence."

Katie had quickly changed her clothes into casual jeans and T-shirt before she picked up Cisco at the sheriff's department K9 kennels. Her energy heightened Cisco's concentration as he whined and spun in circles on the back seat.

"Easy there, buddy," said McGaven as they returned to the house on Garden Way for the second time that day.

Katie jumped out of the vehicle and hooked up Cisco's long search leash with a padded harness. McGaven watched quietly, keeping a good distance behind them so as not to intermingle his scent with the one she wanted the dog to find.

Cisco was amped, taking in everything around him.

When they walked around the house to the back door Cisco hesitated and backed away slightly, obviously catching the scent of death. But Katie urged him on, directing him to the bloody towel, careful not to touch it, while she encouraged Cisco to catch the scent. Her plan was to allow Cisco to search the large property to find anything connecting the scent on the towels.

Katie decided that they would search the closest areas first. It would be more likely that if someone killed Stiles, they would bury his remains somewhere near to the entrance, to save time.

Katie stepped into the first search area and did a slow three-hundred-sixty-degree turn. There were no houses or barns overlooked from the neighbors. It was a textbook place to bury a body without being seen. Several clusters of trees surrounded the area. It appeared that it would be a perfect spot to grow a garden: flat, lush soil, and lots of sun. She gave Cisco the command to get to work, though she knew from his body language that he was already on to something. Cisco's body tensed, head down, tail down with a slight upward curl at the end. His ears pushed forward and his nose was close to the ground, moving back and forth. German shepherds have a distinct way of searching that is organized and methodical.

Katie kept the dog on a lead about ten feet in front of her, noticing that the soil was soft and sandy, making it difficult to navigate easily. Giving Cisco a bit more lead, Katie wanted to keep him on the same track. They covered the first area and then hurried to the second. She quietly hoped that the dog wasn't tracking a squirrel or fox instead of the scent from the bloody towel.

Katie glanced back and saw McGaven waiting patiently at the entrance of the house, upwind from Cisco's tracks, but watching Katie's back in case there was trouble.

After about fifteen minutes, Katie was about to give Cisco a break and some water when he stopped abruptly and began digging at the soil. She stopped him, commanding "*platz*," to make him get down and stay in his position. She moved closer to the loose dirt as Cisco let out a slight whine to indicate he'd found something of importance. Kneeling down, Katie ran her fingertips through the soil but found nothing. Digging deeper, she paused as something caught the light. She scooped up a handful of dirt, sifting it through her fingers until a shell casing appeared in the palm of her hand. Gold and copper colored with a dark end; it was clearly a .38 shell casing from a gun. Katie kept digging and found two more. She didn't touch them with her hands—not wanting to disturb any evidence.

It was difficult to estimate how long they had been there, but it would be much too close to the road and house for a shooting range or a hunting area. Katie stood up. "Good boy, Cisco," she said and gave him a quick pat. "Found something," she hollered to McGaven.

Jogging over, he said, "What?"

"Looks like .38 shell casings—three of them. I touched one, but left the others for CSI."

"Do you think that Stiles's body is out here—or buried here?"

"Don't know, but I think there's enough evidence now to warrant digging for it," she said. "Let's put in the call—it's time for the three-ring circus. I guess our cold case is hot again and we're going to have to sit this one out."

"You don't know that for sure," he said.

"Oh yeah. The first thing they'll do is tell me to go home."

They walked back to their car and McGaven put in the call for a homicide detective and forensics. All Katie could do was stand there and wait for the sheriff's department to show up—and then helplessly watch as they investigated her crime scene.

CHAPTER 20

Tuesday 2145 hours

Just as Katie predicted, Detective Hamilton was officially assigned to the homicide case and Katie's and McGaven's assistance was no longer needed—they were ordered by Undersheriff Martinez to turn over everything they had on the case before the end of the day.

Katie went home not long after Hamilton and John arrived and got to work. John had suggested that he could use a GPR machine—a ground penetrating radar that could be run on the surface of the ground to see any anomalies underneath—to search for Sam Stiles. He would look out for any disturbance of soil resembling the approximate size of a human body.

Now home curled up on the couch with a quilt, Katie napped and woke several times. She was mentally and physically exhausted, but her mind still kept running all types of scenarios about Samuel Stiles. She tried to read for a while, but nothing held her interest.

"Oh, Cisco, how can you sleep?" She stroked the jet-black shepherd as he snoozed peacefully next to her. "Such a good boy," she whispered.

Her cell phone dinged to alert her to a text message from John:

Found a body—no ID, but fits the basic description of Sam Stiles. Looks like three gunshot wounds—one to the head and two to the chest. Your instincts were spot on.

Katie set the cell phone down. She was pleased but it wasn't her case anymore. The hard work that both she and McGaven had done now belonged on the desk of Detective Hamilton beside her aunt's case. *How much time was he allotting to each?* she wondered.

Her cell phone rang.

"Scott," she said when she saw it was McGaven.

"Hey, I don't know if you heard," he said.

"Stiles's body was found—but not identified officially yet."

"Yeah," he said slowly. "I turned everything we had over to Hamilton about an hour ago."

"Thanks for that."

"Not a problem. What are partners for?" he said trying to sound upbeat. "You okay? You aren't alone, are you?"

"Nope."

"Why don't I believe you?"

"Cisco isn't nobody."

"If you're up for company, Denise and I can come over. We could watch a movie—I'd even agree to a romance."

Katie smiled. It was a nice invitation, but she wasn't up for company. "Thank you, but I'm going to bed early to get some sleep."

"That's probably the best idea. Then it's back to the drawing board with a new case."

Katie didn't say anything—she wanted to finish the case she had started, but it was reassuring that Mrs. Stiles might, at least, have some closure.

"Katie?"

"Yeah."

"All this will work out. You know it will…"

Katie felt tears welling up but she pushed them back. "Thanks, McGaven, I appreciate that."

"You'll see. If you need anything… *anything*… we're there for you."

"Thanks, McGaven." She ended the call.

Katie was sick and tired of feeling miserable and filled with grief. She wanted to move forward to find out who killed her aunt, to free her uncle and make the right person pay. There hadn't been any word from Nick, but that didn't mean anything. It was going to take time, even more now she knew that Detective Hamilton was working the Stiles case, taking precious manpower away from her aunt's homicide.

The clock was ticking.

Her phone rang again. Glancing at the display it wasn't a number she recognized; she answered it.

"Hello?"

"Ms. Scott, this is Lawrence Ameretti."

"Yes, Mr. Ameretti. What can I do for you?"

"I'm sorry for the late hour, but after hours of negotiation, the court has decided that your uncle can be released and put on house arrest until the trial."

Katie breathed a sigh of relief and closed her eyes. "He can come home?"

"He can, but he's adamant that he doesn't want to go to his own home—at least not now—because of where the tragedy took place."

"He can stay with me. I have space and he's comfortable here."

"That's great. I'll have the papers prepared and I need you to come and pick him up from the jail tonight. Someone will be coming to the house with you to fit the ankle device and to set the parameters."

"I'll be there. Thank you, Mr. Ameretti," she said.

"No thank you necessary."

"Has a court date been set?"

"No, not yet."

"That's good news, isn't it?"

"I can't really answer that. The investigation is still underway and things seem to be changing daily."

"I'll see you shortly."

CHAPTER 21

Wednesday 0745 hours

Katie only had a couple hours of sleep, but she was full of energy. After her uncle had arrived home with her last night, she got him settled in the guest room, which had once been her parents' bedroom. It deeply saddened her that her upbeat and take-charge uncle was now just a shell of what he used to be. He barely spoke to her and averted eye contact. It was clear that he was grieving, not only for the loss of his wife, but also the unknown outcome of what would happen to his life.

When she arrived at the sheriff's department it was barely 6.30 in the morning but her office had already been stripped of all signs of their investigation work; the maps were gone with all the folders from the original case and their reports. It was depressing at first glance, but she kept her mind focused on the fact that she had done her job.

She spent all morning seemingly poring over computer searches for their next cold case, when in fact she was actually trawling cases that her uncle had worked that might have resulted in disgruntled defendants and family members that might want to do him harm. It was exhausting, but it felt important to her to be doing something to help him. She was determined to find something that she could use to clear his name—anything.

There were two cases from fourteen years ago involving a drug ring that resulted in numerous complaints and threats. Four suspects had been arrested and spent eight years of their sentenced fifteen. During the penalty phase, one of the defendants had yelled "Detective Wayne Scott, you won't live to see your next birthday." It caused quite the uproar in the courtroom—and the media had a blast reporting on the incident. The convicted man had sliced his finger across his throat as he spoke. Katie wrote down, *Clarence Warner, 57A 2nd Street* along with the case number #WAR27857. Warner had been out of prison for about five years and had had ample time to stalk, study, and plan his murder—his revenge. Katie knew that it was a long shot, but she needed a list of people who would want to see her uncle framed and in prison for life.

She also couldn't ignore the incident with Paul Patton at the anniversary party. Was it just a drunken disagreement, or something deeper? Helpful as he was, something had seemed off when she had visited Patton to interview him about the Sam Stiles case; but to murder a man's wife over a few heated words seemed extreme. Even so, Katie added him to her list.

Looking at the time, she knew that McGaven would be arriving shortly. She put her things away and continued to search for a case to work, preferably one that her uncle had investigated. It would be a perfect cover for her to keep looking for evidence that might prove useful in solving her aunt's murder. Printing a list of the top cases he worked that had gone cold, Katie also grabbed the top two boxes of cold cases that he had originally prioritized for her. Balancing the boxes, Katie used her foot to open the door to find John on the other side, staring at her.

"John," she said. "You startled me. What's up?"

"Here," he said and took the top box from her.

"Thanks." Katie's instincts kicked in—there was something that was bothering John and he was there to talk to her about it.

Katie put the box on her desk and John followed suit. She shut the office door and, turning to John, she said, "Spill it. There's something that you want to say to me."

"You've put me in an uncomfortable position," he said.

Katie knew instantly it must be something about her visit to her uncle's house. Pressure built up in her chest and she felt a lump in her throat.

"Ever since you've been here at the sheriff's office, I've watched you take hold of these cases with such intelligence and tenacity."

Katie waited. Maybe this wasn't going to be as bad as she had thought.

John continued, "I can't imagine how horrific it must've been for you to find your aunt's body and I don't claim to know how it feels. But, you were given instructions, make that orders, by our highest boss to not meddle in this investigation." He clenched his jaw and seemed to hesitate.

Katie nodded. She didn't know where exactly he was going so she kept her mouth shut.

"I knew you were up to something when I ran into you at the house on Monday. I've been swamped with work so I didn't look at the video until this morning."

Katie frowned, looking away from him.

"I saw you and Cisco searching for clues—and finding something. It wasn't clear in the video what it was but you did find something and you kept it to yourself. There were several blank sections due to the re-recordings."

She had never seen John angry—it was a calm controlled anger, but he was mad, nonetheless. "I was just—"

"You were going to step in anywhere, whenever you wanted, with no regard to anyone else doing their job, so you could find evidence that would prove your uncle's innocence, right?"

"Well of course. Do you know what's at stake here?" She shoved the boxes farther on the desk and leaned against it.

"What kind of question is that?" He moved closer to her.

"An important one."

"I'm the only one who has seen the footage."

"And?" she said, waiting for his answer.

"You're lucky that the video didn't reveal anything of importance. Otherwise…"

"Otherwise what?" she challenged.

He shook his head obviously frustrated with her. "I've never met anyone quite as stubborn as you. Don't push this *maverick cop* routine too far. You're still too new to investigations. I see right through you, and at the rate you're going right now you could really damage this case. Is that what you want?"

His words hit Katie like an arrow in the heart. Her pain and grief weighed against her as her worst enemy. "I can't just sit back and do nothing," she managed to say.

John stepped back contemplating his next words. "Why didn't you come clean to me that day at the house?"

"I… I just didn't want to involve anyone—if I'm going to get suspended for doing something stupid, I'm not taking anyone else down with me."

"Noble, but very stupid. You act like you're the only one who cares about the sheriff."

Katie couldn't meet his hard glare as she realized that she had been so focused on the case from her own perspective that she had been selfish.

"Look." He stopped himself. "Where are the two pieces of evidence you collected?"

"I have them in my briefcase."

"What are you going to do with them?" he asked.

"I… I… was going—" The truth was she didn't know what she was going to do with the evidence, but she wanted it analyzed by a private forensic lab.

"Give them to me. I'll take care of it."

"No, I don't want to cause—"

"Too late, I'm already involved."

"But…"

"Do I need to repeat myself?"

Katie picked up her briefcase and slid out two small evidence bags which held the piece of blue fabric and the small pieces of thread. "Here," she said. "Thank you."

"I'll let you know if they are anything relating to the case."

Katie felt like a student who had been reprimanded by the school principle.

"Didn't the military teach you anything about teamwork?" he said and then appeared to lessen his anger. "I'm sorry, but I don't want to see you make a huge mistake and jeopardize your career. We need more detectives like you."

Katie nodded. She couldn't say anything for fear of breaking down and sobbing. Realizing how close she came to risking her aunt's investigation, it made her sick and disgusted with herself.

John gave her one last look before he left.

Moments later McGaven entered. "Hey, what's up with John? He looks like Rambo on the rampage."

Katie laughed softly. "Well, he's pretty pissed at me about my aunt's case…"

"What? Why?" he said.

"Not important. Let's get another case going before someone else gets on *my* case."

McGaven looked like he wanted to say something, but remained quiet.

"Okay," she said, "I've pulled the top two boxes of cases the sheriff recommended." She flipped the lids off and began pulling out file folders and a couple of binders. "I've already looked briefly through the first one, but I haven't looked at the second one. So here you go," she said and slid the pile closer to McGaven.

It was quiet in the office for almost an hour before Katie said anything. She knew that McGaven was giving her space and time, but the quiet was beginning to get to her.

"Okay," she half blurted out.

"You okay?" he said.

"I'm just frustrated. We take on a missing person's case and then we don't have the opportunity to find the killer."

"Well, maybe let's not pick a missing person's case this time."

"Good idea," she said. "I have a list of cases that my uncle worked and I'm cross-referencing them with these cold cases. I'm going to call them off—let me know which ones you have."

"Go," he said.

"Barren, Christopher Leland—homicide."

"No."

"Nicholls, Sarah—homicide."

"No."

"Curtis, Amy—homicide."

"Nope. Why are you reading off homicides that your uncle worked?"

She ignored his question and said, "Andrews, Cynthia Jane—homicide."

He paused, looking through notes. "Cynthia Jane Andrews. Body found tied and staked to a tree Upper Pine Valley."

Katie got up from her chair and leaned over McGaven's shoulder. "How long ago?"

"It was twelve years ago. Investigating detective, actually detectives, were your uncle and Detective Kenneth Teagen."

"Looks from the notes like Teagen had been assigned to the case and my uncle was assigned later."

"Here's a binder from the crime scene," he said as he pulled it out and opened it. He began flipping through pages.

Katie gasped.

"What?"

"It's just…" she managed to say. She turned the pages slowly, showing the details of the damage inflicted on the body of the victim. "It looks similar to…"

"To what?"

"I don't know for sure, but these wounds look similar to the wounds…" She couldn't finish the sentence, remembering.

McGaven studied the photos from the gruesome and violent crime scene closer, as well as those of the body in the morgue after the blood had been cleaned up. The gaping, slashed wounds were nothing less than disturbing.

"Those wounds and the vertical direction look just like my aunt's wounds," she managed to finally say.

CHAPTER 22

Wednesday 1130 hours

Katie walked through the main entrance of the morgue to the office of the Medical Examiner, Dr. Jeffrey Dean. It was the last place that anyone wanted to be during a homicide investigation, and she knew that McGaven struggled with viewing and examining dead bodies more than most.

The closer Katie studied the photographs taken of Cynthia Andrews' body, slashed and bound to a tree, the more she realized that there might, no matter how small, be a connection between hers and Claire's wounds. There was only a copy of a preliminary autopsy report in Cynthia's file, but Dr. Dean would know for sure.

For the first time in days she felt hopeful and McGaven, though skeptical, had agreed to go along with it. She knew she was walking a thin line, but the Andrews case was indeed a cold case—so within her remit to investigate.

A fair-haired middle-aged man wearing a splashy-colored Hawaiian shirt and dark khakis under a white lab coat appeared out of one of the examination rooms. He smiled at once when he saw Katie, his glasses swinging back and forth on the end of a chain around his neck.

"Detective Scott and Deputy McGaven, hello," he said with almost a whimsical note to his voice.

"Dr. Dean, thank you for seeing us on such short notice," she said.

"Of course. I was curious about the case you referred to because it was one of my first cases here. I was a little bit of a newbie. Please," he said, "come this way." He moved quickly through the rooms and bypassed a few other areas by way of the long corridor which led to his personal office.

Katie tried not to look at the bodies being worked on as she passed. Technicians were hard at work weighing each organ with care and recording the results and it was difficult not to stare at the blood spatters on their plastic face masks. McGaven's eyes were glued firmly to the floor.

Dr. Dean reached an office at the end of the hallway and Katie followed him in, surprised at how big the office was. It was tidy and organized like any other—except it was located in a morgue.

"Detectives, have a seat," he said.

"I wasn't completely honest when I talked to you on the phone about the cold case," Katie began.

Dr. Dean gave her a quizzical expression.

"You see…" she began. "I think looking into the Cynthia Andrews homicide might also be able to assist in the recent Claire Scott homicide."

The doctor's face changed. "Oh my, Detective. Please forgive me for my lack of sensitivity. Working here does that to you, I'm afraid. My sincere condolences about your aunt and the terrible predicament of your uncle."

"Thank you. But I need you to understand that I'm here because I think there's some similarity between the wounds inflicted on my aunt and Cynthia Andrews. If I'm right, my uncle is the link between them." She knew that the cases would be considered conflict of interest for her, but she wanted to appeal to the doctor's sense of compassion.

"I can tell you about the Andrews case," he said and opened a file he had waiting on the corner of his desk. "Cause of death: exsanguination, or acute loss of blood. Andrews had lost more than two-thirds of the blood in her system. An unusual long knife, about six inches long, with a slight hook on the end, was the murder weapon. The victim was sliced down each side of her torso and across the sternum. There was also a wound that pierced her upper torso and lungs. From my examination, the stabbing wounds were from the back and came out the front of the body."

"The file said that the murder weapon was never found," she said, still recalling her aunt's wounds.

Dr. Dean said, "We tried to figure out what type of knife, but nothing current fit the dimensions and depth. It was decided that it was most likely an antique weapon."

"Doctor, I have a very important question," she said.

"You know I cannot comment on your aunt's case. It's an active investigation and you're too closely involved."

"Oh," she said and looked down. She had to know, but didn't know of any other way to get her answer unless she bribed a technician.

"I can't comment on it, but *you* can," he said and nodded his head.

Katie understood. She could theorize and he would not verbally agree or deny in response. She said, "*Theoretically*, the slicing on both Andrews' and Scott's bodies seemed to be consistent."

"Theoretically, both wounds on both bodies might be considered consistent," he said.

"And *theoretically*, the weapon that made those slicing wounds seems similar," she said waiting for his answer.

"Theoretically, both wounds, on both bodies, might be considered consistent and caused by the same *type* of weapon—by same I mean, consistent in length, angle, and depth. But of course that would only be theoretically speaking." He smiled and nodded.

Katie stood up. It was all that she needed to hear, and she had her first solid lead.

"Was there anything else, Detective Scott?" he said.

"No, that was all. Thank you so much for your time."

"Anytime."

Katie rushed out of the morgue and hurried through the parking lot to get back to the forensic unit.

McGaven caught up with her and stopped her in her path. "Wait a minute."

"What?" she said.

"Katie, what's going on? You really think that the killer from twelve years ago is the same person who killed your aunt? I followed your lead because you've always been smart and methodical. Don't you see how far-fetched this sounds?"

"Don't you think I know that?"

"This isn't the right way to go about it."

"The medical examiner said that the wounds and type of weapon were similar," she said. "I'll take that."

"Similar, Katie. Not a slam dunk."

"I can't go backwards now. Let's go ahead and see what shakes out," she said. It was clear that she was losing McGaven and he didn't see eye to eye with her. "It's our job to investigate the Andrews cold case, right?"

McGaven sighed and nodded in agreement. "Of course."

"We need to talk with friends and family. Also, the retired detective Teagen, and my uncle. *Right?*"

"Yes."

"We'll work the case from the beginning, just like we always do—and if it happens to give us a lead in my aunt's murder, then that's two birds with one stone."

"Fine."

Katie could see that McGaven was still hesitant, but she could work with that.

CHAPTER 23
Wednesday 1515 hours

Katie was edgy and filled with nervous energy, which made it difficult to concentrate on the investigation. She knew that McGaven was right and they didn't need to jump to conclusions, but she was impatient—and deeply concerned about her uncle. He was unable to express his feelings and it seemed that he was sinking deeper into a depression.

Taking a step back, she assessed everything and began at the beginning. She reread the file overview for Cynthia Andrews to get a better understanding of the case:

Bio: Cynthia Jane Andrews, twenty-nine years old, single, working on a Ph.D. in Environmental Biology at UC Sacramento, and as an assistant to a botanist at the local college. The interdisciplinary field of environmental biology focuses on the relationships among plants, animals and their surroundings, including their responses to environmental stimuli. She wrote papers, articles, and blog postings about how important the wildlife was to the environment and a sustainable future—and how everything interacted with their surroundings. Her goal was to educate people on certain flowers, shrubs, and native wildlife. She was especially concerned with California shrubs and flora.

In the weeks leading up to her murder, she was researching for a paper about the elusive, some believe extinct, yellow flowered plant—King's Gold. She packed up food and water along with her camera, cell phone, and notebook to hike to the location where the plant grew, and she planned to camp there for several days—alone.

Background: Friends and colleagues of Andrews became worried when she didn't answer her cell phone and didn't come home after a week. With growing concern, family called the state parks and requested a ranger look for her. A park ranger, Rob Stein, found her camp in a state of disarray, and he found her body tied to a nearby tree.

Why would someone murder a budding young scientist? She flipped through the photos again and studied where the body had been located, the extent of the wounds, and the victim's background. It didn't add up. Katie knew that many killers wanted to display their victims in a shocking way just to taunt the police; but in this case, with the victim almost hidden, it wasn't clear why. And the report described how the tent had been intentionally torn—possibly with a knife. The same type of knife?

Katie skimmed through a number of reports from friends, family, and colleagues until they all started to sound the same. No one had a clue why someone would want to murder this sweet, intelligent nature-lover. She had no known rivals, didn't consort with unsavory types, didn't drink or do drugs; she was a shy workaholic by all accounts. She didn't even have time for romance; she was focused on finishing her Ph.D.

Leaning back, Katie glanced at their now stripped-back crime scene board and knew they were going to have to start all over again.

"Okay," said McGaven sounding tired, "we have an appointment with Dr. Brandon Wills tomorrow at UC Sacramento. Wills was her friend and lab partner—they had known each other since they were in high school. He might be able to shed some light on things."

"Yeah, I read his statement. I don't think he'll be able to give us much, especially now that more than ten years have passed," she said.

"Well?" he said.

Katie could still detect some frustration from her partner. "Well, what?"

"I thought you'd have a profile by now, or at least a victimology."

"Well the victimology wouldn't be much. All we know about her was that she went camping."

"Why would she go alone?" he said.

"You're right. You'd think there would be a group of them, or at least another person."

"This is going to be a tough case. Especially given your uncle couldn't solve it."

"Yeah, I'll have to ask him about it." She got up from her chair and began writing a preliminary profile. "So this is what we have so far about our killer."

Killer knew the woods and remote areas well enough to hike to the camping location and to find a suitable place to pose the body.
It appeared that the killer hunted Andrews down—crime was not opportunistic or crime of passion.
It appeared that Andrews tried to escape and run. Two sets of footprints—one size seven (victim, no shoes) and one size twelve (heavy hiking boot).
Wounds were overkill and severe.
Hooked knife used—specialty, hunting, fighting, antique?
Weapon not found.
Nothing was stolen—wallet, cell phone, binoculars, infrared binoculars, and personal items still at scene. Victim's car, Toyota SUV, was still parked in the parking area—nothing appeared missing or interfered with according to forensics.

Katie stepped back. "That's a slim profile."

"You have to start somewhere," McGaven said, sounding more like his usual self. "How long does it take to get to the area where she camped?"

Katie opened an expanding file where there was a map of the county. Her uncle or his partner had marked the camp area as well as two different routes to the campsite. "Interesting. It's an area that I've never been to before, but I'd guess from the map legend it would be about three or four miles from the parking lot at Dodge Ridge. Here." She noted and then secured the map on the wall.

"It's not that far, but it's a rough ride to the parking area—really steep in some places."

"I don't know. Some of the hills are extreme hills and since it's not an area frequented often, the trail is probably almost non-existent," she said. "So…" She updated her profile to include:

Killer an experienced hiker. Park ranger, mountain climber, outdoor enthusiast, mountaineer etc.

"Katie, let's pick this up tomorrow," said McGaven.

"Yeah, you're right. I need to get home to see how my uncle's doing." She was tired and hungry, and wanted to put these crime scene photos to bed for a while—out of her mind. In the morning she would have fresh eyes and they would begin again.

CHAPTER 24
Wednesday 1645 hours

When Katie pulled into her driveway she saw a dark navy pickup truck parked to the far right side. She didn't know who it belonged to and thought it was strange that her uncle had a visitor. Every type of bad scenario flooded through her, stirring her anxiety awake.

"Uncle Wayne?" she said, trying to disguise the worry in her voice as she walked through the front door. Her kitchen had been cleaned and the dishes were drying in her bamboo dish rack.

"Cisco?" she called.

Looking down at the coffee table, as she passed through, she noticed a 9 mm handgun lying on it, along with two extra magazines sitting next to it. Her fear cranked to horror—the gun wasn't hers. She grabbed it up and checked to see if it was loaded and if there was a bullet in the chamber—there wasn't.

"Uncle Wayne!" she cried, walking through the house, panic rising in her chest.

She stopped and strained to listen. There were voices coming from the backyard—men's voices, several high-pitch barks from Cisco. She sprinted to the back door and swung it open ready to fight, only to find her uncle sitting with Nick at the picnic table and Cisco running around with one of his toys dangling from his mouth.

Flooded with relief, Katie tried to regain herself before they noticed she'd been alarmed. She willed her pulse calm and her breathing back to normal. "Hey, what's going on?" she said at last.

"Nick came by and we started talking," the sheriff said, turning to greet her. "We're both in a tight spot in our lives, and well, it's been nice to chat." Her uncle looked tired and worn out. He wore an old T-shirt with dark cargo pants and deck shoes without socks.

"Everything okay?" she said. "I saw the 9 mm on the coffee table and…"

"Everything is fine," her uncle stressed. "Nick brought the gun over here for you to keep it for him. I didn't know where you wanted to keep it, or if you had a special place you kept your weapons."

Katie wasn't sure if she understood why.

"Just for safekeeping," said Nick.

She finally understood her old sergeant didn't want it around him because he was worried about what he might do with it. It was quite common among returning soldiers with injuries and PTSD to wrestle with these types of feelings. It weighed on her heart, but she was happy he was mindful enough to realize that there shouldn't be a gun at his place.

"Okay," was all she could say.

"You look tired," her uncle said.

"Actually, I'm going to agree with you—I am tired."

Cisco ran over and dropped a slobbery ball at her feet. She picked it up and flung it across the yard.

"There's some leftovers in the fridge. Short ribs, salad, and rolls," he said, and Katie observed that his mood had improved.

It was at that moment that Katie noticed the electronic tracking device around his right ankle. Seeing her uncle in his current state, when only a week ago he was the strong sheriff of the county, made her crash back to reality. The facts sat in front of her and there was no escaping it.

"That sounds good," she said and went back in to the kitchen where she pulled out the foil-wrapped food and made herself a plate. The meat was still warm and it smelled fantastic.

The door opened as both men came inside followed closely by Cisco. She never thought that those two would actually be good for one another. Her uncle kissed her cheek. "I forgot how nice it was being in this house again. I spent a lot of time here with your parents."

Katie began eating and tried not to think about how her family was being systematically taken down, one by one—at least that's how it felt to her. Suddenly, she wanted to be anywhere else but home.

"Uncle Wayne? Why don't you let me go over to the house to pack some things for you? Like clothes… toiletries… and anything else you might want."

"I was thinking about that, but didn't want to burden you."

"You're not a burden. Don't ever say that."

"I was going to start ordering some stuff from the Internet."

Katie looked at Nick. "Nick and I can go over there tonight."

"Well… I don't know…" the sheriff said.

"It won't take more than an hour round trip," she stressed.

"I have no problem going with Scotty, sir," Nick said.

"Well, okay. It would be nice to have some fresh clothes."

"I'm sorry, I should have stopped on my way home tonight." Katie finished eating and then grabbed a duffle bag and a tote. "You'll be okay?" She didn't take the time to change from her work clothes into something casual—she still had her gun and badge attached to her waist.

"Of course," he said. "I've got Cisco to keep me company."

They both rode in silence until she pulled into her uncle's driveway. She jumped out and punched in the security code. As they drove up the driveway, Katie noticed that the crime scene tape was gone and surmised that John must've removed it.

"Nice place," Nick said.

"It really is… the property is so pretty up here," she replied, absentmindedly, flashbacks of finding her aunt flashing through her mind at the sight of the house.

"Hey," he said catching her attention and gently touching her arm. "I know that things feel impossible right now, but it's not going to stay that way. Look at everything you've been through… worked through… and survived. You're stronger than you think you are. I find it difficult to believe that after all you've been through that this would cause you to stumble. No way," he said.

Katie always felt safe around Nick. There was no other way to describe it—she felt safe, calm, and at peace. She dreaded going into the house again, but it was important to get her uncle's things. This wasn't just about her—it was about being there and helping her uncle. He was so important to the community and to the employees at the sheriff's department.

She squeezed Nick's hand. "Thank you."

Katie unlocked the front door and immediately noticed something was wrong.

"What is it?" Nick asked.

"The alarm isn't set."

"Who's been here besides the police?"

"John from forensics, but he's such a stickler for procedure."

Katie pushed the door open further. Shrugging off her silly hesitation, she entered. Everything looked the same. She turned on the overhead lights illuminating the entire room.

Nick shut the door behind them. "Everything seems okay."

The face of her aunt flashed into her mind. The wounds. The blood. The desperate bloody handprints on the bedroom door. Blood spatter on the walls and pooling on the floor tripped through her memory as if it were a horror movie in slow motion.

All the hideous depictions from that morning spun through her head.

"No!" she yelled, and then realized that she had uttered out loud.

Nick was at her side. "What's wrong?"

Feeling foolish and unsteady, she said, "I'm sorry. Nothing. Nothing's wrong."

Nick searched her face, trying to decide if he believed her. They were standing at the doorway to the master bedroom. He noticed the blood on the door and walls, and didn't wait to take Katie by the arm, steering her into the bedroom. "You're not alone," he said adamantly. "I'm going to wait right here until you've finished packing."

"Okay," she said shakily. She put down the duffle bag on the stripped bed. Opening the dresser drawers, she began pulling out clothing that her uncle would need. Once she was finished, she went to the walk-in closet and then the bathroom. The entire time, Nick spoke to her, which helped her to relax and pack more efficiently.

"I'm surprised that you haven't asked me about the investigation," he said. With certain words, his southern drawl took over, especially when he spoke slowly.

"I figured you would tell me when there was something to report," she said folding some shirts. Nick's voice helped her to relax as she listened with interest to his update on Detective Hamilton.

"He is quite the talker, which he didn't seem like the first time I saw him. He loves to chat with baristas, waitresses, and he's pretty loose lipped with colleagues. Not a good thing for a cop, but good for us," he explained. "It seems that he's taking all the credit he can from your investigation into the Sam Stiles case. After Stiles's body had been identified through DNA, he completely went full steam ahead with your findings. Appalling, but not surprising. They homed in on the auto garage owner and co-worker. It wasn't entirely clear, but there was some type of fallout between them and the victim. The best I could figure from what he was sayin' was that Stiles borrowed money and then got involved in gambling, losing more money, and the garage wanted it back. It got to the point where the business was in risk of shutting down. From there, it's not difficult to understand what happened next."

Katie listened carefully and in her mind she knew that something had gone wrong, not the way they had planned it, causing the death of Sam Stiles. What didn't make sense to her, at least at the moment, was why kill his wife so many years later?

"Almost done," she said as she grabbed her uncle's cell phone and charger before running downstairs to grab his backup laptop and briefcase.

Back at the front door, she stood for a moment, trying to remember what else he might need.

"Anything else?" Nick asked.

"No, I think that's it."

"Let's get out of here." Katie quickly reset the alarm system.

The daylight had faded and it was night time.

As Katie backed down the driveway and secured the wrought iron gate, she decided to ask the question burning through her mind. "Nick, what made you stop by my house today?"

"I see we're changing the focus from you to me."

"Of course."

"Just what your uncle said. I don't want a firearm around the house right now, so I thought I'd bring the gun over to your house for safekeeping. We had a good talk. The sheriff is a good listener. I like him."

"Did he have some insight for you?" she said.

"Some."

"Like?" she asked.

"A gentleman never tells."

"I figured you might say that."

"What I will say is … he's hurting, I mean *really* hurting right now. Can you imagine someone you loved being murdered—and then to top it off, they blame you?"

Katie drove in quiet solitude, unable to answer and lost in her thoughts. She glanced in the rearview mirror and noticed a black truck that had pulled out from one of the country roads, license plate XLG_344Y. Katie pressed her foot on the accelerator.

"What's up?" Nick asked calmly, reaching for something on the door to hold on to.

"Large black truck following us. I saw the same one the other day when McGaven and I were running down leads on the missing person's cold case."

"Testing to see what their intentions are?"

"Yep. Last time I was in the unmarked police vehicle and now this is my personal car. It's clear this person has been watching me—and following me for a while."

Katie's Jeep took the back road tight corners with ease—she had done it a million times. The black truck followed, swerving over the double yellow lines.

"Still there?" he asked glancing at the side mirror.

"Yep."

"Take a right on the main road."

"That's my next move," she said as she gripped the steering wheel harder. A bus passed in the other direction and blew the horn because the truck was hogging part of their lane. "He's going to get someone killed."

"Is there another way off this road to get to the main street?"

"Yes. It's been under construction, but it's passable."

"Your Jeep should have no problem, but that truck will once the terrain changes."

"I want to know who it is… I can't tell who's behind the wheel or if there's a passenger. The windows are too dark."

Katie took a hard right up the rural road past an apple orchard. To her surprise, the truck followed, taking the corner too fast and fishtailing down one of the orchard rows parallel to the path she was on.

"What the hell?" said Nick.

She reached into her pocket and pulled out her cell phone. Tossing it to Nick, she said, "Here, record it."

Nick didn't waste time. Bracing himself on the bumpy road, he pressed record and, steady as he could, he moved the cell phone around to keep the truck in view.

"You okay?" he said.

"This is easy," she said sarcastically.

The black truck sped up, cut its lights, and they couldn't see it anymore in the darkened orchard. Within seconds, the stealth truck made a sharp turn in front of them.

Katie stomped on the brakes, causing the truck to veer to the right. The Jeep skidded in the loose dirt and barely missed the truck by inches. Both vehicles stopped. Dust rose in the air. Lights suddenly blinded Katie and Nick as the truck shone its high beams directly at them.

Unable to see, Katie dropped her vehicle into reverse and pressed the accelerator. They shot backwards as she cranked the steering wheel left, swinging the front end round so they faced the opposite direction.

"Can you see?" she yelled.

"Not really," he replied.

"Hang on!"

Katie was able to maneuver the Jeep down one of the orchard rows and sped off again, as branches slapped at the windshield and sides. The headlights of the truck appeared behind them, closing in.

"Where does this lead?" Nick yelled.

"I'm not quite sure," she said. All she knew was that they were still up in the first set of hills near her uncle's place, surrounded by gullies and valleys.

The black truck was now inches from the Jeep's bumper.

Katie glanced down at her speedometer: it was pushing sixty-seven miles per hour. The truck slammed her vehicle from behind, causing it to sputter and fishtail, but Katie held strong.

The truck hit them again, whipping their heads forward on impact, and then pulling back.

"I think I know where we're going, and we need to stop," she shouted, slamming her foot down on the brakes and grinding the Jeep to a halt. The black truck screeched to a stop behind her and gunned the engine, as if challenging her, letting her know that he was still there.

"So you want to play?" she said under her breath.

Katie stomped the accelerator and the Jeep charged forward again. She began silently counting backward, slowly, her focus sharp and nerves steady.

5...

The truck started closing the gap behind her.

4...

The truck flashed its headlights.

3...

Closer.

2...

She made a drastic last-second turn to the left without warning.

1...

Engine roaring, and like a black serpent in the night, the truck kept driving straight for a few seconds before there was silence—and the headlights disappeared over the edge.

Katie had overcorrected her Jeep and couldn't slow it; fishtailing wildly it rolled over a few times before landing on the roof between two fully loaded apple trees—wheels still spinning. The engine stopped. Steam rose from the radiator. The one remaining headlight sputtered, slowly dimmed, and finally went out, leaving the apple orchard dark and quiet.

CHAPTER 25

Wednesday 1945 hours

Katie woke with a jerk. Her seatbelt cut into her side; her body was halfway between the seat and the ceiling. Fighting with her door release, she kicked open the driver's door and felt the cool air whip through the cab. She managed to unhook her seatbelt and crawled out on her hands and knees. Sitting down in the dirt, she regained her bearings and calmed her dizziness.

It was too dark to really see anything. She wasn't sure if Nick had crawled out too. Half expecting to see a looming figure climbing up from the ravine, Katie kept her voice low.

"Nick," she whispered. "Are you alright?" She felt something watery on her face as she brushed the hair from her eyes and realized it was blood. She decided to crawl around to the other side of the Jeep, keeping a low profile. She groped for her weapon on her waist, but it was missing. Perspiration ran down her back and face as she made it to the passenger door and yanked it open.

"Nick," she whispered. "You okay?"

She made out his outline still strapped in the seat and reached for his face. "Nick."

He moved and mumbled.

"Yeah, I'm fine," he said.

"Let me get you out of this." She felt for the seatbelt release and finally found it, pressing hard against the side of his stomach. "Ready," she said.

He acknowledged. She pressed the side of the buckle and it instantly released Nick, and he fell on his side. He let out a groan of agony.

"You okay?" she asked.

"I will be. Need a bit of help."

He began to wiggle from his position as Katie put one of his arms around her shoulder, pulling him out of the Jeep and over to an apple tree, leaning him against the narrow trunk for support.

He handed her back the cell phone.

Surprised, she said, "It still works," and immediately dialed the police, giving them her badge number and general location. Turning to Nick, she could vaguely see with the light from the cell phone. His face had blood running down the side.

"You're hurt," she said keeping her voice strong.

"Nah, it's just a scratch."

They were interrupted by a strange sound coming from the ravine area. It sounded like metal scraping against more metal. Something screeched and groaned. Katie's eyes were becoming accustomed to the darkness and she could see outlines of the trees and where the orchard ended, dropping into a valley area.

"Stay put," she said. Getting to her feet, she walked over to where the truck had disappeared, stood at the edge and stared down—heavy tire marks had dug into the earth and ended abruptly. The headlights were still illuminated but directed at the ground while the bed of the truck pointed up at a forty-five degree angle. She could barely make out the driver's door open and what appeared to be the outline of a man.

Katie turned and hurried back to her Jeep, dropped to the ground and dived inside the cab looking for her gun. She didn't immediately find it. Running her hands along the inside of the roof, now the bottom, she searched frantically, knowing that the man was going to return and finish the job.

"C'mon, c'mon," she said under her breath.

Jamming her fingertips under the seats and in every cranny she could, she felt the familiar grip of her Glock. She pulled it out of the Jeep and ran to Nick. "We have to move you now," she stressed.

"What?"

"He's coming," she whispered.

Helping him, she propped him up, making sure he could move with her.

They shuffled up the track and several rows to the left. "Okay, stay here," she said, helping him to sit down in a dark, bushy corner where he would be relatively hidden.

He grabbed her arm. "Don't try to be a hero. Hold him off until the cops get here."

"Yes, sir," she said. She tossed him the cell phone and was gone, running in the opposite direction from her Jeep until she found a good spot to watch and wait, ready to distract her attacker if he got too close to where Nick was hidden before the police arrived. Steadying her Glock ahead of her in a primed stance and moving slightly back and forth, she was ready.

After barely two minutes, Katie saw the outline of a man limping through the darkness. As he got closer she saw he carried a shotgun, but reached inside his long jacket and retrieved a semi-automatic handgun.

Two guns against one...

She waited quietly and watched him, as she tried to decide by his build and how he moved if she had ever seen him before. She couldn't ascertain if he was old or young, probably somewhere before middle age—thirty to fifty-five. That wasn't helping, but she needed to be able to give the police something if he somehow managed to slip away.

He moved quickly toward the Jeep and, without checking to see that she or Nick were inside, he bent over and rapidly opened fire at the windshield. The shots echoed throughout the area. No hesitation. No remorse. Four shots to kill two people.

She watched the dark figure look inside the vehicle. He stood upright, alert, and carefully scanned around. Katie couldn't remember a time where she had been so scared—in the army, perhaps—but here in her hometown, absolutely not. There had been close calls with killers but this situation felt different; it felt deadly.

The figure turned and started to walk in Nick's direction as if he knew that he was there.

Katie considered her move. If she waited, she would leave Nick defenseless, but if she followed, it may be the last thing she ever did.

She crept slowly behind the man, her footsteps practically silent. He was getting closer and closer to Nick with every step. She felt helpless, knowing she would have to act soon or Nick's cover would be blown.

With a sudden move, the man spun around and fired two shots in Katie's direction. She sidestepped out of direct fire and dropped to the ground—a military move that instantly made her wish she had Cisco tucked in at her side. The bullets missed her—but not by much. She heard one hit a tree trunk behind her and the other zinging past over her shoulder. Digging her elbows into the dirt, she steadied her Glock and eyed her target. She wasn't going to fire until it was absolutely necessary.

The man began walking toward her, unhurried and deliberate, but she knew that he couldn't see her. He slowly raised the shotgun waist high. Katie tensed, and her trigger finger slowly squeezed the trigger…

Sirens sounded in the distance, several of them, approaching fast.

The man turned, dropped his gun and ran in the opposite direction. Katie sprinted over to where she'd left Nick.

"Nick," she said softly. Her heart quickened. "Nick," she said again.

The sirens were close now.

Finally, "Here," he said.

She spun around and dropped to her knees. "Are you alright?"

"Shouldn't I be asking that question?" He started to get up; Katie helped him and wrapped her arm around his waist.

"Funny," she said.

Bright blue and white light blinded them as the patrol car approached. Katie raised her other hand to signal, and the patrol car lowered its lights and stopped. A deputy opened the driver's door and stepped out. "Is there an active shooter?"

Katie pointed in the direction the man went.

Two other deputies rolled up and exited their vehicles, and followed the first one into the dark.

"Stay here," they ordered Katie and Nick.

Flashlights strategically swept back and forth, lighting up most of the apple orchard as deputies searched for the shooter.

CHAPTER 26

Wednesday 2215 hours

Katie leaned against a patrol vehicle after she and Nick had given statements and turned over the video that had been on her phone. She pulled the foil blanket closer around her to stop her shivering as she watched the sheriff's department's K9 teams go off in search of the shooter. Nick limped over to her, a bandage on his face and larger wraps around his arm. "Well," he said, looking down, "I keep collecting more scars. They wanted me to get a few stitches and I just laughed."

"Yeah well, I'm catching up to you, I think," she said, touching her forehead. "Ouch."

"It's clear that whatever you're working on is making someone very unhappy."

"Don't tell them that," she said, referring to the top brass now arriving at the scene. The undersheriff was only just out of the car and barking orders to anyone in his eyeline. "This incident definitely has something to do with either one of my cases or my aunt's murder."

For the first time, Nick looked concerned. "Hey, I'm just an army throwaway, but maybe you should take a few days off. Reboot. Reassess the situation."

Katie knew he was right. "You've heard the saying that after twenty-four hours a homicide is more difficult to solve. But after four days, it's next to impossible." Her words hung in the air around them.

"Detective." Undersheriff Martinez, dressed in sweatpants and a leather jacket, was walking over to her. "Glad to see you're okay." His words didn't quite match his tone.

"Thank you, sir," she said, bracing for a reprimand.

"I've been briefed on both of your statements," he said, nodding to Nick. "Sorry about your Jeep, Scott. One of the deputies will give you both a ride home."

"I need to get a bag out," she said.

"I don't see a problem with that," he said and then hesitated. It was clear that he wanted to say something else, but decided against it for now. "I look forward to your report tomorrow."

"You'll have it on your desk at the end of the day," she said.

Martinez walked away.

As Katie and Nick waited for one of the deputies to give them a ride back to Katie's house, they saw John climb back up to the top of the orchard, torch in hand. He had been examining the truck for any evidence.

He approached Katie and Nick. "You guys okay?" he asked.

"Not my finest moment, but we're going to live." Then she couldn't help herself, so asked, "Anything?"

"Nope. License plate belonged to another vehicle. The VIN number had been removed, and there were no fingerprints. Was the guy wearing gloves?"

"I couldn't say. I couldn't see much," she said.

"The gun he dropped was clean—not a print—so I assume he was wearing gloves."

Katie nodded in agreement still dazed by the entire incident.

"Too bad. You guys take care, and I'll see you tomorrow," he said to Katie.

CHAPTER 27
Thursday 1000 hours

After making sure her uncle was stocked with plenty of food and Nick was safe and well at home, Katie got herself together and unraveled the bandage from around her head. She had a full schedule today and didn't need to explain to everyone she came in contact with what had happened the night before.

McGaven's dark sedan pulled around the lane and made the sharp turn into her driveway. Hurrying to get in, Katie settled in the passenger seat, snapped her seatbelt into place, and settled in for the forty-five minute drive to the university.

"I thought you'd be more banged up," said McGaven.

"That took an entire thirty seconds before you could make a joke?" she said and smiled.

"Well, I was going to lead up to it, but what the heck, just go right in for the kill."

"Didn't even need a Band-Aid," she said.

"Heard about all the theatrics from Deputy Moore. Wow. And they didn't even catch the guy. Slick…"

"Yeah, well, if they'd been another five minutes coming, I wouldn't be having this conversation with you right now."

"You have no idea who it was? Couldn't see anything about him to identify him?"

"It was completely dark and the truck had blacked out windows," she said.

"You know, if the guy was that ballsy, he's going to try again."

Katie sighed. "I know."

"What's the plan?"

"Plan?"

"Yes, plan. How do you plan to stay safe?"

"Isn't that always the plan?" she said, keeping her eyes on the road.

He took the turn-off to get onto the freeway. "You know what I mean."

"I don't know…" she said slowly.

McGaven turned to look at her. "You don't know?"

"It's like I'm fighting a ghost. I don't know if it's someone from the Stiles missing person's case, this case, or if it's about my uncle. I'm driving blind here."

"Well I have news for you, you better figure out how to be safer."

"Of course."

"I know that you have an instinct about it, right?"

"I keep coming back to my aunt's homicide—it has to have something to do with that. It would make sense."

McGaven drove in silence—it appeared that he too was thinking about the cases, his eyebrows furrowed as his jaw clenched. Katie looked out her side window as the world rushed past in a blur. If she didn't find a connection or some solid evidence soon, she was lost.

Her cell phone buzzed to an incoming text:

Thought you'd want to know. Officially a positive ID on Sam Stiles.

Katie was glad, but at the same time, she was also sad that Mrs. Stiles would know for sure that her son had been murdered and buried out in a field. She wondered if anyone had spoken with her in person or if she'd had just an impersonal notification. She closed her eyes for a few moments before she opened them again.

As the dense forest made way to more open areas with buildings, businesses, and parking lots, the hazy overcast morning warmed up. They were almost at the main part of the campus decorated with colorful signs, posters, and large banners for meetings, protests, and anything that the student body wanted to voice an opinion about.

"I think we can park over there," McGaven said, referring to the large guest parking area for the science buildings. "You up for a walk?"

"Sounds good," she said.

McGaven eased the police vehicle into a spot on the end and they made their way on foot along a thin pathway with a sign posted every which way to different departments.

"We're looking for building three, room 112."

Katie nodded. It was cooler than it appeared so they briskly wound their way through student parking lots and in between clusters of trees. As the season turned cooler, the aroma of pine trees was unmistakable; fresh, invigorating, and clean. The slight breeze carried the outdoor smell, making Katie think of times when she was young and everything was about being outdoors and having fun.

The parking lots were full and students poured from all directions. Obviously, the classes were out just before lunchtime. No one paid any attention to Katie or McGaven. They waited a few minutes as the last of the students funneled through the doors before entering the building.

It had been a while since Katie had been to school and the familiar sights and sounds came tumbling back. The stark hallways. Assignment and grade postings on the bulletin boards. The different faces hurrying to the next class carrying notebooks and the next necessary text books.

"I think room 112 is down here." McGaven gestured to the farthest end of the hall. "Make you glad you aren't in school now?" he said.

"I had enough school back then—no desire to go back anytime soon."

McGaven laughed. "Here it is." He pulled open one of the double doors.

Katie was surprised to find that it was a lecture hall, and not an office. "Detective Scott? Deputy McGaven?"

Katie noticed a pile of work on the podium and a bottle of spring water, and a box of Kleenex. There was also a pair of glasses folded neatly and a gold pen sitting perpendicular next to a small writing tablet with scribbled shorthand. Still lit up on the large screen from a PowerPoint presentation were chemistry symbols and complex formulas printed neatly.

A young man, lean with dark hair and the shadow of a beard, had come out of an adjoining room. Katie estimated him to be in his mid-thirties.

"Professor Brandon Wills?" said Katie.

"Yes, it's actually Dr. Wills," he said, emphasizing the word "doctor."

"Of course." Katie recognized immediately that Wills was a stickler for the rules.

"I'm Detective Scott and this is Deputy McGaven."

He nodded. His posture was stiff and uncomfortable.

"Thank you for taking the time to see us," she said.

"You said it was about Cindy Andrews. Any news? Did you find her killer?"

"I head up the cold case unit at the sheriff's department. And I'm looking into her homicide." She made a mental note that the doctor called Cynthia, Cindy. Interesting. "I'm getting up to date by revisiting some of her friends and family members."

"I see," he said. "Please, let's go into my office." He gestured stiffly with his hand.

Katie and McGaven followed.

The room was larger than Katie had expected, decorated with conservative wood furniture, a large mahogany desk, credenza, and three bookshelves. Everything was excessively neat and tidy. On his desk was a name sign: Dr. B. Wills, Director of Natural Sciences.

"Natural Sciences include biology, chemistry as well as botany and zoology?" Katie asked.

"Yes, it does. Please, have a seat." He gestured and then sat behind his desk maintaining control—but at the same time trying to appear relaxed. He fidgeted with his tie until he was satisfied that it was perfectly straight.

"Thank you," she said.

Both Katie and McGaven sat.

"I thought it was more environmental studies and physics," said McGaven.

"Yes. Actually, you're both correct."

"That's quite an accomplishment for someone who is your age," McGaven said.

"Yes, I guess you're right. I've known my entire life that I wanted to make a difference, environmentally speaking, and teach others to appreciate these studies and to begin to make the world a better place."

"Well," began Katie, thinking that Dr. Wills was high-minded with a slight delusion of grandeur, "we just wanted to ask a few questions and won't take up much of your time."

"Absolutely. Ask away." Wills clasped his hands on the desk and fidgeted with his right thumb.

Was he anxious, irritated, or was this just a habit?

"You were good friends with Cynthia Andrews," Katie said.

"Yes, we had been friends since the ninth grade. Both of us had the same ambitions and interests. We were like family. She was like a sister to me."

"I see. Were you aware of her camping trip to find the elusive… let me check my notes to get the correct description… King's Gold?"

Wills smiled. It was the first time he had shown any personality or emotion. "Yes, I knew about it. She had asked me to go with her, but I was unable because I was also working on a thesis of my own. And, well, I thought she was spending too much time on that elusive little weed. We both had schedules that didn't allow much free time."

"Who else knew about the King's Gold study?"

"Well, her advisors knew… I can't remember their names but I'm sure you could find out from administration. And I think her family knew about it, but most people, fellow students, didn't know and frankly probably didn't care." His voice became deeper.

"Please forgive me, but why was this study so important?"

"Well, Cindy was a conservationist. She cared about everything natural all around us. She felt strongly that it was a good sign when plants native to California were coming back. It fit a theory she had about all things being connected: trees, birds, the ocean and so forth," he said. He had unclasped his hands and picked up a gold pen similar to the one on the podium.

"Did Ms. Andrews have any problems? At home? Or with another student?"

"No, you would have to have known Cindy. She was quiet and shy, except when she talked about her work."

"Was anything bothering her?"

"No, not that I was aware of. And we spent a lot of time together."

"I see," said Katie. "Was it usual for her to hike and camp alone?"

Wills thought a moment. "I actually can't think of any other time she had camped alone, but like I said, this part of the thesis was *extremely* important to her."

"Did she have a boyfriend?"

"No."

"Anyone that she was interested in?"

"No."

"Forgive me, Dr. Wills, but you seem quite adamant about that," said Katie.

"Well, let me spell it out for you. All of us science types are considered geeks, shut-ins, library nerds, whatever you want to call us—so no, she never said anything about any student she was interested in dating. There wasn't any time for that." He scoffed and stared at Katie.

"Just one more question: When you heard about her death and how she was killed—what was the first thing that came to mind?" Katie watched him carefully as he thought about the question and how to answer.

"I… I was stunned and horrified. I thought it couldn't be true…" His voice trailed off, but didn't seem genuine somehow.

"About how she died?"

"Quite honestly, I thought things like that only happened in horror movies."

"Thank you, Dr. Wills," Katie said and stood up, touching the top of her forehead and suddenly noticing it was bleeding. "Do you have a Kleenex?"

"Oh, take one of these." Wills reached into one of his desk drawers and pulled out a small plastic sheath with new handkerchiefs tucked neatly inside. He handed one to Katie.

"Oh no, I couldn't."

"Please I have a million of these. Call it an obsession." Looking at her head, he said, "You should have that looked at."

"It's already been looked at." Katie glanced down to the lower drawer and noticed a small glass display case inside. Inside the box were three antique knives. "Nice collection."

He looked to see what Katie referred to. "Oh, yes. It's a gift for one of the professors. They collect early American things."

"If we have any further questions, can we contact you here?" she said.

"Of course."

"We'll find our way back out."

Katie and McGaven hurried their way back. Neither said anything to the other until they were seated back inside their car. Katie had more questions than answers, but things were moving forward at long last.

"Okay, I have one word," said McGaven. "*Cindy?* Really?"

Katie laughed.

"Not exactly a smoking gun…" he said.

"I sensed some resentment, or even unresolved feelings between them, didn't you?"

McGaven nodded, drove out of the parking area and eased into traffic to leave the campus.

"We need to talk to someone completely impartial about this King's Gold. It may be the key to finding the person who murdered her."

"I definitely couldn't see Dr. Wills tying someone to a tree and slicing them up. I've never seen *anything* like that before."

"I need you to check out Dr. Wills and find someone to give the scoop on King's Gold from twelve years ago. Maybe there's something about it us non-natural scientist types don't understand. And run backgrounds on everyone who gave a statement."

"And you are…?"

"I'm going to have a look at the evidence from the crime scene and talk to Detective Teagen about the case."

"I don't know him; he was retired before I began working at the sheriff's department."

"He had some problem with his health and had to retire early."

"What about your uncle?" he said.

"I'll have plenty of time to chat with him this weekend."

"Why not talk to the family now?"

"I want to wait and have a better grasp on their backgrounds, what they did right after Cynthia's death, and what they're doing now."

McGaven hit the accelerator and took the ramp to the freeway. "Fair enough."

Katie's cell phone alerted to a text message from John:

Results in on the evidence you found.

"What's that? Any news?" he asked.

"No, just personal stuff."

CHAPTER 28

Thursday 1405 hours

Katie dashed into the office to run down a phone number and address for Detective Kenneth Teagen. She grabbed her notes and jacket and was just about to leave when McGaven stopped her.

"Wait," he called out.

Katie turned and saw the look on his face. He was easy to read with his expressive eyes and wrinkled brow. It was straightforward to see that he was concerned about her.

"I know that you're capable of doing a lot. You can run down leads for any type of investigation and you can lead an army team into action, but…"

"Let me save you the well-intended lecture," she said and raised her hand to halt him. "I know what you're going to say, but I can't just sit idly by and wait for something to happen. No matter what… I have to do this," she said.

"That's all well and good—"

"But—" she said.

"Don't interrupt me. Please… This isn't run-of-the-mill kind of stuff. You've been through a traumatic family loss… you're in the middle of grieving, in case you don't know it. And there's been an attempt on your life. You. Have. To. Slow. Down."

Katie stared at her desk as McGaven put his two cents into the ring. She appreciated having a great partner and good friend, but she was more than capable of taking care of herself. "I'm aware of what's at stake. The sooner we narrow down the suspect pool the better—for everyone."

"I have news for you, Katie. You're not working your aunt's case," he said, on the verge of raising his voice. "Don't think I'm stupid. I know you've devised some way to work her case too. Picking a cold case that has similarities, which gives you access to be somewhere you're not supposed to be. You're not as clever as you think."

Katie sucked in a breath and let it out slowly. "I know everything you're saying is true. But I *have* to do what I *need* to do. And I'm not…" She caught herself before she revealed too much. She had to protect her friends from getting too involved.

McGaven got up from his desk, his huge frame towering over her making her feel small and helpless—it wasn't supposed to come down to this.

"Let me do what I need to do," she said.

"You're taking too many risks. You can't do this alone," he stressed.

"I'll be fine. I'm armed. And if I go anywhere after dark or secluded, I'll take Cisco."

"That's not good enough. With your uncle out of the picture, there are people here that aren't on your side."

"Well… that's too…" She caught herself from saying something that she'd regret.

"Let me help," he said.

Katie turned to leave. "We have our assignments."

He gently took her arm. "Let me help."

"We'll meet back at the end of the shift and work it out. Okay?"

He relaxed somewhat and let out a sigh. "Okay."

She finally left.

Katie felt the burden of everything weighing her down—her heart, her mind, and her investigative load. McGaven was right. Things were becoming too much for her to bear. She stood in front of the forensic examination room contemplating if she should go inside. It would be just as easy to move on and go to her meeting with retired detective Teagen.

"Waiting for me?" said John behind her.

She turned to see him standing close wearing his lab coat. It was unusual to see him dressed officially for the job, but it suited him. His eyes studied her as if he could hear her thoughts.

"Hi, I got your text," she said, lamely.

John moved past her and entered the room, expecting her to follow. "I have some preliminary findings for you." His voice was flat, without his usual personality.

"Great." She tried to sound light, even though she was dying to know what he had found. She moved closer to John and waited patiently to hear what he had to say. He sat in front of one of the computers and brought up a chemical report. He glanced at the doorway before he began. "The blue fiber is a type of polyester, or Dacron."

"Oh," she said. "Ordinary and could be from a million different things?"

"Quite the contrary. This is lightweight material with high tensile strength, superior abrasion resistance, and flexibility. However, it has a low modulus, allowing some stretch. It's susceptible to UV and chemical degradation, and its properties can change due to moisture absorption."

"What is it used for? Athletic wear? Luggage?" she guessed.

"You're on the right track. But this type of Dacron is used for camping gear, like tents, backpacks, and even used for some types of sails for boats. It's difficult to individuate whether it's for one type of use or another. And it's impossible to find out what piece of fabric it originated from without the original to compare it to."

"What about the threads?"

"It's consistent with the fabric piece. Again, I cannot give an exact expert opinion that these came from the same piece of fabric, but it's consistent."

"John, thank you for your discretion and your time," she said, feeling guilty about keeping McGaven out of the loop.

"I can't say I'm happy about this situation, but… I completely understand why it had to happen like this. If roles were reversed, I would do the same thing." He kept Katie's gaze for a bit longer than necessary. "I have one more piece of evidence for you."

Katie waited, praying it would be the missing link she so desperately needed.

"I nearly missed it, but there's a small spot of grease on the swatch you gave me. When I tested, it came back…"

"What?" she asked expecting, or rather hoping, it would be a breakthrough.

"Grease."

"Just… grease?" she said.

"Well, let me put it to you this way. There are three essential components to grease: base oil, thickener, and additives. And this tested as grease. There were no foreign things in it, so that means it was poured right out of a container." He watched Katie's reaction.

"So what you're saying is this grease wasn't the result of some-thing dripping, like from a car."

"Yes, it's in the original mixture form, uncontaminated."

"From a car?"

"Possibly."

"A motorcycle, boat, or some type of machinery?" she asked.

"It's possible, but at this point I can't say where or what this grease was used for."

"I have another question."

He looked at her and waited.

"Did they find out if my uncle had been given anything in his drink?"

John was hesitant. "You'll find out anyway. Yes, they took a blood sample from him and there was a small trace of Diphenhydramine. The glasses had already been cleaned so they were of no use."

"What's that?"

"It's just an over-the-counter sleep aid. He claimed that he didn't take anything to sleep, but this can cause some discomfort, like upset stomach and jitters."

"Where did it come from?"

"That is unknown."

"It could have come from anywhere, the caterers, guests at the party, and even Patton could have slipped something into his drink," she said. "But they didn't know him well, he didn't drink much."

Katie digested everything John had told her and knew it was a clue but it wasn't as dynamic as she had hoped. She knew that someone had come to the property, entered the house, and killed her aunt. And now, they had contact with some type of lightweight polyester used for camping type of items with grease on it. Even though she was disappointed, she knew it would help down the road. That's what she had to believe.

"Thank you, John," she said and turned to leave.

"It wasn't what you had hoped?" he said.

"No, not yet."

As she drove to Detective Kenneth Teagen's house she tried to keep her mind on the Cynthia Andrews homicide and what they knew so far. She had phoned him and he was polite, receptive and wanted to help her with the cold case in any way he could. She thought he sounded a bit lonely, and a visit from someone from the department might be just what he needed.

From what Katie could confirm, Teagen had retired from the sheriff's office eight years ago with health issues. His cases had an average closure rate of about seventy percent and he worked with other detectives on some of the homicide cases. He lived in an unincorporated part of the county and it appeared that he divorced from his wife about a year before retirement.

Driving through farmland and areas thick with trees, Katie finally found a road called Apricot Lane. She turned the sedan down the gravel drive and ended at the retired detective's house. It was a small, box-like house with two small barns in the back. All the buildings were rundown and in desperate need of maintenance; paint chipped on the front and porch, slats in the fence line were missing, and the weeds were beginning to take over. There were several paint cans, buckets, and a ladder leaning against the house.

Katie parked and got out. She thought she could smell honey-suckle, although she didn't see it. She stepped up onto the porch and knocked on the door, but there was no answer. She knocked again and waited.

Katie walked over to one of the barns used for storing tools, boxes, furniture, and what looked like an old car.

"Hello?" she said. "Detective Teagen?"

There was a sound toward the back of the barn, so she followed it to a small workshop area with specialized carving tools and various pieces of wood scattered about. Every tool had a specific place—neat and orderly. It was the only thing systematized in the barn. An old hunting knife lay on one of the tables, bloodied. One of the wood cabinets rattled next to Katie. She watched it for a moment, not wanting to move. "Hello?" she said again.

A blur burst through the opening of the large cabinet and landed in front of her, primed, growling and inching closer to her. "Easy, big guy," she said to the large husky mix snarling at her feet. "Easy…" she said and began to slowly back out of the barn.

"Rambo, down," said a voice behind her. The dog immediately obeyed the command, and Katie turned to see a handsome man in his late thirties to early forties with dark hair, and a tanned face from being outdoors. He was dressed in jeans and a short sleeved T-shirt. "I'm sorry if he scared you. He's trained to guard and bark, not attack. He's got the guard part down but growls instead of barks," he said and took a rope and lassoed the dog for a temporary leash.

Katie composed herself and said, "Hi, I'm Detective Katie Scott."

"Oh, of course, Dad said you were going to stop by today."

"I knocked on the front door but no one answered."

"Oh, damn. He probably took his hearing aid out and didn't hear you. Please, I'll take you to him. I'm Cody, by the way."

"Nice to meet you," she said.

"Dad was excited that someone from the department was going to come out. He gets lonely out here and has been pretty depressed," he said. "C'mon, Rambo." The dog relaxed and padded along with them.

"Oh, I'm sorry to hear that."

"Well, police work was always his life—his *only* life, I'm afraid to say. You should know how cops can be."

"Do you live here?" Katie asked.

"No, I have an apartment in town, but I spend most of my time out here just helping out because there's no one else. Sometimes it's not so convenient. I'm all Dad has now and I want to spend time with him—as much as I can."

They reached the front door and he opened it. "Dad," he said loudly. "Dad, the detective is here."

The house was neat, ragged and worn, but everything had its place. The living room had a small broken down sofa with a folded blanket on one end, one large recliner, and a coffee table with neatly stacked books and magazines. Katie didn't see a television or any type of electronic devices like a computer or cell phone. There was a cane leaning against the far wall.

A large man with a mostly bald head sat in the kitchen reading a magazine next to a small plate with the remains of a half-eaten sandwich on it. A small bottle of oxygen sat beside that, with tubes running up and into the old man's nose. He appeared lost in his own world and didn't immediately look up to see them.

"Dad!" said Cody raising his voice. "You need to wear your hearing aid!"

The man finally looked up, realized there was company and immediately put his hearing aid in place. "Sorry, lost track of time." He released his oxygen connection and turned the canister off. He very slowly stood up and shuffled a couple of steps. "Please, we can talk in the living room," he said with a winded voice.

Katie waited patiently as Teagen made himself comfortable in the recliner chair.

"Dad, do you need anything?"

"No, I'm fine. Quit fussing over me."

"Nice to meet you, Detective." Cody smiled at Katie and left the house. She heard him call for the dog and there was a short yip and a scurry of claws on wood.

"I'm Detective Katie Scott and, as I told you on the phone, I'm heading up the cold case unit."

"Yes, of course."

"Detective Teagen, I just have a few questions about the Cynthia Andrews homicide."

"Please, Detective, just call me Ken."

Katie nodded. "Of course, Ken."

"You must be Sheriff Scott's niece."

"Yes."

"I seem to remember something about you going to the police academy and then army, was it?" he said.

"Yes, two tours as an army K9 handler."

"Impressive. Thank you for your service."

Katie nodded. "I appreciate that." She couldn't help but think that this poor man's body had failed, but his mind was still sharp. It must've been difficult for him to be forced to retire before he was ready to. "I'm getting up to date on the Andrews homicide. Do you remember that case?"

"Yes, absolutely. It was a hard one to forget. In my entire career, it was the most senseless and grisly crime scene I had ever seen. I'm glad that you're taking a look at it. It had always bothered me."

"You visited the actual scene?"

"Yes, I couldn't now, but we all trekked up there at the time. Your uncle and I, as well as the crime scene and morgue technicians."

"I've seen the photos, but can you tell me what your first impression was?"

"Well, we received a call from State Parks with news that a body had been found. When we arrived, we had no idea exactly what we would find. That Andrews girl was strung up to a tree, body gutted. I had never seen wounds like that, not in all my years."

"The medical examiner said the cuts were deep, no hesitation."

"That's right. I assumed it was someone crazed on drugs or something ritualistic, but the footprints we found told us that someone was stalking the poor girl before she was killed," he said, catching his breath. "She didn't have any defensive wounds, so it happened quickly, or she was already unconscious."

Katie hesitated for a moment before continuing, "I have to ask this, but was there anything going on at the time at the department?"

"What do you mean, personally, or at the entire department?"

"In general, at the department. Were there pressures from the community or political issues, anything like that?"

Teagen took several breaths and with each inhale seemed like it would be his last. He finally said, "Nothing big like that. But…"

"But what?"

"You're going to find out from your uncle unless you already know. He and I weren't getting along at the time. He was so intent on running for sheriff and we were at odds on this case."

Katie shook her head. "No, he hasn't told me anything. He's been focused on—" She stopped.

"It's okay, Detective, I know all about the homicide. The entire town knows. I'm so sorry for your loss."

"Thank you." She rethought her next question. "This signature seems specific and not something that was a first time thing. Did you ever find any link to other cases?"

"See, that's where your uncle and I differed. I wanted to spend more time on that angle—it was likely it was a serial killer or some satanic killer. But Scott wanted to concentrate on the family."

Katie frowned.

"I know this isn't what you wanted to hear, but that's how it was. Maybe today, we would think differently." He fought with his breathing. "Could you bring me my oxygen?"

"Of course," she said and went to the kitchen table. Reaching for the oxygen, she knocked off a magazine. Picking it up, she noticed a clipping from a college course sticking out of one of the pages: Introduction to Environmental Sciences, Dr. Brandon Wills as speaker—she then quickly grabbed the oxygen bottle. Going back to the living room, she gave the oxygen and apparatus to Teagen. "Shall I get your son?" she said.

"Oh no, I'm fine."

"I have to admit this case is challenging. So let me get this straight. You thought it had the hallmarks for a serial killer and my uncle thought the family should be pressed more."

"Yes."

"What did he think was the motive for the family?" she asked, thinking of some of her own ideas.

"The usual: jealousy or revenge."

"Jealousy for her accomplishments? She was achieving high grades and was working on this thesis. I don't follow revenge so much."

You see a lot of revenge in this business, Detective. More than there should be. Looking at it now, I guess we were both wrong. Something would have shown up by now."

"I don't necessarily think so. People kill for many different reasons. I'm beginning to see why you both had a difficult time working this case."

"There was very little physical evidence—the slashed up tent and unusual marking from a hooked knife. Evidence, but it wasn't anything we were successful in tracking down. The only thing that stood out was the location and the signature of the killer. That's what we had to work with."

"Well I think that's about it. May I call you for your opinion if I have a follow-up question?" she asked.

"Of course, anything, Detective."

Katie stood up. "Thank you, Ken, for seeing me today."

Katie took the scenic way back to the department even though it was well past 5 p.m. She called McGaven on speakerphone:

"McGaven," he answered.

"Hey, it's me. Just finished talking with Detective Teagen."

"Anything?"

"Not really. I'll fill you in later."

"Can't wait. I have a few things shaking out with the family."

"Good."

"What's up? You sound tired."

"Hey, it's late in the day. I'm going to head home," she said.

"Stealing a cop car, I see," he chuckled.

"I know… I'll add buying a new car to my to-do list."

"Could be fun."

"I guess."

"Take Denise with you—she lives for that kind of stuff."

"Noted."

"Katie?"

"Yeah?"

"Sorry I vented on you earlier. But I want you to take care of yourself. Go home, support our sheriff, and get some rest."

"Okay. I'll write our reports."

"Good. I have my two patrol shifts Sunday and Monday, third watch."

"So I won't see you until Tuesday?"

"Yep. I've left you the evidence boxes locked in the room across the hall, and my background notes on the family on your desk. I saw your notes."

"What notes?"

"For linkage. Searching other jurisdictions and counties about any victims with the same type of signature? I pulled up some articles that might interest you, but I haven't been able to contact the departments yet for details."

"Thanks, McGaven. What would I do without you?"

"With luck, you'll never have to know. See you Tuesday."

McGaven ended the call. Katie listened to the dead tone before her end hung up.

It was the end of the day on Thursday, but her real work was just beginning.

CHAPTER 29

Saturday 0805 hours

Katie woke to an eighty pound dog on her chest. Halfway rolled on his back with his paws outstretched, Cisco wanted her up and ready to do something. She leaned over and saw it was early.

"Cisco, I need another half hour," she whined.

The dog grumbled and spun around in a playful way, bouncing on the bed.

Katie moaned and turned her attention to the sunshine peeking between the shades. It was obviously a beautiful morning and she wanted to take advantage of it.

She got a whiff of bacon cooking. Her uncle must've made breakfast. She rose slowly, pulling on her sweats and robe to venture into the kitchen only to find it empty. Noticing the oven ajar, Katie opened the door and saw a plate with bacon and eggs sitting under the warmer.

Her uncle had to be close because his electronic ankle device would alert authorities if he ventured too far from the house.

"Uncle Wayne," she called out.

Katie looked out the window and saw him sitting at the picnic table staring in the distance. Her heart broke. He looked older. His hair had grown out a bit and a heavy shadow of stubble weighed down his face. She had been so caught up in clearing his name, she'd hardly stopped to think about her uncle's grief. Perhaps because she wasn't willing to address her own.

Adjusting her robe and cinching the sash tighter, she went outside to speak to him. He turned to see her walking across the yard and smiled. It was genuine, but she could see the extreme hurt behind it—in his eyes, his posture. He had lost hope. Katie knew that she must find it for him.

"Morning, Katie," he said forcing a relaxed smile.

"Thank you for the eggs and bacon," she said. "What are you doing out here?"

"It's a nice morning. I thought I'd enjoy some of it."

"You haven't told me much about what the attorney has said or what you're going to do."

"Not much to tell," he said never looking directly at Katie. "Not yet anyway."

"Are you prepared to fight?"

"It's hard to fight when all the evidence seems to be against me."

"I've never heard you sound fatalistic before." She frowned as her concern for her uncle increased.

"Well, nothing is final yet." He took another sip of his coffee, looking at his surroundings, obviously trying to focus his mind on something else. "This is such a great piece of property. Brings back so many memories."

"Uncle Wayne, I'm worried." Her voice choked up. She reminded herself to stay strong and not break down.

"Katie, I don't want you to worry," he said and took her hand. "You can't take everyone's burden as your own."

"I'm worried about you," she stressed. "I'm going to do everything I can. We're family. You're my family—I can't lose…" She couldn't finish the words. Tears welled up in her eyes. She couldn't think about what could happen—the worst-case scenario.

"Katie, I'm still here. And don't think I don't know what you're doing."

"What do you mean?" she said.

"I've known you ever since you were a little girl—and I know you better than you think. Always trying to solve problems, taking on big things just because you could." He laughed. "You were a serious little girl and you always knew what you wanted—and went after it."

"I can't help it," she said.

"I've had a lot of time to think. I'm more worried about you and whoever this person is that came after you than I am about being thrown behind bars. It's obviously someone who is intent on making *me* pay by taking those I love away from me."

"Do you think it's the same guy?" she said, shuddering at the thought of the man shrouded by darkness and firing off four rounds into her Jeep like he was shooting fish in a barrel.

"I don't know."

"Speculation?"

He hesitated. "Of course, there's a high probability that it is. But *who* is the question."

"And why?" she said.

"It's someone committed to hurting me at any cost. Their hatred is overflowing and they want me to pay. Instead of killing me, they are taking away everyone and everything important to me." He turned to face Katie. "I won't allow you to put yourself in danger."

Katie sat quietly.

"You will keep me informed, right?" he pushed.

"Of course. I can handle myself—you know that," she said. "And, you seem to forget that I led an entire army team through bomb-infested areas ten thousand miles away from home." She tried to sound lighthearted, but she knew that she didn't.

"You'll understand someday when you have children. Even though I never had any, you were like my own. But, it's difficult not to see our children as children anymore. You're always going to be that spunky little girl running with boys, climbing trees, and riding motocross bikes." He laughed in spite of himself.

"Uncle Wayne…" she said and hugged him tight as tears fell down her face.

"Now, Katie," he said, wiping her cheeks, "just because there isn't a quick fix to all of this, doesn't mean there isn't a solution. And we may not like the outcome. We have to stay strong."

Katie nodded, keeping her breath easy. "I've been meaning to talk to you again about what all that was about with Detective Paul Patton at the party. I know what you said before, but…"

"Just like I told Detective Hamilton, Patton is still steaming over the past—he cannot seem to let it go. I had to take him off certain cases before he retired and he was angry—and now obviously bitter."

"Do you think he's capable of murder?" she asked.

Looking away, her uncle said, "I think everyone is capable of murder at some point in their life—but there's a thin line that most will not cross."

"Uncle Wayne, I'm not the press." She hated pushing him on this matter. "Do you think he could be capable of murdering Claire?"

After a moment or so, Katie didn't think he was going to answer her question, but he finally said, "Yes, I think he's capable. But I don't think he did it."

Katie thought about what her uncle had told her and then she thought about the figure in the dark in the apple orchard and wondered if that could've been Patton.

"I get the feeling you wanted to ask me something else?" he asked now staring at her.

"I'm working on the Cynthia Andrews homicide case."

Her uncle studied her and she could tell that he was unhappy, even bordering on angry. "Why did you pick that case? That wasn't in my original selection."

"Well, I…"

He stood up. "I know why you picked that case. You think that the same person who killed Andrews killed Claire."

"Wait a minute. First, it was in the cold case file—just not the top priority cases. And two, it was one of *your* cases. I thought that if I could look at some of your old cases maybe something, anything, might pop up as to why someone would want to bring this much heartbreak into your life."

"I see where you're going but there's no proof that the signature is identical."

"Actually, I spoke with Dr. Dean and he said he couldn't say one hundred percent, but there are definite consistencies of the wounds in both crimes. There's a chance it was committed by the same person. Tell me, how could you, or anyone, think it's a coincidence?"

"Katie, you don't know what you're getting into."

"I hope it leads us to the real killer. If this person killed Andrews twelve years ago, and has come after you by killing Claire… we're dealing with an organized, violent psychopath who knows how to not get caught. There must be other cases, not just these two."

He sat back down and chose his words before saying, "This is too dangerous."

"I'm not ten anymore. I have McGaven working with me on the Andrews case."

"Does he know why you picked that one?"

"I haven't told him, but he knows I'm up to something, and believe me, he has already lectured me on it."

Her uncle smiled. "I always liked him. I'm glad he's worked out as a great partner."

"The best," she said. "I spoke with Detective Teagen yesterday."

Her uncle didn't immediately answer and she couldn't read his expression.

"What did he say?" he asked flatly.

"He just talked about the case and how it was the worst crime scene he had seen on the job. Nothing more than I could obtain from the reports and statements."

Her uncle listened.

"Uncle Wayne, he's in really bad shape. He can barely get around, has to be on oxygen. Why do I get the feeling that he wasn't being completely honest with me about you?"

"You picked that up? Yeah, well, sometimes you have to make tough decisions about people that doesn't make you friends."

"I didn't get the feeling that he has a problem with you."

"Oh he does, believe me. And it'll never change."

"Why?"

"We were never good friends, but we respected each other, as most do on the job. As his health began to go downhill with his heart condition, the sheriff at the time assigned me to work with him on his cases. You can just imagine how well that went over. Teagen thought I was his babysitter, overseeing every move he made." He paused as if remembering specific conversations.

Katie listened with interest, comparing Teagen's account to her uncle's of him.

"Well, the Andrews case was the last one we worked together and it was difficult. I was trying to run for sheriff in the next election. We both had different opinions on the case: I thought the family needed a closer look and he thought that it was possibly the work of a serial killer."

"He told me that, but he didn't seem like he held a grudge against you or anything."

"You had to have known Teagen in those days. He was ruthless, often combative with other officers who didn't agree with him. There were a few times he acted like a bully. He was clever about making himself look good in a bad situation, like he was the hero."

"Wow," Katie said.

"Don't let his weak condition fool you," he said like he had heard her thoughts. "His body may be failing, but his mind is always working the angle and he's still that ruthless guy."

"So, what about the case? You two had different angles, but couldn't you check out both?"

"We kept running down leads, but nothing panned out."

"What about the friend, Brandon Wills?"

"The friend? Supposedly the *best* friend? We spoke with other students and many said that Brandon was very jealous and he would say mean things about her when she wasn't around. Typical immature kid stuff."

Katie remembered how Dr. Wills referred to Cynthia Andrews as "Cindy" as if it was an endearing name for a close friend. But if he did kill his friend, why would he also kill Claire?

"I can tell that you have a lot on your mind," he said.

"Just balancing two cases at once," she said. "Let me ask you a question: How would you approach the Andrews case today?"

"Besides re-examining everything—the evidence, the statements, and finding out what friends and family had been doing since the murder—I would study the killer, like you do with your profiles, and then talk to the closest people to the victim."

"Would you search for similar cases in other jurisdictions?"

"Sure. To cover all bases if nothing is turning up. But that's a lot of work."

"That's what McGaven does best."

"I know that I can't stop you from doing your job—but I can't stress enough to be careful. Take extra precautions even if it seems silly, okay?"

"I will, I promise. I have another question and I don't want you to be mad, okay?"

He sighed, obviously bracing for the worst.

"I did a bit of a background check on anyone who had threatened you publicly and swore revenge. I don't know what Detective Hamilton is doing about that—but I thought it was important to widen the suspect pool."

He laughed. "That's probably a long list."

"That's not funny," she said. "There were more than I thought, but the name that stands out is Clarence Warner."

Her uncle leaned back and he nodded. "He was certainly angry and he threatened to end my days in every way possible, but like so many criminals, after they get out of jail they have so many other things that they are focused on—"

"Still, I think this guy is worth looking into. He's been paroled. Did you know that?"

"No."

"Well…"

"I know what you're thinking… and, Katie, I forbid you to go after this guy."

"Don't worry, I know what I'm doing."

"Katie, I'm not kidding. Take all the extra precautions. Understand?"

"I know. I hear you loud and clear. I will be careful."

CHAPTER 30

Saturday 1330 hours

Clarence Warner hated Sheriff Scott and hadn't learned his lesson from perpetrating crimes—he spent most of his life in and out of prison. He had committed almost every type of crime except for murder. He was angry, and was considered a felon that would reoffend by the criminal justice standards. It was clear he wanted to make someone pay for everything he had had to go through.

The unmarked police car Katie had taken home was retrofitted with a back door release and internal fan system for police dogs. It had proved extremely helpful in the past, so she was glad it was available. Cisco was happy too, panting and circling in the back seat.

"Easy there, Cisco, you're just the backup. All eyes and ears."

As Katie drove, she knew that she was breaking protocol, but the way everything was escalating, she felt she had to do something. It seemed that her uncle was going to wait and see what was going to happen to him, and that wasn't good enough. She needed to be proactive for him.

Dressed in jeans, black T-shirt and lightweight leather jacket, she had her backup gun, a Beretta, concealed in her ankle holster. She'd told her uncle that she needed to get out and run some errands. She hated lying to him, but she had little choice. She had to find out more about Clarence Warner, the man who had vowed to get even with Sheriff Scott at all costs.

According to police parole records, he had been released from prison two weeks ago to a transition residence, nothing more than a halfway house, until he could obtain a job and rent an apartment. The address indicated that the building was near the old train station and it had been some type of boarding house from the 1920s.

Katie entered the old train yard and drove around to get a feel for the area. A few people loitered around but no one seemed to pay her much attention. Cisco watched the people move about, eyes and ears alert. He didn't make a sound as his excitement evolved into his serious training mode.

The area was known for a lot of drugs and prostitution, but the statistics at the police department had shown a decrease over the past two years due to diligent police sweeps and busts. Katie kept driving around and decided to park near the building where Clarence lived—or was supposed to be residing, at least according to the court papers from the parole board. Before she had left her house, she made sure that she had an up-to-date photo of him, so she glanced at it now on her cell phone; his dark features and deep-set scowl made his face unforgettable.

Outside it was overcast with a light drizzle breaking through the fog common in Pine Valley and throughout Sequoia County. Katie ruffled her hair, keeping it loose and messy to try to fit in to her surroundings. She definitely didn't want to look like a cop. As an extra precaution, she secured a small retractable police baton inside her jacket.

She had parked near an old drainage area where she could see her vehicle from the housing units and Cisco would be safe and comfortable with the interior fans set to a thermostat. Feeling a twinge of guilt leaving Cisco behind, she didn't look at him before she stepped out of the vehicle. The damp breeze pushed against her skin. She squinted as the drops of moisture blew into her eyes.

Two men were leaving the building. One tall man was smoking a cigarette, and the other, short and stocky, was looking back and forth as if he expected someone to jump out at him at any moment. They both hesitated, pulling their jackets tighter, and then decided to move on down the road.

Katie made her move, crossing the street. She knew that Cisco watched her every move. She opened the door and the old wood plank floor creaked under her boots. Two older men sat in folding chairs playing cards at a small table. Each looked up from their hands curiously, but must've decided that Katie wasn't that interesting, as they went back to their game.

Bookcases covered each side of the room behind two small green-colored sofas facing each other. They were so old that there were permanent indentions where people often sat. A large door to the right was most likely the kitchen and laundry area. Straight ahead was an old dark wooden staircase that went up to the second and third floors.

Katie turned to the men at the card table and said, "Hey, I'm lookin' for Clarence." She made sure that she sounded relaxed and informal.

One of the men, face creased beyond recognition, answered, "Up the stairs, second floor, to the right." He nodded his head in the direction of the staircase and then went back to his game.

"Thanks."

Katie climbed the staircase and nonchalantly checked to make sure that she had the car release button attached to her belt underneath her jacket. On the top landing the narrow hallway went to the left and the right, so she went to the right towards an open window and what looked like a fire escape.

The doors were labeled with what she assumed were the first three letters of each occupant's last name. She saw "WAR" for Clarence Warner and a shiver ran down her spine. She knew she shouldn't be here alone, but her stubbornness and fear about something happening to her uncle pushed her to continue.

A door opened behind her from the other end of the hallway and a heavyset man with a towel in his hand made his way to the bathroom. "Hey, baby, maybe you can do me next." He grunted as he passed and laughed all the way into the next room.

She rolled her eyes, relieved when he was gone. Alone again, she touched the doorknob and gently turned it, surprised to find it was unlocked. She looked back and forth again before she slowly pushed the door open. "Hello?" she said softly. A twin bed, battered dresser, wooden chair, and a small table with a lamp were the only things in the room. A closet with a wooden sliding door was open; a few items of clothing were hanging inside on old wire hangers.

Katie stood at the threshold, shocked by what she saw. Clicking the door shut quietly behind she tiptoed over to the closet where articles from the newspaper and printed from the Internet were tacked to the wood with push pins. All were local stories about Pine Valley, and all of them featured Sheriff Scott.

Glancing back at the door, Katie pulled her cell phone and took several photos, making sure she got every article. Most were ones she had seen before, but there were a few that she didn't know about that must have taken place before she returned to Pine Valley. There were several photographs of her uncle giving press conferences and entering the sheriff's department.

Tough on Crime Sheriff Scott Wins Election for Second Term.
Keeping Reoffending Criminals off the Streets
Sheriff Scott Testifies in Clarence Warner Burglary Case
Niece of Local Sheriff Receives Commendation for Solving
Toymaker Serial Case

Katie briefly skimmed the articles and looked closely at the photograph of Warner being led away by deputies after the guilty verdict was read; his face contorted, mouth forming hateful words, and the look in his eyes that of a wild animal.

Katie tore her eyes away and began to look around the room for anything that might connect Warner to her aunt's crime scene.

A duffle bag, camping equipment, blood; anything that would be suspicious or an outright admission of guilt. She slipped on a pair of thin crime scene gloves from her pocket before opening drawers; patting down clothes; looking at the bottom of a pair of shoes; slipping her hands underneath the mattress, under the bed and lamp. She checked everything she could think of, then looked up, trying to see anything that didn't look like it was part of the room—a secret hiding spot. There was nothing unusual except for the newspaper articles, which though incriminating, didn't prove anything.

Damn...

Stepping closer to the wall inside the closet, she looked at the condition of the articles; some had been folded and others had been printed recently from an inkjet printer. There were also some heavy black smudged fingerprints with some red mixed in.

Blood?

Blood from her aunt?

Katie couldn't take the chance that the articles could be thrown away, lost, or destroyed before she could get the police to investigate. There were two areas with the red stains, so Katie made a rash move and carefully tore off a few small pieces of the article. She didn't have CSI bags or containers, so she decided to put the pieces into one of her gloves and rolled the end to seal it, and then put it in her pocket.

She was just walking back towards the door when the doorknob turned. There was no way she could hide or explain why she was in his room, so took a couple of hurried steps toward the bed, sat down, and waited for the inevitable.

A tall man stepped inside, tattoos covering his arms and up the sides of his neck. He carried a sandwich and a bottle of Coke. It took a couple of seconds before he saw her sitting on the bed.

"Hey," she said, "I was looking for Brandon." Katie stood up. "I can see that you're not Brandon, are you?"

"What do you want? Who are you?" he said, shutting the door.

"Hey, it's an honest mistake, baby," she said. "Just lookin' for Brandon."

"There are no Brandons here." He moved closer to Katie. "You reek of a cop, bitch," he said surprising her. "This is bullshit. You're a liar."

"Hey, there's no reason for name-calling, sweetie. Just here for a good time and I was told to see Brandon." She tried to step past him, but he stood in her way.

"Oh yeah?" he said, pushing her back against the bed. "You're going to do what I want, bitch."

Katie stopped the cute girl routine and stared him right in the eye; she had to act quickly to defend herself. "Oh yeah…" she replied with sarcasm, trying to squirm out of his grip as she pulled her telescoping baton from inside her jacket and expertly swung it at his neck.

Warner dropped to the floor, seething and spewing vile curse words at her.

Katie didn't wait another second, she ran for the door, flung it open and headed for the stairs, but the two men she'd seen leaving the building earlier had returned and were in her way.

"Hey," yelled Warner. "Stop that bitch!"

The two men stood their ground. The only other choice was towards the window.

She ran—at full speed.

Warner had just managed to get up and out of his room to catch Katie, but just missed her as his fingertips grazed her jacket. She saw her destination, accelerated towards the end of the hallway, covering her face as she crashed through the window. She hit the fire escape landing hard, clambered to her feet, jumped down two steps and then dropped to the ground, jarring her teeth. Not waiting to find out if Clarence had followed her down, Katie ran around the alley and across the street until she reached her car.

Cisco was barking wildly. Within seconds, Katie was inside and driving off down the street praying no one saw her leave the boarding house. She kept driving for ten minutes before, finally, pulling over into a shopping mall parking lot in a different neighborhood. Cisco, worried out of his mind, had managed to squeeze himself into the passenger seat and was trying to lick Katie in the face.

"Take it easy, Cisco," she said.

Her pumping adrenalin was easing off, allowing her to calm down and realize that her forearms and the side of her face were burning. She glanced at herself in the rearview mirror and saw a trickle of blood. Her immediate thoughts were that she got what the case needed: a small piece of evidence to put him directly in the line of fire of the investigation and take the focus off her uncle.

Katie got out of the car and ran to the nearby gas station. The light in the restroom was dim but when Katie looked at herself in the mirror she was somewhat shocked. Her face looked drawn, greyish, peppered all over with nicks and grazes. Her blood dripped into the dirty sink.

She shed her jacket and assessed the wounds on her arms, which were sore but thankfully minimal. Cleaning her forearms and dabbing her face, she looked better within a few minutes. She picked some small glass shards from her jacket, dropping them into the trashcan.

She let out a noisy breath, not realizing that she was holding it inside. Anxiety often held her breath hostage, allowing all the symptoms of fear and panic to trail along behind with sweaty hands, chest pressure, tingling extremities, dizziness.

You are not welcome here…

Go away now.

NOW!

Katie averted her stare from the mirror and splashed more water on her face, and then headed back to the car where she sat a moment in the driver's seat with Cisco huddled at her side. She felt strangely better and somewhat relaxed despite the circumstances.

Katie turned the key and her vehicle roared to life just as her cell chimed for an incoming text from Chad:

Missed you at the house. Can we meet in about an hour?

CHAPTER 31

Saturday 1645 hours

Katie rushed home to take a shower, steady her nerves, and get ready before Chad arrived. She had been so wrapped up in the cases, her uncle, and trying to keep everything in line that she had forgotten about the most important person in her life. She knew that he understood that it was a rough patch, but she didn't want to ruin a great thing.

As the heat of the water cascaded down her body, she felt her cuts sting and was reassured that they were temporary and insignificant, not like the psychological wounds she hid, sometimes even from herself. Her mind wandered to her first encounter with Dr. Carver. *Was this the answer? Would therapy heal all wounds?* Katie knew she needed to give it another chance. It was difficult to be vulnerable and talk about raw emotions, but something would break if she kept things the way they were going.

Katie saw movement in the bathroom and for an instant her senses went into high-alert. As the steam cleared from the glass door, she saw the black nose accompanied by tall ears of her best friend pressed against the glass. Cisco's shiny coat and light brown wolf-like eyes peered at her, his tail wagging. She shut off the water and opened the shower door. "Cisco, you startled me," she said, quietly impressed that the dog had somehow worked the door open.

Since Chad didn't tell her what they were doing, she dressed casually in jeans and a light sweater. She took the extra minutes to put some makeup concealer on her bruises. From everything on her mind and physical exertion from early in the day, she was exhausted. Hearing voices in the kitchen, she stepped into the hallway and listened. It was Chad and her uncle, but they were talking in soft tones, which was unusual. She strained to hear, but could only make out a few words.

She walked through the living room and stood at the kitchen door where both men were huddled together.

"Well, are you figuring out what to buy me for Christmas?" she said jokingly.

"Just talking guy stuff," said Chad.

"What? Like man caves and sports?" she said leaning in to kiss him.

"How did you know?" said her uncle. His complexion was back to normal with color in his cheeks as he was beginning to look more like himself. The conversation with another guy must've helped.

Katie noticed that Chad was dressed casual as well.

"You look fantastic given you totaled your Jeep," he said.

"Didn't take five minutes before you brought that up!"

"Well, everyone at the firehouse was talking about it, and I got the opportunity to say yep, that's my girl."

"Where are you two going tonight?" the sheriff asked, obviously not wanting to talk about Katie's accident.

"I thought something informal and easy," he said. "You up for it?"

"Absolutely. As long as I'm not driving." She smiled.

Katie's uncle went into the living room and made himself comfortable on the couch. "Just me and Cisco tonight." The dog's ears perked up at his name. He padded over to the couch and jumped up next to him, moving one of the throw pillows before settling down.

Chad hugged Katie and took her arm. She winced. He looked at her with concern.

"Still a little sore from the accident," she said, still smiling. "Goodnight, Uncle Wayne." She gave him a quick peck on the cheek.

"Don't worry about me," he said and picked up the television remote.

The night had turned colder and the sun had finally completely disappeared. As Chad eased his large SUV down the driveway, Katie was suddenly struck by how lucky she was and how she wanted all the drama to go away.

"Babe," Chad said.

Katie looked at him and realized that he had been talking to her, but she was lost in her deep thoughts. It was difficult for her to turn off her work load. "Oh, I'm sorry," she said. "It's been a rough week, that's all."

"I would say so. That's why I wanted to have a relaxing evening without all the reminders of what you've been dealing with."

"So what are we going to do?"

"I thought it might be fun to go to the movies. You know, eat popcorn and those chocolate drop things you like."

"Yeah, that would be fun."

"But no," he said. "Then I thought I could make you dinner at my apartment. All nice and romantic. Quiet too."

"Sure, that would be nice too."

"Yeah, well no."

Katie laughed. "What are we going to do?" She played along and absolutely loved to watch his eyes light up with that same mischievous expression he had when they were growing up.

"So, I had to really think about it. And as it so happens, Rick, who is the firehouse cook, made us a special dinner for two. Even I don't know what's in there," he said and pointed to the back seat where an insulated bag sat.

"Wow, what a great guy to do that."

"Well, I kind of tell stories about you and the guys are impressed."

Katie was surprised and a bit flattered. "Like what?" she said.

"Don't forget they can read, you know. Those cases you've worked have been in the paper. Not to mention your heroics."

"Hardly me, I had help."

"Well, everyone is entitled to their own opinions."

Katie observed the area as Chad turned off the main road and took one of the back roads. He flipped up the headlights to high and the entire forest came into view. The moon peeked between the tall trees, lighting up the area even more.

"Is it a full moon?" she asked.

"Yep," was his reply.

It seemed like an eternity since Katie had just enjoyed the evening outdoors with a full moon. "I remember those camping trips we had."

"Those were the best, weren't they?"

"Yeah. They really were."

Katie surveyed the road and it seemed a familiar area. Since she had been home, there had been so little time for her to enjoy the area again. It was as if she had been thrown right into the serial killer and missing persons' cases.

Chad drove the SUV around a popular scenic point, but then took a little-known road and stopped. He then backed up and maneuvered his vehicle so that the back end faced the view.

"Wait right there." He jumped out and jogged around the front and then opened Katie's door. "Here you are."

Katie said, "Is there anything I can do?"

"Nope."

She noted as he hurried around the vehicle and pulled out the insulated food container and another food basket, blanket, two pillows, and extra jackets. He opened the back where it had been cleared out and cleaned. "Wow, you know how to plan and pack. Not to mention it's so clean."

"I know, right?" he said. "I actually cleaned out the entire cargo area. Not sure when I've done that before."

Katie gazed at the view in the valley of trees and rolling hills. Normally you wouldn't be able to see it at night, but the moon illuminated the breathtaking view that rivaled an artist's interpretation of perfection.

"Here," said Chad as he put a comfortable long jacket around Katie's shoulders.

"Thanks. It's colder than I thought it would be." She noticed the way he looked at her as he helped her pull the jacket around her shoulders. His expression was deep and soulful. It was the way that every woman wanted to be looked at by the man they loved. Emotions hit her like a fire in her heart, heavy and smoldering.

"You know, I think this is the best light," he said. "It makes gardens look like they are glowing. Trees are another deeper shade of green."

Katie looked down, taking everything in.

Chad pulled her close to him and she could feel the heat from his body. She still felt like a teenager whenever she was with him and remembered the first time they took the leap and slept together. In her mind, she would always be that teenage girl with her first love.

He leaned in and kissed her slowly and passionately. She felt his lips soft against hers, longing and wanting to be with her. Katie let all her passions loose and felt all her trauma and responsibility disappear, even if it was only for a little while.

The cool evening contrasted with the heat between Katie and Chad. The moonlight was picture-perfect, lighting up the landscape all around them as they stood together at the hilltop. All the creatures in the forest were quiet except for the sudden screech of an owl.

Katie's mind resurfaced and she slightly pulled away from Chad's warm embrace. It was an amazing romantic moment, but it was leading to something much more intimate that would be more appropriate with the comforts of the indoors.

"You cold?" he asked.

"No. But I have to admit…" She hesitated. "I'm a little hungry and curious about what's in those bags."

He laughed. "Of course, I'm hungry too. I skipped lunch today." Chad moved to the vehicle where he pulled out the blanket and smoothed it out in the cargo area. With the back open, it made a perfect place to sit and eat while watching the moonscape.

Katie arranged the soft pillows before taking her seat. "This is great. The true meaning of dinner by moonlight." She smiled and felt more relaxed than she thought possible.

Chad made himself comfortable. "Let's see what the master chef has prepared for us. There's definitely enough light out here to see everything." He opened the insulated bag and there were two large bowls with heavy lids. "What do we have here?"

Katie leaned in as Chad carefully removed the lid. The fantastic aroma of beef stew filled the air between them. "Wow," she said. "That smells so awesome."

"Perfect for the cool weather." There were fresh baked rolls with butter to accompany the stew. He then pulled out two rolled up cloth napkins with silverware.

Katie and Chad ate and were quiet for a few minutes as each of them enjoyed their meal.

"Oh, I almost forgot." He retrieved a bottle of wine, uncorked it, and filled two glasses.

"Your chef thought of everything," she said.

Chad raised his glass. "To us, to justice, and to happier adventures…"

"Cheers," they said in unison.

They enjoyed their meal and wine, chatting about work and mundane things, enjoying each other's company.

"Now," said Chad. He jingled the keys in his hand and then returned them to his pocket. "Now that I have you here and I have the only means to get home, you need to come clean."

"What?"

"I'm not joking. What's going on with you?"

"You've been talking to Uncle Wayne again?"

"Maybe."

"McGaven then?"

"Maybe," he said again.

"What's going on?" she said suspiciously.

"I may not be a first-rate detective, but I know when something hinky is going on."

"Hinky? Really?" she said.

"Look, everyone is worried about you, including me."

"Why?"

"It's not just working these cases or the fact that someone came after you the other night. But that does concern me. It's what you're *not* telling anyone. Look, give us all some credit, we know you; we know how you're not going to back down when you want to get to the truth."

"Wait... wait a minute."

"Tell me I'm wrong and I won't bring it up again. Look me in the eye and say it."

Katie started to deny it, but she wasn't going to base her relationship with Chad on a lie. "Alright. I'm looking into a few things, but nothing that is dangerous."

He sighed and said, "I knew it."

"What would you do if it was your family? Sit around and expect everyone else to put the kind of time and heart into it you would? Or, would you do everything you could to find out the truth?" She watched his reaction. His face clouded, and she knew that he would fight for his family.

"Of course that's true, but… this case is bigger than anyone thinks it is, except maybe your uncle. There's something *big* at work here—this doesn't seem like a small-town murder. Framing a sheriff for murder, and brazenly going after his niece."

"I know," she said softly. "Believe me, I've agonized over it. I don't want to bring anyone else in on this—"

"You mean McGaven?"

"Yes. I know he's annoyed, probably angry at me too. He wants to help."

"I want to help," said Chad.

"It's not your job," she said softly.

He stared at her. It was unclear to Katie if he was insulted or never thought of it that way before.

"I love you. I love you more than I ever thought I could. So you need to trust me. I'll be fine," she stressed, not sure if she was trying to convince him or herself. "I keep saying this a lot lately, but you do know that I headed an army team through combat zones, navigating around improvised explosion devices, right?" She forced a smile.

"Who you are, and all the multi facets to you, are what make me love you so much. Just promise me before you do something that's not according to your job assignment—just let me know."

"I will, I promise." She squeezed his hand and kissed him. "I will." She hated not telling him what she was planning and hoped that he would understand.

He stroked her face and kissed her again. His eyes conveyed his concern and worry, but he trusted her abilities. She could always read his emotions—he wasn't adept at hiding them.

"Okay, I was going to save this for later, but…" he said playfully.

"But what?"

"There's something with chocolate for dessert."

CHAPTER 32
Monday 0745 hours

Katie arrived at her office shortly before 8 a.m. She expected to see McGaven already at work in the office conducting background searches, but his chair was empty. She had been so immersed in her own complications and how she would proceed with her uncle's case without getting noticed that she had forgotten about McGaven working his patrol shift and he wouldn't be working investigations until tomorrow.

Stacked in the middle of her desk were reports on Cynthia Andrews' family. A neatly printed note attached read:

Interesting reading. You now can begin your criminal profile.

On a three-by-three inch yellow sticky note were the words:

AND 377 and AND 377-A located in the office across the hall. Have fun.

McGaven had pulled the evidence on the Cynthia Andrews case, which helped to jumpstart her Monday morning.

Katie smiled, looked at McGaven's empty chair and listened to the silence in her office, and wondered what would ultimately happen if things didn't go the way they were supposed to.

Suck it up, Scott…

She went to the office across the hall, pressed in the security code and entered. There were two large plastic bins with heavy-duty attached lids, which had the corresponding identification affixed to the outside.

She hefted both boxes into her office, putting one box on McGaven's desk and the other on hers so she could examine each one with ease and spread anything out. Glancing at the board, she reread everything in detail she already had then opened the first bin and sorted out the bagged evidence: rope, clothing (T-shirt, socks, and shorts), tent, miscellaneous camping supplies, sleeping bag, backpack, notebook, canteen and food, and a binder with copies of published papers.

Katie took out the notebook first and slipped it out of the evidence bag—the notes with it explained it was found just outside what was left of the tent. It was one of those lab books with a black hardbound cover and college ruled paper inside for about hundred pages. Both sides were well-worn and the entries were meticulously entered with small printed letters and numbers referring to times, dates, and types of foliage native to California. Cynthia had further referenced their appearance and size, which wasn't helpful to Katie. She turned each page but nothing jumped out to her except an out of place doodle or two.

Katie finally reached the last entry Cynthia had written before she was killed. Instead of data, she had written:

> *This camping trip was perfect timing to get away. I don't want to think about the aftereffects of my research once it becomes common knowledge. It would surely fast-track my application and I will be on my way to a teaching position at the university. I left a message for Celeste Harper, the head of my Ph.D. board, with all the details.*

Katie sat back and thought about all the implications of sci-entific breakthrough: grant money, speaking engagements, and a position at the university. She thumbed back through reports from Detective Teagen and her uncle. There was a mention about the journal and that Dr. Celeste Harper was out of the country at the time Cynthia was murdered, which had given her an airtight alibi. Katie wanted to speak with her all the same, to see if she could shed any light on the investigation. Keying in a search for Dr. Celeste Harper on her computer, Katie found a website that described her as "the Mother Nature of the science world" and listed speaking engagements all over the world and an office at the university.

Dialing the number, Katie waited.

"Hello Dr. Harper's office, may I help you?" greeted a very pleasant woman's voice.

"Hello, is Dr. Harper back in the country?" Katie asked.

"Yes, she's back here for about two weeks."

"Would it be possible to set up an appointment with her?"

"Let me see… Yes, she has one appointment tomorrow at noon."

"That would be fine."

"Affiliation?"

"Pine Valley Sheriff's Department."

There was a pause on the other end of the line. Finally, she asked, "Name?"

"Detective Katie Scott."

"And this is regarding?"

"A former colleague."

"Okay, Detective Scott. Your appointment is for tomorrow at noon."

"Thank you," she said as the phone disconnected.

Katie took the notebook and made a photocopy from a small copy machine she had requested and finally received a few weeks ago. She took the reproduction of Cynthia's last entry and taped it to the cupboard next to an eight-by-ten photo. She was an attractive brunette with long hair, sad eyes, and a pleasant smile.

Katie stared at her for a moment thinking about who would want to kill her—and why.

Stay focused…

Katie pulled out the remnants of the blue tent; it had been reported that there were no bloodstains on it. She studied them inside the bags and read the notations of testing the unknown stains, and she also noted that there'd been no tests for the usual culprits like blood, saliva, semen, or anything associated with camping. The testing had concluded that the dark stains were a type of grease similar to the grease found on the material outside her uncle's house. There was nothing more recorded about it in the report.

Moving the boxes and clearing both desks, she pushed them together and laid out the tent material like pieces of a jigsaw puzzle. The poles and supports were in the other box, but she didn't need them at the moment. Looking closely at the slices, she realized that the knife was sharp and it appeared to cut at an angle. Referring to the forensic report—it wasn't John's because it was before he was hired—the conclusion had been that the slicing was from a blade that was more than three inches and less than twelve. Katie frowned. The information wasn't what she had hoped and was annoyingly unspecific. There was no way of knowing if the weapon that killed Andrews and sliced up the tent was modern, or antique.

Next, Katie opened the binder with the crime scene photos of Cynthia tied to the tree. The slashes on the bloodied white T-shirt in the evidence bag matched the photographs of her body taken at the morgue. They were neat and proportional, having a terrifying note of self-control to them.

As hard as she tried, Katie couldn't separate this murder from her aunt's, the vicious attack, overkill slicing, and the type of weapon used.

What's the connection?

She quickly looked at the rope, sleeping bag, backpack, and tent supporting poles before beginning to pack everything away. Suddenly, she paused, remembering the sliver of blue fabric she found in her uncle's yard. Could it be from a tent, or backpack? She looked to the note on the profile of her killer: "comfortable hiking and camping and even climbing if that were necessary."

She picked up the folder that held the background information on Cynthia Andrews' family. McGaven had done preliminary backgrounds for Andrews' mom (Sarah B. Andrews), sister (Tara Anne Andrews O'Conner), cousin (Charles F. Harding), aunt and uncle (Mr. and Mrs. Robert S. Harding). No one had a criminal background, though some had minor citations including one trespass, two disorderly conducts, and a dozen parking tickets. It appeared that her dad and grandparents were deceased.

McGaven had taken the background checks a step further to find out what everyone did for a living and their special interests. He managed to pull some personal information using the main police database. It gave a better picture of who they were along with the statements they gave to the investigating detectives. Andrews' mom worked as a marketing associate, her sister was a kindergarten teacher, her cousin managed a car rental company, and her aunt and uncle owned their own sporting goods store.

A red flag went up for Katie when she saw the mention of a sporting goods store. She read further to find they'd owned the store for almost fifteen years and were avid outdoor adventurers. They probably would be able to hike, climb, and camp with little difficulty. But why would they kill their niece? Financial gain? Deceit? Jealousy? Katie didn't see it. Maybe it was a coincidence that they had a camping and sporting goods store? Did Cynthia buy her equipment there before her trip? She stared at the map.

How did the killer know Andrews was going to be there?

Was he already there and waited for the perfect moment to strike?

Was the killer following her so closely that he knew where she was going to be?

Katie scrutinized her lists and the maps. The killer had to have known where she was going. The only people who would have known she was going camping to get research on the King's Gold based on their statements were:

Dr. Brandon Wills (best friend)
Dr. Celeste Harper (Ph.D. head of the board for Cynthia Andrews)
Possibly Aunt and Uncle Harding (owners of sporting goods store: Everything Outdoors)

Katie pulled out her personal iPad with notes about her uncle's case. Persons of interest included:

Clarence Warner (arrested and swore revenge, saved every newspaper article)
Retired Detective Paul Patton (crashed anniversary party, felt cheated out of working cases)
Retired Detective Kenneth Teagen (worked cases with Uncle Wayne, felt cheated/disrespected, health issues but blames Uncle Wayne)

Her office phone rang, startling her back to the present.

"Scott," she said.

"Hey, it's Denise."

"Hey there," said Katie as she smiled.

"Just a quick piece of information that I thought you'd like to know. The license plate XLG_344Y that was on the car that chased you is registered to a Robert Stanley Harding, but the truck actually belonged to a Mark Steven Messinger and he reported it missing days before."

"Harding?" Katie reveled. "Is that the same Harding who owns Everything Outdoors Sporting Goods?"

"Yes. How did you know that?"

"Denise, you've just helped to put another piece into the puzzle. Talk to you later." She hung up. Moments later, her cell phone alerted her to a text message from Nick:

Meet me at the Night Owl at 6 p.m.—Don't dress like a cop.

CHAPTER 33

Monday 1815 hours

Katie drove to the Night Owl, a dive bar located in the most historical area of Pine Valley. With its flashing neon sign advertising its name, the bar was in stark contrast to the beautifully restored buildings that surrounded it. It was a place known for havoc that attracted some of the roughest characters around. Katie had never been there, but there were plenty of stories over the past five years about knifings, brawls that ended with someone getting thrown through the window, and several homicides. It was obvious Nick felt the area's worst bar would be the best place to sit and talk without anyone knowing or caring who they were. If anyone did recognize them, they were two ex-army military personnel who could handle themselves. Katie hoped that it wouldn't come down to that.

Pulling into the parking lot, Katie parked in a dark corner so no one would spot her unmarked police vehicle. She untucked her sleeveless blouse, tossed her work jacket in the backseat, and let her hair down. For good measure, she darkened her makeup and doused her lips with burgundy lipstick. It was the best she could do. Ready, she sat in the car listening to the sound of the cooling engine, surprised not to hear music blaring from the bar. No loud voices. No jukebox. No arguing in the parking lot. With her Glock safely locked in the trunk, Katie slipped her backup weapon into her ankle holster. It was a bit uncomfortable, but knowing that she had something to protect herself at all times gave her peace of mind. She grabbed her small purse and exited the car. Glancing around the parking area, she didn't see Nick. She was almost twenty minutes late, so she assumed he was inside waiting for her.

She pulled the front door open and walked inside, glancing from one side of the room to the other searching for Nick. Most people were huddled over their drinks at the bar. The bartender, an old man with a heavy grey beard, stood behind the bar pouring a double Scotch on the rocks. Several small tables were spread out around the room and an attractive middle-aged woman wearing a T-shirt two sizes too small was going from table to table flirting with patrons.

In the corner, drinking a bottle of beer, sat Nick. She had to squeeze by a couple of tables to get to him and could smell the nauseating mixture of whiskey and cheap aftershave.

"Well?" she said, barely loud enough for others to hear. "Are you going to invite me to sit down?"

He didn't say anything but gestured to the empty chair, playing it cool.

Katie pulled the chair out and made herself comfortable.

"You want a drink?" he said chewing on a toothpick.

"Do I have to ask?" she said, keeping up the performance.

Nick waved to the waitress and indicated he wanted another two beers. He leaned forward, smiled and gave her a wink. "You look too good to be in a place like this, Scotty." He spoke in low tones. "I wanted to talk to you away from anywhere someone you know might come in. It couldn't be at your house or work."

"No one would *ever* find me here," she said.

Nick's expression changed. It was obvious that something was troubling him.

The waitress delivered their beers.

"Thank you," he said.

Katie moved her chair closer to his. "What is it? Just tell me, okay."

"The department is planning to formally arrest your uncle and charge him with first degree murder."

Katie felt her blood run cold. "I... I don't understand. What motive do they have? They have to prove *mens rea*, the defendant's intent. What? What could they possibly have?"

Nick took both of Katie's hands across the table. He gently squeezed them. "Apparently it was for money."

"Money? That's ridiculous."

"Your aunt had a significant amount of money in investments, more than three million dollars."

"That can't be right," said Katie, reeling from the information. "Are you sure?"

"Yes. I heard it from Detective Hamilton and then later it was verified when my brother took over from me and he heard other detectives talking about it."

Katie was speechless, not knowing what to say or even how to process this information.

Nick let go of her hands. He looked grim, so Katie braced for the worst.

"Your uncle knew about the money," he said.

"He wouldn't care about it—he's not like that and never has been."

"Maybe so, but there are two witnesses who will testify that they heard your aunt and uncle arguing about money. So that means—"

Katie interrupted him, "So that means that they have motive and opportunity. Not to mention that his fingerprints are all over the murder weapon," she said, trying to keep her emotions in check.

"I'm sorry, Scotty—I am really sorry. I wanted to be the first to tell you in case someone at work decided to tell you. It doesn't take a genius to know that he didn't do it."

"What are they waiting for? Why don't they arrest him now?"

"The DA needed to verify the witness statements and your uncle's attorney wanted to get an independent to lab test the evidence. You've got a few more days."

"In which time they'll prepare a firing squad—it's going to blow up in the media. I can't let this happen," she said, moving to get up.

"No. You can't act on emotion here. You're smart, Scotty. You have time to plan and make your moves—strategically."

"No. You don't understand." Her voice cracked. "He is the *only* family I have now…"

Her words simmered for a moment before he finally said, "I can't say that I know how you're feeling now, but I do know about family. And you brought me back mine. But don't ever forget, Scotty, you have more family than you think."

As his words hung in the air Katie kept his gaze and managed a small smile. She knew what he meant; family was more than blood. As lost as she felt at that moment, she knew that her family would give her all the strength she needed to save her uncle.

CHAPTER 34

Tuesday 0930 hours

Katie had been in the office for two hours on the phone to both Cynthia Andrews' mom and her sister. They did more than answer her questions: they wanted to do whatever they could to help, and were more than a little surprised that someone was picking up on the case after all these years. They told her that Cynthia's death had left a gaping hole in their family that could never be filled. Something that Katie could relate to.

McGaven arrived and gave a warm hello. "You look like you've been here all night."

"Nope, just this morning. I've been doing background checks with Andrews' mom and sister, nothing we didn't already know, unfortunately."

"Then why do you sound so chipper?"

"Being pissed off hasn't helped me or the investigation so far, so I thought I'd change tack."

"Fill me in," he said, taking his coat off and hanging it on the back of his chair.

Katie turned her chair to face him and thought long and hard about the night before, realizing that she needed to stay positive and constructive. "I went through all the evidence boxes, pieced together the tent, examined the T-shirt she was wearing and photographs of the scene. The wounds were absolutely horrific, but deliberate. It didn't look like the killer was out of control or acting on impulse."

"Okay, so a strategic killer. That slims down the suspect pool a bit."

"Oh, and I found something interesting," she said and pointed to the journal entry from the victim's lab book. "This was the last page of her notebook, dated the day she was killed. As you know, she had only been camping for three days. And the medical examiner had estimated that her body had been tied to the tree under twenty-four hours."

McGaven examined the photocopied journal entry.

I don't want to think about the aftereffects of my research once it becomes common knowledge. It would surely fast-track my application and I will be on my way to a teaching position at the university.

"We didn't initially think that her plant research held any significance, but obviously it does. Whether it's grant money, a university position, or notoriety."

"Is it worth killing over?" he said.

"Anything can be worth killing over if you want it badly enough."

"That's true."

Katie got up and scribbled beneath her profile of the killer: *jealousy, greed, revenge.* "From the statements and my conversations with Andrews' immediate family, I don't see that there are any red flags. But… I want to know more about her aunt and uncle who have the outdoor sporting and camping store. That's worth checking out."

"Undercover?" he said.

Katie laughed. "I think that might be a good idea."

"True enough," he said, reading the board. "So I see that you've also included the retired Detective Teagen."

"If we don't include everyone who might have some connection besides the obvious, we could miss a clue. I know it's not the usual thing to put fellow law enforcement officers on the list. It doesn't necessarily mean that they are killers—it just means that there might be clues pertaining to the case we're missing." Katie paced the room as she spoke.

"Detective Scott, how much coffee have you had today?"

"Not enough."

"What's next?"

"I have a noon appointment with Andrews' Ph.D. supervisor, Dr. Celeste Harper. She's an interesting character. She travels all over the world giving lectures on environmental issues and climate change, and how California is *apparently* leading the charge with its research." Katie rolled her eyes in sarcasm.

"You don't believe in helping the environment?"

"No, that's not it. Our environment is important, but you still have to look at motivations for everything."

"That's it. Only decaf tea for you from now on."

"Seriously, I think this woman has figured out a way to make a handsome living on just talk. Whether it's for saving the planet or fear mongering, I take pause when it comes to these types of people—that's all."

"Fantastic, well, we'll know for sure when we meet today," he said smiling. "They always said you would get to meet interesting people as a cop."

"I was meaning to ask. Is it possible to take another car?"

"Not the unmarked patrol vehicle?"

"Yeah, normally that's fine and when I have Cisco, but I think we should blend in."

McGaven thought about it for a moment, then, contemplating, he said, "I think I can work something out with the guys at impound."

"That would be great."

"Speaking of cars… what are you going to do about yours?"

Katie let out a breath. "My Jeep is totaled and I've got to get a new one at some point, but when do I ever have time?"

"Let me go to impound and ask around," he said.

"Okay."

"Meet you back here in about an hour?"

"Great. I'll meet you out front," she said.

McGaven left and Katie searched the Internet for more info on Dr. Harper.

As Katie rounded the building and crossed the parking lot, she heard voices and saw several news vans parked in a huddle outside the station, and Undersheriff Martinez getting ready for a press conference on the steps. She stopped to watch the media frenzy from afar as Martinez fidgeted with his tie, reveling in the spotlight, before he signaled for quiet and began to speak.

"Thank you, ladies and gentlemen, for being here today. Pine Valley Sheriff's Department has an update we would like to share with the community. Five years ago, one of our residents, Samuel Stiles, went missing on his way home from work. We put our very best men and women on the case, but after months of tireless work the case went cold." He paused for effect. "But we never gave up on the search. We will never give up on anyone in this community. And through the incredible investigative efforts of our detectives, we were able to find Mr. Stiles…"

McGaven appeared at Katie's side, equally intrigued to hear if their names would be mentioned, expecting them not to be.

"Excuse me," interrupted a reporter, "our sources tell us the victim's body was buried on his property. How did you find him?"

"Diligent and relentless detective work. Rolling up our sleeves and following every lead."

"My source said it was the cold case unit. Was it Detective Katie Scott?"

"It's a collaborative effort. We offer our sincere condolences to the family. I wish this were under more positive circumstances. I should add that we also found the body of Natalie Cross, Sam's wife, through the diligent and expert investigative skills of Detective Bryan Hamilton and his team. We have arrested both Dennis Palmer senior and Dennis Palmer junior for one count of first degree homicide, one count manslaughter, kidnapping, illegal gambling, racketeering. Thank you. That's all for now."

McGaven said with sarcasm, "A group effort—please!"

"Are you surprised? Sorry to say but you're now guilty by association to me," she said.

The news reporters had all started firing questions and demanding answers.

"Please," Martinez said holding up his hand, "one at a time."

A young woman from a local network pushed her way to the front. "What about Sheriff Scott? When will he be charged with his wife's murder?"

"We will update you all when there's news. For now—no comment," he said and made his way back inside the office followed by the two lieutenants and two deputies.

"Let's get out of here. Where's the new ride?" said Katie as she pushed the reality of her uncle's fate from her mind.

"Your chariot awaits…"

"Really?" she said, walking with him to the farthest side of the building's parking lot. "Couldn't think of a better line?"

"I'm old-fashioned."

"You know," she said and stopped to look at him, "you are. That's what I love about you."

"You really love me?"

"Shut up, McGaven. Where's the ride?" She smiled.

"It's right there," he said and pointed to a navy four-door sedan.

"It looks like our other car."

"Not really, it's foreign and it's one of the most popular family cars in America."

"Okay, give me the keys," she said.

"What?"

"I'm driving us up to the university."

"Why?"

"Do I have to answer that?" she said.

He sighed and gave her the keys.

Katie got behind the wheel and it felt like the downgraded version of her police sedan. It made her miss her Jeep.

Both Katie and McGaven rode in silence until they reached the university. Instead of going to the teaching area and labs, they were instructed to go to the administration building, where Dr. Harper kept an office that had more security and better parking.

"May I help you?" the woman at the main desk asked politely.

"We have an appointment with Dr. Harper."

"Oh, she's wonderful, and I believe she's only been back a few days. You're in luck."

"Could you point us in the direction of her office?" asked McGaven.

"Of course. Take the elevator to the third floor, turn right and follow it to the end."

"Thank you," Katie said.

Katie was relieved when the elevator doors opened to a long narrow hallway on the third floor; the air inside had been stifling and smelled of musty carpet and stale food. They quickly approached the office and Katie took a deep breath before knocking, then tried the door handle when there was no answer from inside… "Dr. Harper?" she said, opening the door and walking in to the office. "Dr. Harper? It's detectives Scott and McGaven."

The office was large, a corner room that looked out over the campus and into a pretty wooded area. The furniture was modern and inviting, as was the artwork that hung alongside certificates of all of Dr. Harper's accomplishments and a pin board with flyers for her upcoming speaking engagements.

"Nice office," said McGaven.

"Yes, I like it too," said a female voice behind them.

Katie turned to the impeccably dressed blonde woman. She was wearing a burgundy suit that fitted perfectly on her slim frame, and three-inch strappy shoes.

"Dr. Harper. I'm Detective Scott and this is Deputy McGaven."

"Yes," she said walking over to her desk and glancing down at a crowded appointment calendar. "You have half an hour. Will that suffice?"

"Yes, that should be fine," said Katie.

"Please, have a seat," she said as she took her place behind her desk. "What would you like to know about Cynthia Andrews? Such a terrible tragedy."

"Dr. Harper, thank you for seeing us. We've been reinvestigating Ms. Andrews' homicide as part of a new cold case department within the Pine Valley Police Department. You were her doctoral advisor?"

"Yes."

"What do you remember about her?"

"Well," she began, "she was bright, extremely driven, and passionate about her work. She was the type of student that any advisor would hope for."

"Did you guide her on all her research?" Katie asked.

"I don't recall all the research, but yes, generally I help students across all their subjects, refining their work to give them the best chance of earning their Ph.Ds.," she said, looking from Katie to McGaven and back to Katie again. "She was writing about native California plants which have once been extinct, or thought to be extinct, and then have made a comeback. Her idea was that we could solve some of our environmental issues based on the return and resilience of plants, foliage, and even small wild animals. I don't really expect you to completely understand."

"Something like King's Gold?" Katie watched the reaction from the woman, her eyes, hands, and demeanor.

"You've done your homework, Detective. I like that," she said. "Yes, the King's Gold was thought to be long extinct, but Cynthia said that she had seen it up in the mountains round here. I remember her telling me all about it—she was excited about documenting it."

"You don't sound convinced," said McGaven. He seemed calm and collected once the doctor's personality showed itself to be high-minded and bordering on narcissism.

"Well, you would be correct."

"Why is that?" asked Katie.

"One native plant coming back from extinction will not save our planet," Dr. Harper answered. "It's much more complicated than that."

"It is worthy of research and further investigation. Wouldn't you think?"

"There is no proof of its return," Harper said.

"But wasn't that the point?" Katie pushed. "You could see why she was so excited about it. If one native plant has found its way back—more could follow. Couldn't you, in the environmental biology field, use this information for future studies and research?"

Dr. Harper shifted in her chair and tapped her hot pink fingernails against her appointment book. "Am I being accused of something?"

"We're simply trying to get to the truth. This is a homicide investigation and I don't need to remind you how brutally she was attacked. By trying to uncover facts, we realize there might be some unpleasant things exposed, too." Katie kept the doctor's gaze. She wasn't going to let the woman off the hook so easily with partial answers, she wanted the facts.

"I see," she said and sighed. "During that time, I heard all kinds of theories that students were researching for their dissertations.

It was my job to make sure they were on the right track and help them with their topics." She leaned back in her chair, her elbows resting on the side arms. "Writing a dissertation to earn your Ph.D. can take years. *Years*, Detective. It's an extremely important part of these students' lives, and it is my job to guide them, help them, and be the best teacher I can so they can succeed."

Katie changed tack to keep her on her toes. "Did you know of any of Ms. Andrews' close friends, or boyfriends?"

"It's been a while now. No, not that I recall."

"What about Dr. Wills?" said McGaven.

"Oh yes, of course. I had forgotten they were friends."

"Was there anything bothering Ms. Andrews at that time?"

"Not that I recall."

"Did she ever confide in you about anything personal?"

She shook her head. "No, she was driven and her research was the only thing she talked about."

Katie thought a moment how to word her next question. "The day she left to conduct her research, do you remember it?"

"Yes, she stopped by to see me before she left."

"Was she supposed to go alone?"

"I think Dr. Wills, who was just Mr. Wills at the time, was supposed to go with her. I don't know why he didn't."

"She mentioned that she had left a message for you before she left. Do you recall that?"

Dr. Harper paused. "No." She shook her head slowly. "I don't remember that. Maybe she was going to leave me a message and didn't? Or, it didn't get to me. I'm sorry."

Katie flipped her notebook shut. "Thank you, Dr. Harper. We appreciate your time. If you happen to remember anything pertaining to what we've discussed today, please call me." She handed her a business card.

"Of course. I really do hope that you find what you need to solve this homicide."

Katie and McGaven left Dr. Harper's office. They walked back to the new car before speaking to one another.

"What do you think?" asked McGaven.

"It's like chasing our tail with her, but I don't think she knows anything about the murder. She might be guilty of stealing her students' ideas as her own, or something, but she's not looking like our killer."

"Okay."

"At least that's what it appears for now."

"And?"

"And? I'm hungry."

CHAPTER 35

"Okay," Katie began, "our suspects are few and weak, but we're building a better picture of Cynthia's life before she died." She added to the board *Robert Stanley Harding, age 57*, and his wife, *Carol Ann Harding, age 54*, with a notation that they were her aunt and uncle, owners of Everything Outdoors.

McGaven studied the names and associations. "So you're saying that Andrews' aunt and uncle likely knew that she was going camping? Why would she tell them?"

"I studied the tent and the poles from the evidence box. They looked brand new. And where else would she go to buy a tent for her trip? Especially on a student budget."

"I see where you're going with this."

"And the most unusual part…"

"I'm listening."

"The lovely Denise called me about this bit of information."

"I'm really listening," he said.

"The license plate that was taken off the truck that ran me down…" she said, reading her notes. "XLG_344Y was registered to a Robert Stanley Harding."

"Owner of Everything Outdoors and uncle of the victim. Wow. What the hell is going on with this case?"

"There are so many pieces to this puzzle," she said, trying to see how everything she knew fitted together, and slumping into her chair as the last of her energy drained out of her.

"Everyone has said she was a loner and focused solely on her work and article writing."

"Right, so who was around her on a daily basis? I'm just thinking that she went to classes several times a week."

"We have her school schedule. So?"

"Can you get a list of students who were in her classes, including any labs?"

"Your uncle and Detective Teagen did a pretty extensive canvass of students at the time of the murder," he said.

"I know. But, I want to see who attended the classes. We can then cross-reference any of the names on the statements if needed. They certainly didn't talk to everyone."

It was just before 5 p.m. when Katie pulled the car up opposite Everything Outdoors, where they had a prime view of the store's front window and entrance.

McGaven unclipped his seatbelt to get out.

"Wait," she said.

"For what?"

"I just want to watch for a bit. Do you have your stakeout kit?"

"It's in the trunk."

"What do you need?"

"Binoculars."

"There are some in here," he said and opened the glove box, where a small pair of binoculars rested inside.

"Let me see," she said as McGaven handed them to her. Focusing the lenses, she studied the people inside the sporting goods store. There were three customers and a middle-aged man was behind the counter.

"Anything interesting?" asked McGaven.

"Not really. I think that's the uncle behind the counter. The store is bigger than I thought."

"I wonder how they compete with the big corporate guys?"

"I think they've had the store for quite some time and must have loyal customers." Katie scanned from left to right; fishing poles, paddles, canoes, tents, shoes, tennis rackets, and a myriad of other supplies. "Looks pretty ordinary to me."

As she spoke, a white pickup truck pulled up and parked two spots away from the front door.

Katie lowered the binoculars. The truck, which had various items in the back covered partly with a dark blue tarp, looked familiar. It took her a moment to realize where she had seen it before.

"Wait a minute. It can't be."

"What's up?"

"That man who just entered the store."

"Yeah."

"That's Paul Patton," she said, amazed.

"The retired detective who originally investigated the Sam Stiles missing person's case?"

"And he's the one who crashed my uncle's anniversary party." Katie ran through several scenarios in her mind.

"What do you want to do?"

"Let's sit tight. I want to see where else he goes."

CHAPTER 36
Tuesday 1630 hours

Katie and McGaven watched as retired Detective Patton moved around the store as if he had done it a million times before. A middle-aged woman appeared beside Cynthia's uncle and then all three of them conversed, laughing and chatting like old friends.

"What do you think they are talking about?" asked McGaven, who was clearly intrigued by the situation.

"I don't know."

"Do you want me to go in?"

"No, let's sit tight. I'm more curious to see what Patton does than hear what he says." Katie felt chills down her spine: Patton was connected to everything; to Cynthia, Stiles, and her uncle and Aunt Claire. She thought back to the scene at the anniversary dinner.

McGaven peered through the binoculars. "I think he's buying some type of tarp and... it looks like a camping lamp and stove."

"He's going camping?"

"I think he's picked up some of those freeze-dried meals... maybe ten or so."

"Quite the shopper," said Katie with sarcasm.

McGaven looked at Katie and said, "You know, it isn't against the law to buy camping equipment—"

"Here they come," she interrupted.

Katie and McGaven watched as Mr. Harding helped carry Patton's things out to the truck and waved goodbye.

"Here we go," Katie said and started the engine. "This is not the way to his house."

"Interesting," was all McGaven had to say.

Katie eased the car in behind Patton, careful to leave plenty of room to avoid being noticed. "Let's think this through. He investigated the Stiles missing person's case… he disrupts my uncle's anniversary party … and now he shows up at the family business connected to our current homicide cold case… Something's up," she said, gripping the steering wheel tighter.

"You know it could be…"

"Nope. I'm not buying the whole *coincidence* thing." They were heading for the freeway out of town.

"Katie," McGaven began softly, "I know you're working overtime on this case because… well because, you think it ties to your aunt's case."

"I'm focused on the here and now—that's all."

"But you're running both cases through your head at the same time," he said.

Katie didn't say anything. She knew that he meant well, but he didn't know everything: her uncle's time was running out.

"Where's he going?" he asked.

"Not sure, but he's taking a left here," she said.

They were now leaving the main part of the city and heading towards farmland areas. The daylight was almost completely gone and Katie switched her headlights on.

"What's even out here?"

Katie knew immediately. "I can't believe this! He's going to turn onto Apricot Lane. *Apricot Lane!*" she said, barely able to contain her excitement.

"What?"

"See, he just turned," she said and slowed her speed. She didn't want Patton to get suspicious.

"How do you know?"

"This is where Kenneth Teagen lives. What do you think now?"

McGaven stayed quiet, taking it all in as Katie pulled to the side of the road near a grove of trees that slightly obstructed the view of his house.

"Why are you stopping?" he asked.

"I don't want them to see me. You don't know how much I want to search that house and property. I know this means something..." Katie pulled out the binoculars and watched Patton walk to the side door of Teagen's house, and knock. Teagen appeared, moving fast and without his oxygen tank. "I can't believe it."

"What?"

Katie gave him the binoculars.

McGaven said, "That's Teagen in the navy sweatshirt?"

"Yep. And he wasn't moving like that when I visited him. I thought something was up, but he was pale and wheezing, so I gave him the benefit of the doubt. I'm so stupid. I knew I should have listened to my gut."

"Like what? Two ex-cops who worked at the same department hanging out? Where's the coup? There's nothing suspicious about that. We don't know what this means."

"Yet. We don't know what this means *yet*."

CHAPTER 37

Tuesday 2115 hours

Katie sat in her backyard on her patio on a small padded outdoor couch, a blanket wrapped around her, trying to process her day. The weather had begun to turn colder and soon she would have to pull her outdoor furniture inside for winter. She didn't bother to turn on the outside light, preferring the dark quiet solitude. The chilly air blew against her face and awoke her senses. She found that her mind was clearer out here. She could solve problems and come up with new ideas.

Cisco grumbled as he moved to make himself more comfortable snuggled up against her, hogging a portion of the blanket. His warm body was like an outdoor heater. He hadn't wanted to leave her side recently—obviously sensing her heightened level of stress.

Katie saw her uncle's bedroom light go out and it pained her to think about how hard it must be for him to sleep alone, knowing that Claire wasn't ever coming back. Nothing that she and McGaven had uncovered was good enough. There were some interesting clues and strange correlations, but nothing substantial. How was she ever going to figure out who killed her aunt?

Katie was exhausted. She tried to focus her mind on the case in hand; Cynthia Andrews was as obsessed with her work as she was, but what drove her? Her need to be correct? Her deep desire to make a difference? Was she just as arrogant as her doctoral advisor? Was she as needy and jealous as her best friend? Overwhelmed with unanswered questions and dead ends, she took herself right back to the beginning. These questions plagued her and she knew that she was missing something—something important.

Who would want Cynthia Andrews dead?

What did she stand for that someone would want her to die?

What did she do that got her killed?

Nothing. Absolutely nothing came immediately to mind.

Katie needed to look at it from a different perspective: maybe it wasn't about what she was doing, but about the people that surrounded her.

Katie sat up straight, bothering her comfortable sleeping dog. They were looking at this cold case all wrong—the murder was either committed by someone who knew her—or someone who had *profiled* her. The crime scene had the signature of an organized offender. It was like something she had seen before—or something that had been perpetrated before.

She felt like she was being squeezed. There was chatter around the police station that they were going to officially arrest her uncle anytime and that would make the case that much more difficult.

Time was running out for her uncle. Though she knew she had most investigative clues at her disposal, none of it was helping to identify the killer. There were too many questions that still needed answering.

Taking a deep breath, Katie made a decision: to get results, and quickly, she would have to perform a Hail Mary and do the craziest thing. She still had some details to work out, though, because she would have to make sure it was within the law and within the protocol of the police department. But time was ticking down: it was time to implement a plan.

Katie was willing to risk it all; she would set a trap for the killer—and expose everything.

I can keep going…

CHAPTER 38
Wednesday 0745 hours

Katie entered the forensic lab, but instead of heading straight to her office where McGaven was most likely already hard at work, she turned right and walked up to John's private office. The door wasn't completely closed, which usually meant that he was inside catching up on paperwork.

She hesitated at the door. Last night her thoughts were clear to her, but in the light of day, she thought maybe she was being hasty, bordering on reckless. Then she remembered her uncle's behavior this morning—quiet, grief-stricken, worried.

She knocked and slowly opened the door. John sat at his desk with two high piles of file folders. His office was neat and organized, though full of paperwork. John looked up, and didn't seem to be surprised to see her. "Come in, close the door," he said flatly, scribbling his signature on the last few reports.

Only when he had slipped the papers into the appropriate folder did he finally make eye contact with her. He didn't say anything at first, but leaned back and waited.

"Can we speak in confidence?" she said.

"Of course. That goes without saying. Nothing you say will leave this office. But first, I need to tell you: that newspaper article with the dark red marks that you left for me from Warner's room…"

"Yes?" she said.

"It's paint—more specifically spray paint. Generic and anything you could get in a hardware store."

"Oh," Katie said, disappointed it wasn't blood.

"Sorry."

"Time is running out for the sheriff," she began. Her voice sounded strange in the office, but maybe it was just in her own mind. She felt her hands sweat and a peculiar tingling in her arms and legs.

No, you're not welcome here...

Her mantra could not fail her now.

John leaned forward, sensing that she was having difficulty saying what she needed to. "How's he handling everything?" he said with genuine concern.

"He's stoic, the usual tough exterior. But... I've never seen him like this... he's pulling away and seems to be giving in." Katie tried to sound matter-of-fact, but she knew that her voice was quaking. "He's waiting for the inevitable and once they officially charge him... that's when..."

"Katie, I know it's difficult for you to ask for help."

She let out a breath. He was right. She didn't want anyone to feel sorry for her, but she had to trust someone on the inside and John was someone that she felt she could.

"Just tell me what's on your mind. Would it be easier if it were soldier to soldier?"

Katie smiled. "It might be. Okay, my uncle is going to go to jail for a crime he didn't commit. I would bet my life on it. I haven't figured out yet who is framing him—but I'm getting close."

"What makes you think that?"

"From the cold case homicide I'm working. I picked it because the victim's injuries were similar to my aunt's. I believe the same person committed both crimes, but we're talking a twelve year span between killings. I know there are a lot of things that need filling in but—"

"The victim's name?"

"Cynthia Andrews. It was a case that happened before you took over."

"I see," he said as he loaded up some files on his computer. "These databases are limited, but I can see there were some major lacerations on the torso."

"I've studied the photos of the crime scene from every perspective. And I asked Dr. Dean about them in comparison to my aunt's wounds, which he couldn't confirm, but also didn't deny—if you get what I mean? I know that I'm not supposed go anywhere near Claire's case, but I can't let politics, hatred, jealousy, and whatever else ruin my uncle's life. I won't."

John studied Katie closely, making her feel a bit self-conscious. She liked John and respected his work, but there was also some chemistry bubbling away beneath the surface. "You've done more than prove yourself. Don't think for a moment everyone at the department believed what Undersheriff Martinez said about the Stiles case and giving Hamilton all the credit—most people know that it was you and McGaven who found that missing man." He smiled.

Katie looked down, knowing she had to ask John a favor. "I know that there must be evidence that doesn't just show my uncle's guilt—but his innocence. I know there's something, somewhere, that would exonerate him."

"What did you have in mind?"

"Did you confiscate his laptop from the living room? He had three computers—his work one and a personal one, and an old one he kept in the living room."

"Yes, though we took just one."

"Is there also another way to check the security footage—like an automatic backup? Would that be on his personal computer?" She knew that John was an expert with security cameras as he installed the one in her house not long ago.

"It's possible."

"The house is no longer a crime scene, so anything that gets examined or discovered wouldn't be going against the active police investigation. As long as it's turned over to the police at some point, is that right?"

"That's correct."

"One more thing… actually there are two more things."

"I knew there was more," he said trying not to smile.

"The knife bothers me. When I found my aunt, the knife was in the sink because my uncle said he put it there. I remember seeing it lying flat on the bottom near the drain, and it appeared that the knife was saturated with blood—nothing out of place about that. There were so many things that were horrifying and overwhelming that day—but the knife placement has really stayed with me; I think it's because I knew subconsciously that something was wrong. It was too symmetrical, as if someone had carefully placed it there. I don't think my uncle did—I think he was mistaken."

"Okay, so what is it that you need?"

"Two things. You tested the knife and it was my aunt's blood, right?"

"Yes."

"Was there anything else? Someone else's blood? Any contaminants?"

"I tested a fair amount of the blood and it was all your aunt's, and the sheriff's fingerprints were on the handle—smudged, but enough to make a 9-point ridge comparison."

"I believe if tested further you will find someone else's blood—there must be something we can use to steer the investigation away from my uncle. Something,…"

"You said there were two things."

Katie relaxed a bit and her slight dizziness dissipated. "My Jeep."

"What about it?"

"I expect that there were no fingerprints on the truck that ran me down, right?"

"True."

"But, did you dust for prints on my Jeep?"

"Yes, around the exterior."

"But not inside?"

"There was no need to. At least, I was instructed to not bother. We pulled two of the bullets from the interior. The other two bullets had struck one of the apple trees."

"When I saw the man come up from the hillside, I saw him reach inside his jacket for the semi-automatic before he aimed inside my Jeep." Katie paused. "I remembered this later because he bent over slightly and put his left hand inside the cab and then fired the four bullets. It was a weird move. He curled his fingers with his palm up like this," she said and demonstrated. "That would be near the floorboards in the car. Maybe there's some type of contaminant or something that he left behind?"

John leaned back and studied Katie. She thought for a moment that he was going to tell her that he couldn't do anything for her. "So what you're saying is you want me to check your uncle's personal laptop for any security footage that might have been backed up, because it might shed some light on the murder, retest the knife for foreign matter, and dust the inside of your Jeep?"

She nodded in agreement, knowing she'd overdone it and asked too much of him.

"Katie, I've been wondering why you haven't asked before."

"I don't want anything to do with me to interfere in your job—or worse."

"The testing will take a bit of time for the knife. I need to go to the impound for dusting of prints on the Jeep. But… I do have about an hour I can spare for the laptop. Do you have access to the house?"

"Yes, yes, we can go right now. I'll let McGaven know that I will be in the office later this morning."

*

Katie drove up to her uncle's house once again in dark and dreary weather, which matched the situation and her mood. She sat for a moment remembering how light and happy she had felt at the anniversary party. It was almost too much to bear to go back inside again—heavy heartache gripped her chest.

"Katie? Everything okay?" asked John.

"Yes," she said tensely, exiting the car as John followed carrying his small satchel with computer tools and backup flash drives.

At the entrance, Katie unlocked the door and walked inside. She noticed again that the alarm wasn't set.

"What's wrong?" he asked.

"I thought that the alarm would be set, but I guess that I didn't reset it the other night. I was anxious to get out in a hurry." She raced over to the corner desk her aunt would use as a small office. There were accounting items with receipts, check books, bills, spreadsheets, and thank you cards. Everything was spread out in disarray from after the police search. Her aunt had already started writing out thank you cards to the caterers and gift givers ready to send the next day, her writing as beautiful as she had been.

"Where's the laptop?" he asked as if sensing Katie's sadness.

Katie rolled out the three-drawer filing cabinet and pulled open the bottom drawer. There was a special hiding place where it was kept—he always wanted his personal stuff to be out of view. It was extremely difficult to find unless you knew where to look for it. To her relief, the compact portable computer was still there. She put the small computer on the desk, opened it, and waited for it to completely start up. "I think Uncle Wayne just used it for the security cameras, nothing else. I can't believe that you didn't find it, John." She smiled.

"Do you know where he would keep backup discs?" John put on his crime scene gloves and began checking each book on the shelf above the desk until he came to one that actually wasn't a book.

"I didn't know that was there," she said. "I guess it's a new hiding place."

John slid the pretend book down and opened it where there were backups from the security cameras. Looking closely, he read the dates. "None of these are for the dates we're looking for. They are really old."

Katie was discouraged. If the cameras had been recording that night, they could almost immediately place doubt on her uncle's involvement and give credible evidence that someone else could have murdered her aunt.

"Footage still could be in the computer. I don't know the storage capacity right off, but usually people fill them up and then record over it. People keep rerecording until the clarity is terrible. I have a feeling that's what the sheriff did." He spent some time finding the files and looking at the data files and usage. "Okay, this was time stamped earlier that evening, probably during the party." He pressed the play/enter key.

There were four cameras around the house and they showed up on the monitor screen dividing it in quarters: backyard, one on each side of the house, and the front. The screen was small so Katie and John leaned in closer.

"The time stamp appears to be accurate," said John.

They watched as guests began to arrive. John fast forwarded the feed and would stop every so often. They saw several people go outside in the back and some meandered to the side of the house, but no one neared the other side where the laundry room door was located.

"I don't know what I expected to see, but it doesn't look like anything suspicious," she said.

"Wait a minute… let's see later…" He forwarded the time until everyone had left the party. It was past 1 a.m., then 2 a.m., nothing and then the cameras went blank.

"I knew it was too good to be true." Katie sighed and was just about to turn it off when there was a flash on the camera from the side of the house. She gasped and pointed to the screen. "Look."

A dark figure had appeared, clearly a man by the build, with a dark ski mask covering his face and carrying a duffle bag. He dropped it on the ground near the area where Katie found the blue fabric. The man looked around suspiciously before he retrieved an electronic screwdriver from his bag. And then the picture went dark.

"Is that it?" she said. "Can you get it back?"

John took some backup flash drives from his satchel, inserted them into the laptop before he began to rewind the footage. Once again, the same twenty-seven seconds appeared and then it was gone. "I'll copy this footage and also copy what's on the computer. Give me five or ten minutes. It will be added to the evidence list when I get back to the lab."

Katie turned away and walked around the living room trying to concentrate on anything that would take her mind off what she'd just seen. It was a good and bad clue. Good that it showed there was someone sneaking around the house that same night, but that didn't prove anything. The blue fabric must've ripped from his duffle bag. Any attorney could say that the burglar decided not to break in, could say there's no evidence the burglar killed Aunt Claire.

"Got it. Ready to go?" he said.

"Yes, more than ready." She walked to the front door and hurried to lock and secure the house.

John looked solemn and it was difficult to read his face or what he might have been thinking.

"John, in your professional opinion, do you think this helps my uncle or not?"

"It's not the smoking gun, but it's a start: it could cast guilt in another direction," he said. "Hey." He touched Katie's arm, making her look at him. "There's more to test… I'll do whatever I can to help."

Katie forced a smile and said, "Thanks. I really do mean it."

"I know."

CHAPTER 39

Wednesday 1115 hours

Katie left John to his work and continued to her office. She opened the door to find McGaven doing what he did best—running down clues and finding out background information.

"I come bearing gifts," she said and set down a tall black coffee.

"Just in time," he said and took a sip. He looked at Katie curiously. "Things okay?"

Drinking her coffee, she said, "As best as can be. So what's up with the backgrounds?"

"You know our lovely doctor?"

"Dr. Harper?"

"Yep. Seems that she had been involved in a couple of lawsuits for slander and stolen intellectual property."

Katie raised her eyebrows. "Intellectual property refers to patents and trade secrets?"

"And copyright."

"I see where you're going… like articles and books?"

"Seems our gorgeous blonde likes to take credit for other people's work."

"Gorgeous," she said and rolled her eyes. "Don't let Denise hear you say that." Katie's gaze traced the names on the investigative board. "You think that Andrews was onto something worth stealing?"

"Who's going to argue about it now—or sue?" he said.

"Okay, show me what this King's Gold looks like. I need to see it, since we're talking about it."

McGaven keyed up several sites and stock images of the plant. The bush was a yellow green color and looked ordinary—most would walk right past the plant and never notice it.

"That's it? It's not really gold in color, more yellow."

"This is a type of King's Gold created in a nursery—not the native plant supposedly coming back in California. There are variations—and anomalies."

"What could be so important about this plant?" she said. "My gut tells me that Andrews' murder wasn't about the plant, it was more about the circumstances."

"You mean like a random thing? Someone who happened to be at the place where she was camping and decided they should kill this student?"

"As far as we know, she's picture-perfect. There's no jilted boyfriend, no issue with her family members, no life insurance. Just a little bit of professional rivalry over a plant?" She let out a breath. "It's clear that her so-called best friend, Dr. Wills, who still refers to her as 'Cindy' had some issues. But to kill her—and kill her in such a brutal way? I'm not buying it unless there is strong evidence to suggest otherwise. Even though there was a set of antique knives in Wills's drawer—there's still not a strong enough motive to have that type of outcome."

"I know there's something churning in your profile," he said.

"Let's just look at this, like you said, in a random way, from a different perspective."

"Okay. What do you suggest?"

"Let's broaden it a bit, do a strategic search of homicide cases, most likely cold, of course, in the three surrounding counties. I'll look at my database for any case that looks remotely similar."

"From what dates?"

"Any time within the twelve years," she said. "We're looking for victims who have been sliced in a systematic way and left in a staged position, not just dumped, similar to Cynthia Andrews' murder scene."

"Got it," he said, instantly losing himself in the computer.

When she first started the job, Katie had begun working on a database of all the cold cases so she could easily narrow them down by the crime, event, scene, available evidence, workability and solvability. All of these aspects would help her to choose her next case accordingly or make comparisons. She printed out the several sheets with all the sheriff's department's cold cases. They would grow in number each month as old cases from upstairs become cold cases.

There were four possible cases in the county that might closely replicate the type of injury she was looking for, but none were exact matches. And after searching through boxes and reading more autopsy reports and viewing more crime scene photos than she would have liked, Katie came up with zero possibilities.

She went back to her office. "No luck," she said. "What do you have?"

"Some reports are coming in and I've double-checked them with any articles written on the Internet about the crimes. There are two possibilities."

It piqued Katie's interest. She leaned over McGaven's shoulder to see what information was coming in. The first case was from Washburn County, a case where a young woman, Anna Blake, had disappeared from her home only to be found outside at the creek located on her property. She had been sliced up around the torso and left nude sitting against a tree.

"Those injuries do look consistent," he said.

"Absolutely. How long ago was this?"

"Nine years ago."

"What about the other one?"

"It's from Moreno County from about eight years ago. Dillon Masterson was found murdered at his favorite fishing area. His torso was gashed similar to the other victims and his body was left nude and spread-eagle at the edge of the Themes River."

"This is the problem with jurisdiction separations. No one shares information or talks to one another," said Katie, annoyed. "It should be mandatory that anytime there's a cold case, especially a homicide, it should be followed up with at least surrounding areas or county police departments."

"That's all for now, but look at those wounds on the bodies," he said, studying crime scene photographs of the long gashes down each side of the torsos.

"We can't say with absolute certainty unless Dr. Dean has a look at the wounds, but I'm going to add them to the board." Katie took her pen and wrote the names of the victims and plotted them on the map in the general area. "Wait a minute," she said. "What age are they?"

"Anna Blake was 21 and Dillon Masterson was 22."

"Both so young. Do me a favor and see if they were registered at Sacramento."

"Excellent idea," he said and began keying in details furiously.

"So our killer targets college kid ages?"

"Wait a minute… I'm getting some preliminary info from the university admissions. It looks like both of the other victims were attending UC Sacramento. You're right, Katie!"

Katie felt a twinge of excitement, they were making progress, but she couldn't stop there. "Okay, we're still back to square one. Who is the killer?"

"I'm still waiting for the student list for all the classes that Cynthia Andrews attended." McGaven said. "It will be interesting to see if the two other victims were in her classes. They would probably be undergrads, but let's see if there's any connection."

"Are you on patrol tomorrow?"

"No, I'm here tomorrow and then patrol Friday and Saturday," he said.

Katie nodded.

"What do you think?"

"About?"

"What does your board tell you now?"

Her cell phone chimed with a text from Nick that simply read:

They are rounding up the troops.

"We'll have to wait and see," she said.

McGaven wrinkled his forehead and stared at Katie. "I thought we were full steam ahead. We're finally getting somewhere. As you say, keep fighting until everything shakes out."

"Sorry, I've got a bit of a headache and I think I might be coming down with something." She lied, hating it, but it was the only way she could keep him protected. Katie was working out the details for the trap that would begin tomorrow.

CHAPTER 40

Thursday 0745 hours

Katie had been preparing everything she would need since 4 a.m. and was just about finished. Making sure her uncle was asleep, she had packed food, water, her laptop, remote cameras, weapons and extra ammunition in two duffle bags and loaded them quietly into her police sedan. Cisco followed about as she worked, knowing instinctively that he was coming along for the ride. When she returned to the living room, her uncle had appeared and was making himself a cup of coffee.

"Hey, honey," he said sleepily. "Busy day?"

"Yes, we're running down some leads and checking more statements," she said, hating the lie but knowing that after everything was over, and her uncle was free, she would explain everything to everyone.

She headed back towards her bedroom, but took a b-line to the spare room where her uncle slept to swipe the keys to his large SUV and drop them in her pocket. Back in the living room with Cisco in tow she said, "Bye, Uncle Wayne. We'll be back late."

"Oh, you're taking Cisco?" There was some sadness in his voice and he looked disappointed.

"Yeah, I'm going to a rural location so thought he might enjoy exercise."

"Okay. Bye," he said.

Cisco jumped in the back seat alert and ready to go, as Katie got in and started up the engine. She waited a minute before backing out of her driveway contemplating if she was doing the right thing. A twinge of guilt for not telling McGaven or Chad niggled at her, but she pushed on, wanting to free her uncle more. As she drove to her uncle's house to switch vehicles, she left a message for McGaven explaining that she wasn't feeling well and she might be in later.

It took her twenty minutes to get to her uncle's house. Now when she arrived it represented something horrible and traumatic instead of all the wonderful memories that had been shared there. Pushing those thoughts from her mind, she pulled up and parked. It took her less than ten minutes to transfer what she needed into her uncle's SUV. She quickly took inventory and found that he had stocked the car with quite a few things that might prove useful such as tools and some camping equipment.

Before Katie climbed into the driver's seat, she slipped on a few more layers over her tank top and cargo pants and switched out of her boots to hiking shoes. She had a jacket if she needed it.

The large vehicle felt a bit strange to begin with, but she needed a four-wheel drive where she was going.

"You ready, big guy?" she said to Cisco, glancing into the rearview view mirror and seeing his eager face with his ears pointed forward.

It was time to set the trap.

She pulled up to Everything Outdoors at 9 a.m., just as they were opening up the store. It was a good time to shop and there wouldn't be many customers—making it highly unlikely that anyone would recognize her. Inside her pocket, she found the folded piece of paper with four names and corresponding phone numbers. She dialed the first number and waited. "Yes, hello, may I speak with Dr. Brandon Wills?"

The assistant, by the name of Gina, said, "I'm sorry but he's in class at the moment. May I take a message?"

"Yes, please. This is very important. My name is Detective Scott from the Pine Valley Sheriff's Department. Please relay to Dr. Wills that I'm about to make an arrest on the Cynthia Andrews case. I'm going up to the crime scene area now to recover something that Andrews hid and revealed in her journal."

"Okay."

"Could you read that back to me?" Katie asked.

The assistant read it back to her verbatim.

"Thank you," she said and ended the call.

Katie took a deep breath, expecting to smell gunpowder and hear the sound of gunfire deep inside her head, but was surprised to find just the odor of the leather seats and Cisco's breath. For the first time, her debilitating symptoms were strangely absent.

She dialed the second number, not expecting anyone to answer. Katie waited for the beep and said, "Dr. Harper, this is Detective Scott from the sheriff's department. I thought you'd like to know that I'm about to make an arrest. I found Cynthia Andrews' journal and she made a note about where she'd hidden some evidence. I'm going back to the scene of the crime right now to retrieve it. Thanks so much for your help." She ended the call.

She dialed the next number and waited as a couple of cars passed by. The cell phone was abruptly picked up, "This is Paul," retired detective Patton said.

"This is Katie Scott, did I catch you at a bad time?" She tried to sound like there was nothing wrong.

"Ah, Detective, what can I do for you?" he said.

"First, I haven't had a chance to thank you for answering questions about the Stiles case. It really helped and I probably wouldn't have been able to find the trail of evidence without your input."

"Of course. Glad I could help."

"I just had another question," she said, looking at the sporting goods store, remembering seeing him buying camping gear. "I read the notes you wrote about ideas for a book. And it reminded me of a new cold case I'm working on."

"Oh?"

"You talked about how killers take journals and keepsakes from their victims. Well, I'm working on a homicide case from twelve years ago. I won't bore you with details, but what you wrote got me to thinking about a victim's journal I found, one that the killer left behind. It led me to an important clue about the killer, a clue she says she hid. Can you believe it? I wouldn't have given the journal another look if it wasn't for your notes. I just had to thank you."

"Well, I'm glad that I could help. Just curious, which homicide was it?"

"Oh, a young woman, Cynthia Andrews," she said.

There was a silence on the line.

"Paul, did I lose you?" she said lightheartedly.

"No, I'm still here. So you found a journal?"

"Yes, she was able to leave a clue about the killer, which she says in her journal she hid back at the original crime scene. I'm heading up there in a little while to retrieve it. I should be making an arrest shortly."

"Well good for you. Sounds like you're closing some difficult cold cases."

Katie forced a laugh. "That's the whole idea. Anyway, I just wanted to thank you for letting me see your notes."

"Anytime. Good luck," he said, but his voice wasn't as cheerful as at the beginning of the conversation.

"Thank you," she said and ended the call.

Katie leaned back against the seat thinking she may have made a huge mistake. If her plan didn't work she would have quite a lot of explaining to do.

She dialed the last phone number and waited.

"Hello?" said a man's voice, strong and clear.

"Hi, Mr. Teagen?" she said.

There was a pause before he answered. "Yes."

"This is Detective Katie Scott from the sheriff's department."

"Hello, Detective. What can I do for you?"

"Thank you for seeing me the other day to discuss the Cynthia Andrews homicide," she said.

"Of course," he coughed.

"I just wanted to thank you for your insight."

"Insight?"

"I agree with you on your instincts about it possibly being a serial killer."

"Oh."

"Anyway, it got me thinking about how I had found the victim's journal and it referred to evidence she had hidden right before she was killed."

"Really?"

"I can't go into detail until there's an arrest, of course, but I'm on my way back to the crime scene to retrieve the evidence," she said and paid close attention to his response.

"I'm glad that you're able to close the case."

"I feel confident. Again, I just wanted to thank you for seeing me."

"My pleasure," he forced and he ended the call.

Katie sat for another moment before exiting the vehicle. She had set the bait, but there was one more piece to put into play before she would drive up to Dodge Ridge and then hike more than three miles to where Andrews had camped.

The bell jangled as she entered the shop. Within a few seconds, a tall thin man with glasses came out from behind the counter. "Hello," he said. "Can I help you?"

"Hi, are you Mr. Robert Harding?" she asked.

"Yes, that's me. And you are?"

"I'm Detective Katie Scott with the sheriff's department. I head up the cold case unit and I'm currently working on the Cynthia Andrews case," she said and watched his reaction closely.

"I wasn't aware that anyone was working the case anymore."

"I've been reviewing it and following up on leads."

"I see," he said. "I don't know what more I can tell you."

"Oh no, I'm sorry, that's not why I'm here." Katie moved closer to him. "I'm here to buy some camping gear."

"What type of gear?" he said, a little frostily.

"It's been a while since I've been camping, so I need…" Katie looked around. "I need a tent, sleeping bag, and a good hiking backpack for starters."

"Come this way, I can show you some items that would be appropriate. Where are you going to be camping?"

"Oh, I'm going to the Dodge Ridge area where your niece camped."

Mr. Harding turned to her in surprise. "Why on earth would you do that?"

"Well, I don't want to get your hopes up, but I'm following up on a lead. I'm quite confident that it will lead to an arrest."

"Really? May I ask who it was from?"

"Your niece," she said.

"I'm sorry, I don't follow."

"Well, it happens that I found her field journal and she left a clue to her killer's identity—a clue she hid up at her campsite before she was killed."

Mr. Harding's face paled and he couldn't look Katie directly in the eye.

"I'm sorry, I don't mean to upset you, but I would hope you and the family would want closure."

"Of course. It's… just a surprise, that's all."

"It's the best lead I've had and I'll be heading up there today to retrieve it. It may take some time, so I wanted to be prepared in case I needed to spend the night before hiking back down."

"Yes, of course."

She was in the store for about half an hour as Mr. Harding helped her to pick out everything she needed. She paid and thanked him.

Katie was back behind the wheel of her uncle's SUV and on her way to Dodge Ridge. She hoped that it wouldn't prove to be her biggest mistake—or a fatal one.

CHAPTER 41

Thursday 1145 hours

McGaven worked alone in the office as he waited for backgrounds and miscellaneous reports to come back. He studied the investigation board tracking the information that they had so far against Katie's preliminary profile. Something about the board bothered him. There was something that they were missing.

He glanced back at the computer and noticed he had received several new emails, including one from the university admissions with the list of Cynthia's peers. Sitting down, he opened the file and clicked download. "Let's see what we have..."

He quickly scrolled through the roster of names, which were for five classes that Cynthia Andrews had taken. There was also a free lab and students up for doctoral assistance. It wasn't in alphabetical order, so it took a bit more time to read through.

"What? It couldn't be," he muttered.

McGaven pulled a file and looked for the name, but it didn't give him what he needed. He used the police database and entered the name to find out who it was...

John burst into the office holding a printout.

McGaven looked up.

"Where's Katie?" John asked. He was clearly agitated.

"She wasn't feeling well and was taking some time today to rest at home," McGaven answered. "What's up?"

"You think she's really at home?"

"What do you mean? Of course. Why not?" McGaven said.

"I tried her cell. No answer, straight to voicemail."

"So she's probably sleeping."

"Call the sheriff."

"What's the problem?" McGaven asked.

"Just call the sheriff to confirm she's there," John said again, this time he wasn't polite.

"Okay, okay." McGaven picked up the phone and dialed the landline at Katie's house. He waited.

Finally, the sheriff picked up and said, "Hello."

"Hi, it's Deputy McGaven."

"Deputy, what's wrong?" he said.

"Well, nothing, sir, but is Katie there?" He looked at John who was pacing.

"No, she left for work a few hours ago. She's not there?" The sheriff sounded worried.

"No, she told me that she was staying home because she wasn't feeling well."

"Deputy, find her now," he said. "And call me back." The line disconnected.

McGaven slowly hung up the phone.

"What is it?" John said.

"She's not there. She pulled a switch—told the sheriff she was coming here and told me that she was staying there. Dammit!"

"Where is she?" John demanded.

"I don't know," he said.

"You must have some idea?" he pushed.

McGaven wavered, not knowing if he should explain what had been going on or not. "Wait a minute; I know how we can find her." Picking up the phone and pressing two digits, he said, "Hi Denise, do you have access to the GPS on the patrol cars?"

"Yes," she said.

"Even the unmarked lieutenant and detective ones?"

"Yes. What's going on?"

McGaven calmly stated, "I need to know where the vehicle is that Katie and I are using—it's the one that had been retrofitted with a K9 release. Okay? Call me back." He hung up.

"Is that going to work?" John asked.

"It should unless it's somewhere where a signal can't get through."

Looking at the board, John said, "You know she's trying to solve her aunt's case at the same time as your cold case."

"I know," McGaven said quietly.

The phone rang.

McGaven snatched it up. "Yes."

"The vehicle is located at 12788 High Mountain Terrace," Denise said.

"High Mountain Terrace is the address for the sheriff's house. Thanks, Denise," he said and hung up.

McGaven stood up and grabbed his jacket.

"I'm going with you," John said.

McGaven was going to object, but he said, "C'mon."

*

McGaven drove the navy sedan up to the sheriff's house, where they saw the unmarked police car parked at the far left side of the driveway. McGaven called the sheriff again to update him and get the access code of the gate.

Both men jumped out of the car and ran to different areas of the property calling Katie's name, but it was deserted. McGaven ran around the back and didn't see anyone. He received a phone call.

"McGaven," he answered.

"My keys are gone," said the sheriff. "She took the keys to my SUV."

CHAPTER 42

Thursday 1445 hours

Katie navigated the long uneven road and finally made it to Dodge Ridge. The journey had bounced her and Cisco almost senseless. As she drove in quiet solitude, so many things rolled through her mind; her relationship with Chad, what she had accomplished with the cold case unit, and the tragedy of what had happened to her aunt and uncle. No matter how this turned out, she knew that nothing would ever be the same again. It was an axiom she had always lived by since she had lost her parents: hope for the best and prepare for the worst. Katie's only hope was that she wasn't adding to grief the people in her life were already suffering—if something were to happen to her.

Katie turned her phone to silent mode and noticed that there was little signal. She didn't want to talk to anyone in case they had already figured out she had given everyone the slip. If she were to chat with anyone, McGaven or her uncle, they might be able to change her mind. That wasn't going to happen.

Up ahead, Katie saw the parking area. It was much bigger than she had first thought looking at it on the map. It was long and flat without the usual divots and washed out areas from the previous season. She chose a parking place at the end, which was the most level and the most visible.

She had given herself forty minutes to prepare her pack, change her clothes, and ready Cisco with his working vest before she began the long hike up to the location where Cynthia Andrews had died. She also took a few minutes to acclimate herself to the area, referring to all of her senses. Sight could be deceiving. So closing her eyes, she listened intently to the silence around her. A light breeze caressed her face, but she knew that it would get colder as the sun set. It was too soon for any of her suspects to follow her, but her internal intuition told her that the killer was coming.

"Cisco, stay here," she commanded as the dog took a few trips around the large SUV. He then stayed at her side curiously sniffing everything as it went inside her pack. Organizing her camping gear to be ready for transport came naturally to her—she had done this hundreds of times getting ready to go to the battlefield. Inside her jacket, she put extra magazines, nylon gloves, ski hat, cell phone, and extra cell battery. She attached a leg holster and secured her Glock, and secured a small Beretta .32 caliber in her ankle holster. Around her neck, on a thin leather rope, she wore a knife tucked in a cowhide sheath. The four and half inch blade would prove useful under many different situations. Attaching a Remington rifle to the outside of her backpack as a precaution against wild animals, she was ready to go.

The fast-moving clouds covered the sun, casting a dark shadow over her. It seemed fitting, but she pushed past the usual jitters. "Okay, buddy," she said and took out Cisco's bulletproof vest and wrapped it around him, putting some of her water bottles into his side pockets to lessen her load. His demeanor instantly changed; he was now in combat mode. Ready to serve. Ready to go.

She hoisted the backpack and made sure everything was fitted properly before she headed up the trail.

CHAPTER 43

Thursday 1545 hours

McGaven and John stood in Katie's living room talking with Sheriff Scott for almost a half hour trying to figure out what to do. They debated between calling it in to the sheriff's department and putting out an all-points bulletin for the sheriff's SUV. In the meantime, McGaven kept calling her cell phone and then it finally went straight to voicemail—either she was out of range, or she had turned it off.

"Did she take anything with her?" McGaven said.

"Like what?"

"I don't know, like weapons or clothing, anything out of the ordinary."

"I'm not sure," the sheriff said.

The sheriff searched her bedroom and found her closet raided and her firearms missing. He looked around the rest of the room and couldn't decipher what she had taken.

"Anything?" McGaven said as he stood in the doorway.

"I'm not one hundred percent sure, but it looks as if she took extra weapons, ammo, and a heavy coat."

McGaven thought about it and it occurred to him. "What about a duffle bag or backpack?"

"I don't know. When she left she wasn't carrying anything and Cisco was with her."

"Is this window always open like this?" said John as he ran his fingers along the sill. There was a slight crack opening where it wasn't shut all the way.

"I don't think she would leave it like that," he said. Realizing, he continued, "She must've packed some stuff and then dropped it out the window so I wouldn't see it, and then picked it up when she got to the car."

"Then she drove to your house and swapped cars?" added McGaven.

"Why?" the sheriff stated.

McGaven and John looked away uncomfortably.

"What's going on? Tell me everything right now!" he said, his voice rising in anger. "Don't bother denying it—take me through what you've been working on."

McGaven and John followed the sheriff back into the living room.

"I don't know what Katie has told you about the cold case," began McGaven.

"She said it was a case that I worked on with Ken Teagen. The young woman that was sliced up and left in the woods near Dodge Ridge."

"Yes," said McGaven. "We've run down most of the witnesses, family, friends, and her doctoral supervisor."

"Okay."

"Katie began a preliminary profile of the killer, citing that they were experienced with the outdoors, like a hiker or climber. The killing was up close and personal—someone who knew the victim or hated them. The weapon was never found."

"I know this."

"Katie then talked to Teagen and she said he was in rough shape. And we talked to Dr. Wills, Andrews' best friend, who seemed odd, controlling, but not violent. And we also chatted with her doctoral supervisor who was clearly hiding things and might have profited from her research," he said.

"That's still not telling me what you two are keeping from me," the sheriff stated.

McGaven didn't want to tell the sheriff about the two retired detectives, but he had no other choice. "Katie and I were going to speak with Andrews' aunt and uncle. They own a sporting goods store, but when we got there we saw Paul Patton go inside to buy some supplies. We followed him to find out where he was going—he went to Teagen's house."

The room was quiet.

"There could be many reasons why two retired detectives remained friends," the sheriff said, trying to maintain his calm. "What did Katie say?"

"She thought there was something else going on because Teagen didn't appear to be as incapacitated as he was when she had visited him."

"Go on."

"Katie felt that the killer wasn't someone in the victim's family or friends."

"And?" The sheriff turned to John who had been extremely quiet.

"I guess it's my turn. Katie came to me after she searched the outside of your house."

"I'm guessing she found something?" Katie's uncle said.

"She found a piece of fabric just outside the laundry room and video footage for just a few seconds that evening of a man outside acting suspiciously."

"What?" said both McGaven and the sheriff in unison.

"Look, Katie has been trying to figure out your case, trying to do everything she can to help without getting anyone else involved."

The sheriff thought a moment. "Have you been able to find out who that person is on the tape?"

"No, but Katie had a hunch and asked if I would test the knife for any other blood or substances," John said. "I found another blood type that didn't belong to you or Mrs. Scott. It's being tested for DNA as we speak."

Sheriff Scott took a seat at the breakfast bar. "So where is Katie?"

"My guess would be that she's somehow trying lure the killer out," said McGaven.

"How?"

"I think she's feeling the pressure of your arrest and murder one charge coming soon, so she's…" McGaven couldn't say it.

"Going rogue…" said John, finishing the sentence.

"What would you do if you had several possible suspects but not the evidence to back it up?"

The sheriff thought a moment. "She must think that she can make the killer reveal themselves somehow."

"She wouldn't do that, would she?" said McGaven.

"Setting a trap," John said. "That would make sense with the time restraint and multiple potential suspects. She would have to come up with some type of ruse for them to go to… the scene of the crime?"

"That's crazy. There are so many things that could go wrong somewhere that remote." The sheriff got up. "We have to contact the undersheriff and get a team up there right now to search for her."

"Wait, we don't know for sure that she's there," said McGaven. "We also don't know who she's talked to and if she's really trying to entice a killer out."

"She would have to somehow let them know that she had some revealing evidence, or some reason they would want to confront her." The sheriff looked worried. "You're right; if we send a team up there it could expose Katie and get her killed."

"Sheriff Scott, she has Cisco with her."

He nodded.

"I think, speaking from experience, she went up there prepared. She's had plenty of training out in the field. She's smart and capable. She knows what she's doing," John said, keeping his voice steady.

"What do you suggest?" the sheriff asked as he looked at both men. "I know you both care about her but I can't go anywhere; otherwise, I'll jeopardize my temporary release." He referred to his ankle monitor. "Do you really think she's right? The killer will be walking into her trap. Then what?"

McGaven frowned. He knew how driven Katie was; she had gone to a considerable amount of trouble to get away and try to catch a killer. "I think she went because we weren't solving the Andrews case fast enough. She believes her case is related to yours. We're close, but nothing is concrete yet."

"Okay, you both are going to be my eyes and ears. McGaven, check to find out if my SUV is near the crime scene area; I'm assuming Dodge Ridge. John, you don't have to do this, but I need your previous military expertise to be McGaven's backup. Are you both sure that you want to take the risk to search for her? It could mean a suspension or worse if Katie is wrong about this. Her judgment may be biased because of me. This could all be a wild goose chase."

Without hesitation, both men agreed.

"Get prepared. Anything you need. Get it. It's going to be getting dark soon. You need to get up there ASAP."

McGaven and John turned to leave.

"Wait," the sheriff said. "Thank you. I... I don't know what I would do if I lost her too."

CHAPTER 44

Thursday 1645 hours

Katie had been hiking for an hour and the trail wasn't as bad as she thought it was going to be from the descriptions by hikers on the websites she'd checked. By her calculations, she had made great time with only two short water stops for both her and Cisco. At a few points on the trail, it reminded her of hiking through rural towns and higher plains areas with her team. The memories kept her company as she continued, reminiscing about conversations and camaraderie from another life.

The cooler air made her sinuses burn and eyes water as she continued to climb. The area had been without rain for a couple of weeks, giving the ground time to harden—it would soon be a muddy mess as the rain came. She trekked onward, navigating around overgrown bushes and trees, noticing that the ground in the denser areas was getting softer, causing her boots to sink.

She stopped and looked at her map again—another fifteen minutes and she would be at the top point where Cynthia Andrews had made camp. Maybe she was too optimistic thinking that someone like one of the retired detectives would tackle the hike—but if her instincts were correct, she would be seeing Patton, Teagen, Dr. Wills or Dr. Harper very soon.

Katie jogged up a short steep hill to the next level and saw something fluttering attached to the bushes. Upon closer inspection, she realized it was the washed out remnants of what was once yellow crime scene tape.

"We're close, Cisco…"

CHAPTER 45
Thursday 1655 hours

McGaven and John met back at the forensics unit having changed their clothes. McGaven borrowed one of the deputies' SUVs and transferred his duffle bags and weapons from the trunk of the blue sedan into the off-road-friendly vehicle. As McGaven zipped up his heavier deputy coat, he thought he would be feeling guilty or worried that he might be suspended or fired, but nothing was farther from the truth. He felt strong, confident, and ready to do whatever he needed to do to make sure Katie was safe—and hopefully, he thought, they will have captured the killer, too.

He looked up and saw John, who had transformed from the cool science geek to a battlefield commando in SWAT pants and jacket.

"Everything ready?" said John.

"Yep," he said. "Tried to get a signal on Sheriff Scott's SUV, but it says it's out of range. I guess that's our answer. Let's go."

CHAPTER 46

Thursday 1800 hours

The calm before the storm was my favorite time—it was the segment of time before the battle began and after the previous struggles dissipated. It was after the dust had settled and your mind became clear, but before all hell would break loose. It was the time to prepare, mentally, physically, and spiritually before the enemy put its sights on you—again. Make no mistake, it would come at you full force. So let the battle begin…

Katie walked the entire camping area to acclimate herself to her new surroundings. Dropping the tent and some of the gear, she imagined what had most likely happened that night. The original detectives assumed the murders happened at night based on body temperature and the fact the victim was in her T-shirt and panties. It made sense if the killer wanted a surprise attack. She spent fifteen minutes systematically moving around the areas finding entry and exit locations as well as the best vantage points to the site, where someone could have watched without being seen. The fading sunlight flickered between the trees and branches like a beacon, hurrying Katie to work faster. She was running out of light…

She quickly set up the tent and organized everything just like a holiday camper would, padding her sleeping bag out as a decoy to give the appearance that she was tucked up inside. She then mounted small motion cameras generally used for wildlife spotting in several locations around her tent. When she was satisfied she had all areas covered, she hurried to find somewhere she and Cisco could safely watch from a distance.

Tucked away in a hiding place with an unbroken view of her tent, she settled herself and Cisco in for the night. The temperature had dropped and she put on her gloves when she noticed that her hands were shaking. In her pocket, she had forgotten about a canister of mace she had and grasped it thinking it might prove useful. She removed the extra water bottles from Cisco's packs and made indentations in the ground to store them. From where she sat, Katie was able to see more than one hundred eighty degrees, and with her infrared binoculars, she could zero in on any area hidden in the shadows.

Next, she checked her cell phone, glad to see she had a connection with the cameras and infrared alerts. Happy, she leaned back against a large tree trunk and tore open a high protein energy bar for herself and a packet of savory chicken for Cisco. Waiting was the hardest part.

CHAPTER 47

Thursday 1900 hours

The mid-size SUV bounced around, bobbing, weaving and rattling everything inside including McGaven and John as it crawled up the mountain road. The high-beam headlights maintained a full scope of vision, but it didn't help avoid the potholes.

The nauseating swaying made McGaven's stomach grumble. He realized that he hadn't eaten anything in a while, so he drank from his water bottle that was balanced in the cup holder. McGaven had never been here before, but it appeared few other vehicles had either. If he could track and read signs in the road, he might be able to ascertain if Katie had been through there. For now, he had to assume that she was already at the twelve-year-old crime scene. He hid a smile, thinking about how she would have the area figured out.

"Do you think Katie's found the crime scene?" asked John as if he was listening to McGaven's personal thoughts.

"Found it. Walked it. And figured out what the killer did, and why," he said.

John smiled for the first time. "Somehow I think you're probably right."

"I never met any cop like her and it was by pure chance that I was chosen to work with her on that first missing girl case. I absolutely hated the assignment…"

"Yeah," John said, looking at McGaven and holding the safety handle to maintain his balance as they hit bump after bump.

"Oh yeah. But that didn't last long; she put me in my place and then we worked things out from there."

"I could see that."

The road leveled slightly and they saw light tire tracks pressed into the soft dirt indicating that an off-road vehicle had recently come through there.

"There," he gestured to the tire tracks. "New tracks."

John nodded.

McGaven relaxed a bit as he realized that he had a death grip on the steering wheel.

A loud *bang* interrupted the quietness of the outdoors and the SUV listed to the driver's side. They had a flat tire.

CHAPTER 48

Thursday 1930 hours

Katie woke suddenly to the sound of Cisco's low whine next to her. She had been concentrating so much on relaxing her breathing that she must have dozed off for a few minutes. With so much adrenalin and anxious energy flooding her body, it wasn't uncommon to feel drowsy after a while.

Without saying a word Katie used hand signals to communicate to Cisco to be quiet. The dog obediently complied and kept watch, staring into the dark woods. Katie waited a moment as her eyes adjusted to the darkness. Nothing moved. Nobody appeared. No sound echoed or interrupted the natural sway of the trees.

Shielding her cell phone screen from view, she watched the infrared cameras. Nothing had triggered them. There were no indications that anyone moved past the security points. She kept her visual checkpoints and continued to survey with her naked eye and cameras. Over and over she made these visual rounds, slowly and methodically—until…

Movement detected on her second camera.

Another two minutes passed.

Katie shifted her weight silently and kept her eyes tracking—making sure her vision wasn't fixated on any one thing for too long. That's when she saw it again. Movement. At first, Katie thought it was the slight swaying of the branches, but the black mass moved deliberately, like a predator searching for its prey.

Katie slipped her Glock from her leg holster—quietly—ready for anything. She leaned forward, away from the tree trunk and into a squatting position. Cisco crawled forward next to her, alert and ready.

The black mass morphed into the outline of a male figure—similar size and build to the man who attacked her at the apple orchard. He swiftly advanced out of the tree-covered area and into the open, but his face was covered. It was clear to see he had a semi-automatic gun, which was down at his side. He kept progressing, only stopping every three feet or so, and then inched forward again. He moved with practiced precision—he had been trained.

She watched him approach her tent. Slowly unzip the entrance. Bring up his right arm, and fire four shots inside. The bullets echoed all around her.

CHAPTER 49

Thursday 2000 hours

"What was that?" said McGaven.

John listened intently and looked upward toward the camping area. "Sounded like four gunshots. Probably semi-automatic."

They had managed to put some quick air sealant into the flat tire and drive the vehicle the rest of the way to the Dodge Ridge parking lot, where they found the sheriff's white SUV.

"We have to get up there," McGaven said.

"Wait. It doesn't mean that was Katie."

"Then what?" said McGaven said. "Night hunters… no way. What else could it be?"

"Here," he said. "Take a pair of these night goggles. If someone is already up there, then we'll come in the back way and flank them."

"Okay." McGaven wasn't so sure, but John knew what he was doing.

"Get a hold of yourself. We've got this. I'm sure that Katie has everything under control. We're just her backup." John continued to ready himself for the hike as if he was getting ready for work.

McGaven watched in awe how calm and focused John was. He took a moment and calmed himself. If John could do it, so could he. He grabbed his flashlight, extra ammunition, the night goggles, and zipped up his heavy jacket tighter to keep the cold out.

"You ready?" asked John.

"Absolutely."

CHAPTER 50

Thursday 2030 hours

Katie watched as the dark figure jerked open the tent opening only to be greeted by—no one. He stood up straight, tense, looking to every side, now realizing that he had been deceived.

Would he leave as quickly as he had appeared? Katie didn't think so. She moved from safety giving Cisco the hand signal to stay until she released him from his hiding place. Hating to leave him, she turned and looked at the dog's dark outline, perfectly pointed ears facing in her direction, eyes reflecting in the dim light, and then she turned away and headed toward the enemy.

She kept to the areas where she knew the dirt was loose making her footsteps almost entirely silent. She inched closer. Keeping a close eye on the figure, she saw him begin to move away from the campsite. She kept on his tail, hoping to flank him. She had to make her move—no matter what it was—she had to make it now, while he was off balance.

The figure stopped suddenly as if he knew there was someone behind him. Was it Teagen? There was something familiar about how he moved. His body structure, the way he positioned the gun, and how he carried his upper body. It seemed familiar, but not recognizable.

She crept closer with her gun trained forward.

He slowly turned, realizing there was someone following. Strangely, he raised his hands in the air. Katie stopped her approach, expecting some type of trap, but she had him trained in her sights. Nothing would make her miss her mark.

With a sudden burst of speed she ran up on her assailant, yelling her demands, "Drop the gun! And turn around slowly! Now!" Gripping the gun hard, she readied herself to fire at him. "Drop the gun!" she repeated again.

To Katie's amazement, he dropped his gun.

"Turn around slowly!"

The man turned around and at last she saw his face clearly.

"You?" she managed to say.

CHAPTER 51

Thursday 2045 hours

McGaven felt burning in his calves but he had to keep moving.

"Pick up the pace," said John. He moved with ease as if the hike was merely walking in a park.

"I know," said McGaven, panting a little.

"Hey," said John as he stopped. "I saw on the map that there was another way up to the camping area. Maybe the best way there would be for us to split up?"

"Good idea. You have your cell?"

"Yeah, but there's no signal right here. Maybe at the top?" said John.

McGaven surveyed the area and as much as he hated the thought of hiking alone in the woods at night, he had to agree with John it was best that they entered the crime scene area from two different directions in case there were any problems. The sound of those gunshots still rang in his ears.

"The other trail actually runs parallel to this one after about a mile or so. Keep your guard up," John said.

"Alright, once there's a signal, we'll check in. Otherwise, I'll see you at the top," McGaven said, trying to sound like it was a walk in the park.

John gave him a reassuring look, and then he disappeared into the darkened terrain without making a sound.

McGaven knew that John would reach the camping area before him. He was much faster, but that still didn't make him feel any better. He trudged onward hoping that everything was worth the effort—and that Katie's trap would go down without a hitch.

CHAPTER 52

Thursday 2050 hours

The enemy was not always what or who you thought it would be under battle and war conditions. You were always tempted during the hunt to jump to conclusions, which allowed illusions that made you look in the wrong direction. What seemed the most obvious or likely—could be overlooked. But what was the least likely still had the same effect—except it had the most impact throwing you off your game. And that's when it was most deadly. Nothing was ever as it seemed...

Katie was shocked, but kept her position firm and authority in check. "You," she said again but kept her eyes on his hands for any sudden movement. Reaching into her top pocket, she ran her finger over her cell phone and hit the "record" button.

He laughed. "You win fair and square. I give you that," he said. The man who had stalked her and was ready to kill so effortlessly without any remorse—was Cody Teagen, Detective Teagen's son.

"*You* killed Cynthia Andrews?" she said. Her mind instantly ran at high speed to her first meeting with him; skilled with ropes, a collection of antique weapons in the barn. There was even the clipping of Dr. Wills's courses at the university on his dad's kitchen table. The clues were all there and Katie had missed them.

"That was just kid's stuff when I was in school." He laughed again. "She was actually my first…" he said, as if visiting a happy memory. His dark eyes pierced Katie like a caged wild animal waiting for that perfect moment to pounce. He was the most dangerous kind of killer, the one you never expected.

"But, you killed Aunt Claire," Katie managed to say, resisting putting a bullet in his head right then and there. She would get the confession, officially read him his rights, and bring him back to the county jail. The right way.

"No one could have guessed it was me, but you, Detective Scott, are different, aren't you?" he mocked her with his compliment.

"Why?" she said.

"Why not?" he countered.

"Turn around, get on your knees, hands on your head. Do it!"

He laughed like it was a prank, but he did as she instructed.

Katie took a small silver whistle from her pocket and blew it. Within seconds, Cisco was at her side.

"Good boy," she said. "*Platz…*"

The dog instantly obeyed and pressed his chest to the ground.

"Nice touch, Detective… oh, that's right, you're some kind of veteran… tracker… IED searcher. I guess some would consider you a war hero. Some, but not me."

Katie ignored him, suspicious of his quick surrender. Something wasn't right. She didn't want to involve Cisco, but she had no other choice. She was certain Cody had something else planned. She approached him and patted him down. He had two magazines and the gun he had dropped. She quickly retrieved them and put them inside her coat.

"Pretty ballsy coming up here alone," he said.

"Who said I'm alone?" she replied.

"You mean Fido here?"

Katie pushed him onto his stomach, jumped on his back, and quickly bent his arms behind his back so she could slip the zip ties over his wrists and yanked hard to tighten them.

"Hey, I'm not going anywhere. You don't have to rough me up, Detective."

"Get up!"

"Why?"

"Get up!" She moved forward and pressed the muzzle of the gun against his cheek. "Do it now," she said, gritting her teeth as she could still see her aunt's body on the laundry room floor.

"Okay, okay. I'm not going to escape, if that's what you think."

"You don't want to know what I think," she said.

Cody bent his legs and wriggled into a kneeling position and then pushed himself up.

"I'm going to ask you one more time. Why did you kill Claire Scott?"

"You really want to know… it seems to me you would have already figured it out."

Katie could hardly look at the man. The man who cleverly sneaked into her uncle's house, took the antique fighting knife, and butchered an innocent woman. Her aunt. Her beautiful, loving Aunt Claire.

"Well, okay," he said as if he was explaining the errands he had to run. "My dad was a great police officer. It meant the world to him. When he started having trouble with his health the department ignored him… abandoned him… made him feel weak… unnecessary… forgotten. That's not right under any circumstances."

Katie realized that she was staring into the eyes of a serial killer and would bet her badge on the fact that the victims from other counties, Anna Blake and Dillon Masterson, were murdered by him. His lack of empathy exposed him. His hatred. His callous attitude. His enjoyment and fun of butchering innocent people.

"Sheriff Scott pushed him out of the department. My dad was his friend. What you don't know was that Sheriff Scott didn't care about the endless suffering my dad had gone through. Every. Single. Day. And all because of your uncle. I leveled the playing field. One life for another. It was brilliant. The mighty Sheriff Scott would go to prison for the life of someone he cared about. You were going to be collateral damage. I amaze myself sometimes. Easy as that," he said and shrugged his shoulders like he didn't care. "It was too easy to sneak in to the house from the laundry room. Claire was working in the kitchen, so I crept into the living room and took one of the knives. Dad had mentioned them on several occasions. They were really special... special enough for a murder. She must've heard something because she came out and saw me, so she ran toward the master bedroom to alert the sheriff and that's when she... well... you know... got her first..."

"Go," she said not wanting to hear any more details.

"What? You don't want to hear more?"

"Start walking now." There was no one she hated more than Cody Teagen at that moment. There was no forgiveness in the near future for someone who would take one of her family. She ignited a glow stick to illuminate their path.

"Fine." He pretended to pout.

"Keep moving until I tell you to stop." Katie couldn't look at him anymore—he disgusted her.

"You were watching me in the orchard, weren't you? I could feel it. Sorry that I didn't get the opportunity to kill you then. You were smarter than I originally thought. You're a woman, but an intelligent one. I'll give you credit."

"Keep moving," she said. Katie was done talking with him. She wasn't going to let him get into her head. She wasn't going to fall for his manipulations.

They began walking down the trail. Katie kept her distance, Cisco tight to her heel.

"Aw, you're not going to talk to me anymore?"

"I'm sure that the police are going to love hearing everything you have to say."

They kept walking.

Something felt off. There were many questions that needed answering, but it made sense that he would kill Claire to make the sheriff pay for his dad. Still, something was misaligned about the profile—missing.

They kept walking. Katie's adrenalin subsided and her head began to pound. Suddenly, Cody turned to face her. "You just don't understand. I pity you," he mocked. His eyes seared into her with a blazing hatred.

"Keep moving," she said.

"You have no idea, do you?"

"Move!"

"You're just as clueless and—" He didn't finish his sentence.

A crack of a high-powered rifle blazed from a distance and hit Cody directly in the back. The bullet burst out of his chest and then grazed Katie's shoulder.

Katie fell backwards; her shoulder burning, and Cody fell on top of her, pinning her momentarily with his dead weight.

Cisco began barking and tried to attack his lifeless body to save her.

Katie realized that the shooter wasn't her backup, or the police. They would have identified themselves. That was what her instincts were telling her: there were two killers, that's why she couldn't get a complete profile—two different people with two different motives.

Another shot rang out nearby.

"No," she whispered. Cisco was in prime view of the unknown shooter. The only thing she could do was give the dog a command to get him out of the line of sight. "Cisco return! Return!" Katie yelled. "Return."

The dog hesitated, licked her face still pinned under the body.

"No. Cisco, return!" she cried.

The dog looked at her and then ran as fast as he could and disappeared into the darkness. The command was a last resort that told the dog to "return," which meant to return to the vehicle or wherever the handler had first started out for their mission that day. Katie prayed that the dog would make it back to the SUV and not circle back to her. She would get to him when it was all over.

A couple more shots blasted, zinging by Katie and hitting higher in the trees. The weight of Cody pushing hard against her made her sick as his warm blood spilled against her chest. The dead weight was difficult to push away, but with pure determination she wriggled out from underneath him. Her left shoulder was now numb; she was able to reach her Glock that had fallen during the scuffle.

She half-crawled and half-ran, staying low until she could get to safety. The huddled trees and darkness hid her—but for how long? She took cover behind one of the large pine trees, pressing her back against the trunk but alert to everything around her.

The firing had stopped.

She didn't know where the person was or who had been shooting at her. It was clear that the person wanted Cody Teagen dead, but they seemed to be almost toying with her. Was it the second killer? Was Cody a decoy? Was someone else pulling the strings?

*

McGaven froze in his position and took cover. There was no mistaking the sound of a high-powered rifle. He knew it well. Someone was shooting and he didn't believe it was Katie. The echo bounced all around the hills, trees, and valley below. Glancing down at his phone, there was still no signal and there was no way to contact John. Even though he knew that John could take care of himself.

McGaven kept moving forward to get to Katie. He knew that she would need help and that the person shooting was most likely the killer. He had forgotten all about how tired he was and how strained his muscles were. He pushed on.

*

Katie moved from tree to tree, keeping an eye out for anything moving in the darkness.

"Detective Katie Scott, where are you?" a man's voice called out. He wasn't close, but he was headed her way.

Katie froze.

"Detective, I know you're out here. I guess you finally met my secret weapon."

Katie went through every interview, statement, and person that she and McGaven had spoken to but...

"Still don't know who I am? It's pretty obvious, really," he said. "I should've been your first suspect." The man laughed.

Was he disguising his voice somehow?

"Is there some reason why you don't want to talk to me? You seemed so interested before when you and your partner had so many inquisitive questions." He sniffed loudly and Katie instantly remembered speaking to Dr. Brandon Wills with his box of Kleenex and wadded up handkerchiefs on the podium and in his office. He was now hunting her like prey. Of course. Like McGaven had said—revenge and jealousy are the usual reasons to kill.

"C'mon now, you left that message for me. Clever, Detective. Actually, much smarter than I gave you credit for. The cops I met twelve years ago were so stupid. Bumbling. They believed what I told them."

"You didn't kill Cynthia Andrews," she yelled back.

"Ah, there you are. Again, clever, Detective. No, I didn't kill Cindy. I hated her. I envied her. I was jealous of what she was going to get—leaving me behind with nothing. I worked just as hard as she did. But no, I didn't kill her."

"So you used Cody to do it. Taking the coward's way out—I can see that." Katie wanted to draw him out, and if he thought he was so much smarter than her—all she had to do was wait for his mistake.

"No, it didn't start out like that. It evolved. Cody was angry, he hated school, but he was easy to manipulate and seemed to become more and more obsessed with death—in fact, he *loved* it. Then I guess he discovered he had a knack for it. He killed students he didn't like, people he crossed paths with…"

Katie kept her calm. "I see… you're drawn to underachievers and psychopaths to make yourself seem better—more important."

"Hardly."

Katie eased her body to another position, keeping herself moving, so her voice wouldn't be coming from a consistent place. "Hey, you can be as high-minded as you like, but you seem to kill people that you can't control. You couldn't control Cindy and you couldn't control Cody—lost cause."

He remained quiet.

Katie moved again, trying to circle back around to find out if she could spot his location.

He didn't answer her.

"Dr. Wills," she said. "Well actually, it's just Brandon because you really didn't earn your doctorate, but killed and stole for it. I think that makes it null and void. That's the way I see it."

There was still no response.

Katie grew nervous and readied herself. She knew that Dr. Wills was coming for her, cleaning up any loose ends that would connect him to the murder of his classmate and her aunt.

She stayed still, not moving until she could get a fix on him. There was no telling where he was. There was a quick flash from the southern part of the trail. Katie wasn't certain if it was something from an animal or if it was coming from the reflection of a weapon.

She decided to move toward it instead of running from it—not wanting to be ambushed.

Another light reflection emitted.

She held her position.

Walking along the path was the outline of a man who moved in and out of the main trail. She saw the man's profile and immediately knew that it was McGaven. He had found her. But then Katie's spirits dashed as she thought about Wills out there roaming with his rifle homed in with a scope. She had to warn McGaven.

Katie finally caught up with him, waving silently to get his attention. The sound of the rifle cracked, echoing all around them. McGaven hit the ground.

Without a second thought she ran out into the clearing to pull her partner to safety, back into a hiding place in the trees. He had a bullet in his leg. She helped him up and took his weight as they disappeared into the grove, shots firing into the air around them. As they ran, Katie could tell McGaven's wound was serious. He was falling into shock and was having trouble staying conscious.

"Stay with me," she whispered as she tore a section of her coat to wrap around the wound, realizing that he needed a tourniquet. Immediately standing up, Katie took off her belt and bound it around McGaven's leg, pulling it tight. He cried out in pain. "Take it easy. How did you find me?" she whispered.

"We tracked your car," he said, breathless.

"Who's we?"

Weakly he said, "Me and John."

"John?"

"Yeah, a real-life commando."

"Shhh… save your strength and don't move otherwise it will bleed faster."

"Where's Cisco?"

Katie didn't want to think about it. "Stay quiet," she said and tried to make him comfortable. "We're sitting ducks if I don't go after Wills."

"Dr. Wills?" he said.

"Yeah, he's one screwed up mastermind. I'll explain later. I think I have most of it recorded."

Katie went to move and McGaven stopped her. "You can't do this… by yourself…"

"Stay here… don't move," she ordered. "Keep holding that tourniquet."

Without warning, gunfire ripped through the tree branches just above their heads. Katie hit the ground as flat as she could, covering McGaven until the bullets stopped pummeling the area around them.

"Stay down!" she said to McGaven.

Katie pulled her Glock, took aim and systematically began firing from the left to right. Before she knew it, she had to replace her magazine. Looking at McGaven, he didn't look good, sweating, pale, and she knew that she had to get him to a hospital. She wondered where John was, and if he was out there somewhere or had circled back to the parking lot to get help.

Bullets exploded again. Branches ripped from the tree trunks. Pieces of bark shredded.

She heard twigs breaking and froze, expecting the worst.

Cisco. He had probably made it to the SUV and then came around the other way through the forest to meet back up. Katie couldn't help herself—she hugged the dog. Cisco instinctively knew that McGaven was hurt and he took his position next to him, keeping him warm.

Gunfire ignited again, but this time it wasn't aimed at them. Rapid sputters of gunfire seemed to be coming from an area in front of them between two different people. A gun battle. Katie squeezed in with McGaven and Cisco, making sure they were safe and shielded behind her. She kept her gun fixed toward the area where all the gunfire began and then suddenly ended. Katie's nerves were frayed and her strength waning, but all she thought about was how she was going to get McGaven medical help.

The valley and hilltop went completely quiet.

Katie waited. Then…

"Katie, McGaven," followed by a whistle.

"John."

"It's safe now. Keep talking, I'll find you," he said through the trees.

"We're over here… McGaven is hurt… please hurry…"

Finally, emerging from the wooded area, John appeared. Katie didn't recognize him at first, dressed like a commando. It didn't matter. She was thankful that he had found them.

"John, we need to get McGaven to the hospital."

He said, "I know… I called in backup when I had a signal."

"Thank you, John," whispered McGaven.

Katie hesitated. "Where's Dr. Wills?"

"Dead."

"Are you okay?" she said.

"He left me no other choice; he had you guys pinned down. I'm fine."

"I know… he killed his partner, Cody Teagen."

"Where is he?"

"A little ways up the trail."

A helicopter flew over using its spotlights searching for them. The blade's velocity blew wind down through the trees as the helicopter made a large circle around the area.

Katie and John used their flashlights to signal them…

CHAPTER 53

A week later...

Katie rushed through the hospital hallway to find McGaven's room. He was being discharged today and she wanted to see him before he left—and before Denise or anyone else came. He had a few complications from his bullet wound, but after two surgeries, he was going to be fine and was scheduled to return to regular work duties in two weeks.

Katie turned the corner and entered the room where McGaven was lying in a hospital bed with his leg in a contraption to keep it stable.

"Hey, partner," said Katie.

"Hey," he said as a big smile washed across his face.

"I thought you'd be on your way out?"

"I will be later today," he said.

"Everything okay?"

"Oh yeah, everything is fine. I'm itching to get out of here that's for sure."

Katie pulled up a chair closer to the bed and took a seat. "Everything has been so crazy, but—"

He reached out to touch her hand. "You don't have to say anything."

"I do. What I did, not trusting you enough to tell you what I was doing. And then you risked everything to find me and to have my back... you risked your life for me."

He caught her gaze. "I know you were protecting those of us who care about you. You were doing what you thought was right in order to protect your family—I know that, and there's no reason for you to feel bad or apologize for anything. Because I would do it all again knowing what I know now."

Katie remained quiet for a moment. "My life has been somewhat unsettling ever since I came home—make that really turned upside down. But, having people like you in my life has made it all worth it. And without sounding all mushy I really wanted to have a moment alone with you to say... thank you..."

"The feeling is mutual," he said.

They sat together quietly for a few moments.

"Well," she said. "You're going to have a really cool scar from a bullet wound."

McGaven laughed. "Yeah, that's true."

"Not as good as some of mine," she laughed.

"What do you mean?" he said playfully. "I have more than you."

"Ah, I don't think so." She stood up and began to show a few scars, one on the side of her belly, one down the side of her jawline, and a nasty one the side of her shin. "See here and here, and let's not forget here."

"Well, I'm catching up."

"What's going on in here?" said Denise at the doorway carrying a small overnight bag. She walked over to McGaven and gave him a kiss.

"Just sharing our war stories," said Katie.

"Oh, is that all," Denise laughed. "Hi, Katie." To McGaven, "I brought you some clothes to change into before coming home."

"Thanks, babe."

Katie smiled. She loved seeing two of her closest friends together. "Well, I'll check in on you before you come back to work."

"Sounds good," he said. "Is there still a cold case unit?"

"I'm going to find out later, but since my uncle will be reinstated, I don't think there's a problem. Don't worry about that. Get better and rest—we have a lot of cold cases to solve."

Katie went to the door, paused, and then turned back to them. "Thanks, you two." And then she left.

The daylight became darker, as if a dimmer switch was turned down. The red and orange sunset reflected in the valley between the trees was breathtaking and indicated the end of another day.

Katie drove up in her uncle's white SUV and parked. She saw Chad sitting on a large rock watching the day end. He didn't immediately turn to greet her.

Katie walked up and put her arms around him. "I love this time of year. These are the best sunsets."

"They are even better when you share them with someone you love," he said.

Katie smiled. "I think you're right about that—it's even better."

The couple remained quiet, watching the sunset turn more intense before slowly dissipating. The end of the day represented the hope for a new even better one tomorrow.

Instead of rehashing the dangerous covert mission that Katie had embarked upon and what could have happened, they chose to move on and cherish each day.

CHAPTER 54

Monday 0830 hours

Katie sat across the table from Undersheriff Martinez, Sergeant Cannon of the internal affairs division, and Detective Hamilton. She had answered questions and updated them on what had transpired during her "unofficial" investigation in addition to her fully detailed report of everything that had taken place, including the voice recordings.

Sheriff Scott sat quietly next to Katie. No one spoke to him, but all charges for the murder of his wife had been dropped by the district attorney's office.

Martinez headed the meeting and announced, "All the new evidence, as well as the confessions, was corroborated in the homicide cases of Cynthia Andrews and Claire Scott. And we are coordinating with other jurisdictions for the two other homicides of the students, Anna Blake and Dillon Masterson."

"Yes," said Detective Hamilton.

"Cody Teagen murdered both Cynthia Andrews and Claire Scott with the guidance of Dr. Brandon Wills," Martinez said. "I just finished reading the forensic reports stating that there were small blood traces of Cody Teagen's blood on Sheriff Scott's knife. He must've inadvertently cut himself. In addition, the fabric strips left on the property were able to be matched to a small duffle bag owned by Teagen. There are a few other pieces of evidence being tested from the Andrews scene as well as the two murdered students, but it doesn't slow down the process or the status of the cases. As far as I can see, these cases are closed."

"Yes," she said, feeling a huge sense of relief.

"Is there anything you would like to add, Detective Scott?"

"Everything was in my report," she said and now was worried that she was going to be suspended for directly disobeying an order from a superior. "What about Detective Teagen?"

"We've done two interviews and are satisfied that he didn't know anything about what his son was up to." He changed the subject; obviously when a fellow officer was potentially involved in such horrific crimes, he didn't want to talk about it. "How is Deputy McGaven doing?" the undersheriff asked.

"He's doing well," she said. "Getting better every day."

"Good to hear. Well, my job here is done. It has been my pleasure to officially welcome back and be a part of reinstating Sheriff Wayne Scott."

Katie smiled and wanted to clap and whistle, but she sat quietly in her seat.

"Thank you," the sheriff said.

"No hard feelings, I hope."

"None," the sheriff replied.

"You can come back any time you like."

"Tomorrow. Katie and I have something important to do today."

"Very well. We'll see *both* of you tomorrow. Oh, Katie, do I have to remind you—"

She interrupted, "No, sir, you don't." She didn't need to be reminded that she had skated on very thin ice and wouldn't disregard an order again.

Undersheriff Martinez gave a hint of a tiny smile as he organized paperwork on the desk. "Very well."

*

Katie drove her uncle to the cemetery to pay his respects to the woman he had loved more than anything. They both walked to the grave site. Katie felt strange, remembering that day when she accompanied her uncle to say goodbye to her parents. They had suffered too many losses for one family. The overwhelming grief filled Katie as she waited for her uncle to say a few words.

Her uncle kneeled down as if his loss weighed heavy on him, physically. His shoulders were more rounded and his stride had been weaker than usual, but he was a strong man and time would begin to help him heal.

"Claire, if I could do anything to bring you back or stop your killer that night—I would. I hope you knew that I loved you more than you'll ever know. You came into my life and made me whole again. And for that I'm truly blessed. I love you," he said and laid a red rose on her gravesite.

Katie kneeled and left a small wildflower bouquet for her. She quietly said a prayer and stayed for a moment before she joined her uncle again.

"You, Katie Scott," he said, "you are going to follow the rules and be careful from now on."

"Of course."

"I love you." He hugged her tight. "It's just you and me, kiddo."

"What are you going to do with the house?"

"Sell it. I can't live in it now."

"You can stay with me until you find another place to live."

"No, you need your space and I don't want to scare away Chad. So I've rented a condo near the golf course."

"You hate golf," said Katie.

"Maybe I'll try it again. What do you think?"

"I think you'll still hate it," she laughed.

"Maybe tennis?" he said.

"I could see you playing that."

"I like the idea of hitting a tennis ball… making an ace… or whatever."

Katie laughed with him as they walked back to the car.

"That's what I want to hear. Laughter. Now when will I get to go to a wedding?"

"Hey, give a girl time to get her life straight first," she teased.

"You know Chad isn't going to wait forever."

"Uncle Wayne, maybe he doesn't want to get married. I'm not sure if I want to."

"Who doesn't want to get married? C'mon, a detective and firefighter… what better team than that?"

CHAPTER 55

Tuesday 0900 hours

What I realized was weakness wasn't the hardest thing to admit. Asking for help was the hardest thing you could do. There was no shame or society stigma attached to it. Everyone had times when they needed a little help. And today was my time to ask for that little bit of help. Sound mind and a firm focus was your closest friend, so treat them with respect and they will repay you three-fold.

Katie sat in the office of Megan Carver, therapist for PTSD and anxiety disorders. This time she was more relaxed, but still guarded.

"I'm glad that you've decided to come back. So what's on your mind, Katie?" said Dr. Carver, her voice calm and soothing as she spoke.

"Losing a family member. Can we start there?"

"Of course, we can start with anything you feel like talking about."

"My aunt was murdered since that last time we spoke."

Dr. Carver remained quiet. She was stoic even if the news had completely shocked her. "What was the best thing you liked most about your aunt? Tell me about her."

"Kindness. She always knew how to treat people and make everyone feel special," she said. "I think we could learn from her. I think everyone could."

"She sounds wonderful. What else?"

"Trusting. She could always keep a secret or be there for you if she said she would. Trust and kindness go together, don't you think?"

"Absolutely."

"I'm having a difficult time processing her death," said Katie. It was strange hearing her voice say that.

"Let's just take it one step at a time, and we'll work through it together. Okay?"

Katie took a deep breath and nodded. "Okay."

A LETTER FROM JENNIFER

I want to say a huge thank you for choosing to read *Flowers on Her Grave*. If you did enjoy it, and want to keep up to date with all my latest releases, just sign up at the following link. Your email address will never be shared and you can unsubscribe at any time.

www.bookouture.com/jennifer-chase

This was a special project and series for me. Forensics and criminal profiling has been something that I've studied considerably and to be able to incorporate them into a crime fiction novel has been a thrilling experience for me.

One of my favorite activities outside of writing has been dog training. I'm a dog lover, if you couldn't tell by reading this book. I've had the incredible opportunity to train with my local police K9 association, which includes several counties in California. My dog is certified in trailing, scent detection, and advanced obedience. I loved creating a supporting canine character for my police detective.

I hope you loved *Flowers on Her Grave* and if you did I would be very grateful if you could write a review. I'd love to hear what you think, and it makes such a difference helping new readers to discover one of my books for the first time.

I love hearing from my readers—you can get in touch on my Facebook page, through Twitter, Goodreads or my website.

Thanks,
Jennifer Chase

AuthorJenniferChase

JChaseNovelist

authorjenniferchase.com

ACKNOWLEDGMENTS

I want to thank my husband Mark for his steadfast support and for being my rock even when I had self-doubt. It's not always easy living with a writer and you've made it look easy.

A very special thank you goes out to my law enforcement, police K9, forensic, and first-responder friends—there're too many to list. Your friendships have meant the world to me. It has opened a whole new writing world and inspiration. I wouldn't be able to bring my crime fiction and K9 stories to life if it wasn't for all of you.

Thank you to Marla Steckwren, LCSW, Cognitive Behavioral Specialist, who helped me address the PTSD perspective and to bring the therapy setting to life.

Thank you, Detective Michael Lyons (Ret.), Yonkers Police Department, who has been an inspiration to me for creating fictional cold cases.

This continues to be a truly amazing writing experience. I would like to thank my publisher Bookouture and the fantastic staff for helping me to bring this book and the entire Detective Katie Scott series to life. A very special thank you to my editor Jessie Botterill—your unwavering enthusiasm, patience, and amazing guidance have challenged me to become a better writer.